D1298558

The Blessed Season

The Blessed Season

a novel

✳ ✳ ✳

by Melanie Lageschulte

The Blessed Season: a novel
© 2020
by Melanie Lageschulte
Fremont Creek Press

All rights reserved.

Kindle: 978-1-952066-10-8
Paperback: 978-1-952066-11-5
Large-print Paperback: 978-1-952066-12-2
Hardcover: 978-1-952066-13-9

This is a work of fiction. Names, characters, businesses, places, events
and incidents are either the products of the author's imagination or
used in a fictitious manner. Any resemblance to actual persons, living
or dead, or actual events is purely coincidental.

Cover photo: doug4537/iStock.com
Cover design by Melanie Lageschulte

Web: fremontcreekpress.com

Also by Melanie Lageschulte

Novels:
Growing Season
Harvest Season
The Peaceful Season
Waiting Season
Songbird Season
The Bright Season
Turning Season
Daffodil Season (coming spring 2021)

Short fiction:
A Tin Train Christmas

❋ 1 ❋

One tiny snowflake landed on the windshield as soon as Melinda turned out of her driveway. A few more appeared before she made it as far as the bridge over the creek, and the white stuff was falling steadily by the time she reached the county highway.

"Right on time. Auggie predicted our first real snow would arrive this morning." August Kleinsbach owned Prosper's co-op, but was also the community's self-appointed weather expert. "This will have him grinning from ear to ear, I'm sure. The fact that all of northern Iowa's professional meteorologists made the same forecast won't dampen his enthusiasm one bit."

Melinda was also smiling as she turned up the radio. Her favorite station's rotation was already heavy with Christmas tunes, even though it was only the middle of November. As she traveled the four miles between her corner and Prosper, the dull shades of the harvested fields were already being blanketed with white.

The holidays stretched out ahead, just like this road, she decided. And, just like the route she traveled more days than not, Melinda was sure she knew what she'd find along the way: glowing lights, beautifully decorated trees, warm greetings from friends and family, and the busiest season of the year at her family's business.

Prosper Hardware had been an anchor in the little town of two hundred residents for more than a century. Melinda Foster had always been proud of her connection to the local landmark, but had never imagined she'd be working behind its counter. Or living on a two-acre farm.

But eighteen months ago, her life in Minneapolis took an unexpected turn. First, she was downsized from her marketing career. Then Uncle Frank had a heart attack, Aunt Miriam begged Melinda to come home to help at the store, and one detour turned into another.

"And here I am." The car bumped and thumped over the railroad tracks as the highway passed Prosper Feed Co., then made a slight bend as it turned into Main Street and began its four-block run through the little town. Only a few vehicles were parked along Main at seven in the morning, and Melinda recognized every single one.

She passed Prosper Hardware, a two-story brick structure with green awnings that stood on the right, then turned past the post office to reach the gravel lot behind the store.

Auggie was already at the vintage sideboard near one of the plate-glass windows, the coffee cannister in his weathered hands.

"What did I say, huh?" His brown eyes snapped with mischief behind his thick-rimmed glasses. "The snow arrived as scheduled. Of course, not everyone's going to be happy about it. I'm sure there'll be plenty of bellyaching down at the co-op today."

Melinda dropped her things on the antique oak showcase that served as the store's counter. "If you don't want to get the grief, maybe you shouldn't blast your predictions across Hartland County."

"But that would ruin the fun," Auggie protested. "Why would I want to do that?"

The little bells above the heavy oak door soon made a cheerful chime, and Jerry Simmons, a retired school principal who now served as Prosper's mayor, wiped his sneakers on the mat.

"Whew, I'm not ready for this." Jerry removed his purple cap, which sported the local high school's logo, and smoothed his gray hair. "I decided to tough it out and not reach for the winter coat. Not yet."

"It'll melt by this afternoon." Auggie's confidence about when the snow would stop matched his smug prediction of its start. "I'm more interested in what's in that bag."

"Cinnamon-cranberry muffins." Jerry was quick this morning, and managed to snag himself a treat before Auggie could elbow him to the side.

"Candace made a test batch for the holiday bazaar over at the school, and she wants our opinion."

"I don't think you have to worry." Melinda followed Jerry to the sideboard, eager for a cup of Auggie's bracing brew and a sweet snack before the hustle and bustle began at eight. "The guys aren't too picky. I'm sure they'll give those their seal of approval."

"But it has to be earned." Auggie chortled as he settled into his favorite folding chair. "Remember those chocolate-chip cookies Frank brought a few weeks ago? Doughy in the middle, burnt around the edges ..."

Miriam had been too busy finalizing Prosper Hardware's holiday plans to do much baking, so Frank had taken the matter into his own, fumbling hands.

"As I remember," Melinda reminded her friends, "that didn't stop you from eating every single cookie."

Veterinarian John "Doc" Ogden soon pulled up out front, his work truck smeared with gravel dust and mud. Despite the flakes still swirling through the town's tiny business district, Doc waited patiently while retired farmer George Freitag, the coffee group's senior member at eighty-three, carefully parked his car in the next space. Melinda noticed how Doc scanned the sidewalk for any signs of ice and held the door for his older friend.

Uncle Frank was on his way up from the back of the store, cheerful as usual. In his wake was Bill Larsen, the store's only other full-time employee, in a far-less-festive mood.

"Merry Christmas," Bill said sarcastically, as his parka hit the coat tree with a swish. "Why couldn't it wait until after Thanksgiving, at least? Frank, should we bring the ice melt up today, stack it by the register?"

"Gosh, I hope not." Frank sighed. "This snow better just be passing through."

"All gone by three," Auggie predicted. "We'll get above freezing sometime midday."

"Well, I'm glad Miriam doubled our ice-melt order." Bill poured a cup of coffee and reached for two muffins. He was in his mid-thirties, with a stocky frame that promised to turn pudgy one day. "The last thing we need is people fighting over the stuff, like last year."

That brought a groan from the group. "Last winter was the worst I've seen in at least thirty years." George pushed down the sleeves of his cardigan, even though his chair was close to one of the iron grates in the oak-plank floor. "I hope I never see another one like it."

"I hate to break it to you, George." Doc stretched out his long legs, his navy wool socks visible beyond the hems of his old jeans. He and Miriam had an agreement: If there was a farm call before coffee hour, his boots stayed on the mat inside the door. "I don't think you'll make it to one-hundred-and-thirteen. Science is making leaps and bounds, but still."

George stared out at Main Street. "You're probably right, but I want to hang around as long as I can. I guess I'll enjoy this snow, then, from a distance. It's sort of pretty, see? Looks like a winter wonderland."

City hall, directly across the way, was a grand tan-brick-and-limestone structure that was on the national historical register. Many of the other buildings were over a century old, with generous windows and charming cornices, but too many of the structures were vacant. George was right; the flakes were sticking to the stones and bricks, frosting the storefronts' dull edges.

The group fell silent, enjoying the scene. Melinda set her cup on the floor long enough to pull an elastic band from her jeans' pocket, and wind her wavy brown hair into a low ponytail. She'd turned forty in March, and had considered chopping her shoulder-length mane, but pulling it back was still the easiest way to keep it out of the way. Besides, her regular beauty routine had long ago been pared down to making sure her sweatshirt was clean.

The furnace kicked on again, and a comforting rumble echoed up from the basement. The guys seemed sleepy, content to sip their coffee with little conversation. Had they run out of steam already this morning?

Melinda, however, was energized by the snow, and nudged Jerry with her elbow.

"When do you think you'll get the lights up along Main? That'll really brighten things up around here."

"Maybe this weekend, depends on how things shake out." Jerry shrugged and paused for a bite of muffin. Being mayor of a town this small meant there were few tasks to supervise, but all of them depended on volunteer labor. "Bill, can you and Nancy get the lights looked over in the next few days?"

"Sure. We changed all the bulbs last year, so the frames probably just need to be dusted off."

Nancy Delaney was the city's only full-time employee, serving as both city clerk and librarian. The snowflake and tree shapes were stored on city hall's second floor, which was packed with odds and ends accumulated over the years.

Auggie polished off his muffin with one last bite. "Let me know what the plan is. We'll get our big star out on the tower's catwalk some day when it's not too icy." He turned to Frank. "Looks like once you put the tree up, there in the corner, the store's ready to go."

The front windows were already draped with garlands and lights, and the display on the other side of the store was decked out with cold-weather gear, shiny-new power tools and a vintage sled for nostalgic charm. It had taken several admonishments from Miriam to keep Esther Denner, the store's part-timer, from smothering every surface with tinsel and bows the moment the calendar flipped to November.

"I'm good with the tree going up soon." Bill shared his unprompted opinion. "As long as we hold off on the holiday tunes until after Thanksgiving. I know Esther can't wait to turn them on, but I can only listen to them so many times."

"I hate to sound like a Grinch, but I agree." Melinda put her drained mug on the sideboard and started for the counter. "At least you can run off to Santa's workshop and shut the door." Bill was a master craftsman, and spent most of his pre-Christmas shifts in the wood shop, cutting special projects for customers.

Melinda almost had the counter polished when she spied Vicki Colton hurrying down the sidewalk. Her husband, Arthur, was the manager at a bank in nearby Swanton, and they'd moved to Prosper in the spring. With their son off at college, Vicki had too much time on her hands. She had plenty of money at her disposal, too, and had transformed the once-vacant building next door into Meadow Lane, an upscale gift and antique shop.

Vicki didn't just walk into Prosper Hardware; she burst through the front door and flung off her designer raincoat in one fluid, dramatic motion.

"Good morning, everyone!" She tossed her highlighted brown hair over her shoulder. "I just had to stop in before I unlocked the shop. Isn't the snow lovely?"

"Depends." Jerry sighed. "Our snow budget is pretty tight this year, since the county raised its rates on us little guys." Prosper didn't have a public works department. Or a police force, for that matter, and its fire and emergency crew was all volunteer. "I hope this melts on its own, and fast."

"Oh, I wouldn't worry." Vicki waved away Jerry's concerns. "Besides, we're just getting started!" Her blinding smile was in stark contrast to Jerry's worried frown. "It's going to be one lovely scene after another around here, filled with festive lights and holiday cheer."

"And customers." Melinda warmed to Vicki's enthusiasm. "It's the busiest season of the year for retail. I'm so glad you got your shop open, just in time!"

"And that's exactly why I'm here." Vicki's high-heeled boots clicked their way to the counter. She leaned toward Melinda, careful to not disturb the vintage garland draped across the cabinet's front.

"I'm so excited! I just had to tell someone, right away, and Arthur's stuck in some meeting."

"Did you find someone to fix that roof leak?" Frank was hopeful. "If they're good, have them stop by when they wrap up. I want them to check out a few spots."

"Oh, yes, he's coming tomorrow, but ..."

"Let me guess." George jumped in. "You got more of those knick-knacks in, the kids with the big eyes. Mary loves those."

Auggie pointed at Vicki. "You found reindeer! Live reindeer for the holiday open house!"

Doc and Frank exchanged stunned looks. *Reindeer?*

"No, that's not it." Vicki turned to face the men and crossed her arms. "Wait. Do you know somebody? I've been calling around. Anyway, it's way better than that! You all remember when that busload of crafters came through on opening weekend? Well, one of those ladies was so impressed with Meadow Lane, she got in touch with a major women's magazine." She rubbed her hands together. "I can't believe it! They're sending a crew out from New York to do a feature on the store!"

Melinda gasped. "Are you serious? Which one? Can you say?"

Vicki whispered her secret over the counter, even though the men had barely blinked at this news.

"That's a game-changer! Wait. If they're coming now, they surely can't get it in print before the holidays. Will it only be online?"

"The piece will run in next year's December issue. A full spread, an interview, complete national exposure! I've been wanting to start an online store, as you know; and now, I can have that going before the feature runs."

"What's the catch?" Auggie was skeptical. "You sure this is legit? How much is this going to cost you?"

"Not a dime. Meadow Lane's a perfect fit for this magazine." Her tone turned persuasive. "However, I am going to need a little bit of help to pull this off."

Bill frowned. "You have plenty of staff."

Jerry eyed Vicki suspiciously. "I think this goes far beyond the store. Out with it."

"Oh, it's not expensive. We just need some lights and greenery, and for everyone to get on board." Vicki pointed out to Main Street. "Can you see it? The windows and doorways bursting with color and lights? The magazine folks aren't coming until the week before Christmas, so we have plenty of time to get this done."

The men stared at her in shock and confusion as she wandered to the sideboard and filled a coffee cup, then settled into Melinda's vacant chair with a satisfied sigh. "OK, first thing, we need to get the town's holiday decorations up."

"That should happen this weekend." Frank said agreeably. "Next week at the latest. Really, if that's all ..."

"Excellent! Now, once the decorations are up along Main, and the whole thoroughfare is aglow ..."

Auggie smirked. "Only two blocks will be 'aglow.'"

"That's all the decorations we have," Jerry explained. "And that's only if we space them out."

"Well, that's too bad. Anyway, some lights would go a long way. And maybe small evergreens in front of every building. You know, the kind that fit in those cute baskets? I'm thinking half with clear lights, and half with colored. It shouldn't be ..."

"Are you going to pay for this?" Jerry blurted out. "That stuff costs money, and then there's the juice to keep all those lights on."

Vicki blinked. "Well, I was thinking I could help out, of course. Give everyone a stipend. I have a marketing budget." She looked to Melinda for support. All Melinda had to offer was a sympathetic smile.

"But I can't cover all of it. There's a Christmas tree farm north of Eagle River, I was on their website this morning. We can get a discount on a bulk order of fresh garland."

"No way." Doc shook his head. "I can't swing it. I'm sorry. I have one fake tree for the waiting room, which I anchor to the floor and ceiling to keep my clients from tearing it to shreds. The animals, I mean."

"We could get faux evergreens, then. It's an investment, they'll last for years."

Auggie glared at Vicki, and Melinda sensed a speech coming. "It's great your store's going to be featured in some fancy magazine, but there's only so much the rest of us can do. It's been a lean year for Prosper Feed Co., that's for sure, with the economy the way it is and the lingering effects of the drought."

"But that's why we need to get into the holiday spirit!" Vicki was becoming frustrated. "Just think how it would cheer people up to have lights shining in all the windows downtown!"

Jerry nearly dropped his muffin. "You're talking about everything? Even the vacant storefronts?"

"Sure, why not?"

"That's fake!" Auggie spat out. "This town may be going through a rough patch, but we're always ourselves, no matter what. Look, I know you're new here, and you don't get it ..."

Auggie was on a roll, and the next thing out of his mouth was sure to be a blistering tear-down of Vicki's winter-wonderland dreams. Even worse, that would probably lead to an allegation that Arthur's prosperous career insulated Vicki, and her store, from the harsher realities faced by their neighbors and friends.

An insult that would be especially wounding, because Melinda suspected it was true.

"OK, what about this?" She came around the counter and leaned against it. "Can we at least find a way to inspire residents to decorate their homes?"

"You mean, like a lighting contest?" Jerry seemed interested.

"That could work." Doc took a sip of his coffee, thinking. "Many residents put up stuff, anyway. But it's different for the empty businesses, those property owners would have to pay the electric bills for any decorating they do."

"You can't make them do it." Auggie eyed Vicki warily. "Don't even ask."

"Some of them don't even live around here," Frank added. "I think you'll have to drop subtle hints, and hope people catch the holiday spirit."

Vicki was deflated, but finally nodded. She was known for her big ideas, but she was smart enough to know when she was outnumbered.

George shifted in his chair. "I think a lighting contest would be a good idea. But I don't know if Mary and I can participate. Ladders and I aren't the best of friends these days. Besides, when we sold the farm and moved to town, we scaled back on that stuff. There's only enough to decorate our little tabletop tree, and maybe one string of lights to spare."

"Hey, there's an idea." Frank perked up. "Miriam and I have so much of that stuff at our house, way more than we could ever put up. Always seem to be adding to the stash, and not getting rid of anything. If there was a way to spread it around ..."

Bill leaned in. "Like a swap meet?"

"A holiday decoration exchange." Vicki gently corrected him, but she was smiling again. "Why haul your leftovers to Swanton or Charles City to a thrift store, when you can just bring it to ..."

"City hall, I'd say." Jerry was warming to the idea. "We could pick an evening, or a Saturday afternoon. Everyone would drop off their extras in the council chambers, and we could organize it on tables."

"There are plenty of outlets to test the lights," Frank added, "make sure things work. We could put the wreaths and trees along the walls."

"Oh, I wish the community center was done." Vicki peered through the tumbling snowflakes to where the former bank building sat just down the street. "That would be the perfect place to hold the exchange."

"We only closed on the building a few days ago," Jerry reminded her. "It's going to be spring, at least, before it's renovated and ready for events."

"The council chambers would do." Auggie bestowed his implied approval, and Vicki was eager to accept it. "If Karen and Josh can neuter cats in there, you certainly could use it for something like this. Besides, the holidays could be a hard sell this year. This might help people get in the mood."

"We'll have to vote on it." Frank was a member of the council. "But I would think the guys would approve. We can't wave a magic wand and turn Prosper into some fairy-tale village, but there's no reason we can't shine it up. Besides, it would be fun to see this town in a national magazine."

Jerry nodded. "It's not every day Prosper gets that kind of attention."

"Or any attention," George added.

"That's for sure." Auggie rubbed his hands together and turned to Vicki. "We business owners always have to put our best foot forward. What do you have in mind?"

Melinda returned to her pre-opening tasks while Vicki and Auggie hashed out the details for the decoration exchange. Those two couldn't be more different, but maybe they had more in common than either wanted to admit.

* 2 *

Melinda's fingers were cold inside her cotton gloves, but at least she could pick through Horace's old toolbox with ease. Sunny, one of her two barn cats, sauntered down the front sidewalk for a curious sniff of the metal container's mysterious contents. There were packets of screws and nails, screwdrivers flecked with paint, and so many other, odd fasteners that Melinda was now proud to be able to name.

"Never thought I'd need this much gear, but there's always something that needs attention around here. This toolbox was a gift two times over." She paused her rummaging long enough to rub Sunny's fluffy orange coat. "The tools themselves, and then Horace's willingness to teach me what everything was for."

The Schermann family's generosity had extended far beyond the cheap rent Horace's nephew named the day Melinda toured the farm. Horace may have left his lifelong home to join his brother at a nearby care facility, but his heart was still tied to the land. Even now, months after Melinda purchased the acreage, his sage advice and unwavering support were just a phone call away.

The white-clapboard house had come mostly furnished, and the outbuildings had been stocked as well. There were several sheep; a flock of chickens; and Horace's beloved dog, Hobo, a former stray in need of a new friend.

"Of course, there was you and your brother, too." Melinda gently pushed Sunny's twitching nose away and dug deeper into the toolbox. "Horace knew you and Stormy were hiding in his barn, but Kevin had no idea. Oh, where are those packets of hooks? This thing is like a black hole! I drop something in, and it disappears. Wait, here they are."

Last year, Melinda had settled for one string of Christmas lights draped inside the screened-in front porch. But with her handyman skills vastly improved and Vicki's holiday enthusiasm so contagious, she'd decided a repeat simply wouldn't do.

With her employee discount at the store, she purchased some sturdy outdoor lights and enough metal hooks to string them under the porch's eaves, where they would be more visible from the gravel road.

She settled the stepladder closer to the porch, careful not to disturb the recently planted daffodil and tulip bulbs. It was a beautiful afternoon, chilly yet bright, and her move up the ladder gave Melinda a better view of the now-brown lawn and the empty fields and pastures around her farm. The veteran oaks and maples were bare-branched now, and the only pops of color in the windbreak came from the evergreens that marched along its north edge.

Melinda had the end of one light string draped over the first hooks when she caught a flash of gray out of the corner of her eye: Stormy had dashed around the corner of the porch to join Sunny by the ladder. A blue jay landed in the large maple in front of the house, and scolded the cats as they batted at the dangling strand of holiday lights.

"Watch those claws!" As Melinda hurried to lift the other end away from the cats' curious paws, the rumble of an engine echoed down the road. "Good, maybe that's Karen. I'm glad I'm home today to help her deworm the sheep. But first, I better get these lights out of your reach."

Karen Porter was Doc's business partner and one of Melinda's closest friends. Being single ladies in a rural community was just one of the many things they had in common. But as Melinda descended the ladder, a red truck emerged from the billow of gravel dust.

"Hmm, that's not her. But it looks like they're slowing down. Are we having another visitor today?" Stormy and Sunny didn't even look up from where they now lounged on the sunny sidewalk. "That truck looks kind of familiar, but ..."

The driver tapped the horn and waved, then pulled in next to the garage.

"Josh? What's Josh doing here?"

Josh Vogel was a veterinarian in Swanton, Doc and Karen's friend and, Melinda supposed, one of hers as well. Just weeks after he'd taken over a small-animal practice in the nearby town, Josh had eagerly volunteered to help with the community cat clinics Melinda and Karen had organized that spring.

But that didn't explain why Josh had just appeared in her yard. The trio hoped to apply for several nonprofit grants before the end of the year, but there was one more clinic next week. Surely they could discuss those then.

"Hey there!" Josh grinned as he closed the truck's door. His short dark hair was obscured by a navy knit cap, but his brown eyes were as friendly as ever. "I know you weren't expecting me, but Karen asked me to come out. She and Doc are swamped today."

Melinda blinked. "You're here to deworm the sheep?"

Her surprise made Josh laugh. "What, you think I don't know how?"

Josh was obviously teasing her, so she gave it right back. "I trust they taught you back in vet school. But don't you have a sweet, docile cat or dog that needs attention? My sheep aren't exactly welcoming to strangers."

Josh dropped the tailgate and reached for a large tackle box. "You mean, back at my spotless, sterile clinic? Yeah, today's been busy, but I have a gap this afternoon, and Karen and Doc could use a hand. It won't hurt me to get a little manure on my boots, for once. As long as I change them when I get back."

"Well, I'm surprised to see you, but I'm glad you're here." Melinda meant it, and not just because it was tough to hold an ewe still with one hand and push a plunger of goo into her mouth with the other. Josh had proven himself to be an invaluable component of the community-cat program and, if Melinda had to be honest about it, he was rather easy on the eyes as well. Karen had said Josh was thirty-eight and divorced, but Melinda didn't know much else about him.

Even so, did it really matter? She'd been right to break things off with Chase Thompson, and the scars on her heart were slowly healing, but starting a new relationship wasn't exactly at the top of her to-do list.

"So, where's this famous dog of yours?" Josh's eyes snapped with humor as he scanned the yard. "I suppose winning that award means he's more discriminating about who he hangs out with these days."

Melinda sighed. "Quite the opposite, actually. He spent most of the morning down at the creek, came home happy but muddy. Took me almost an hour to clean him up. He's inside, napping with Grace and Hazel."

"You know, if you ever want to foster more kittens ..."

"I know, I know, you've got an in with the Swanton rescue group." Melinda switched her decoration-hanging gloves for the sheep-wrangling pair waiting on the back-porch steps. "But I think I've got my hands full, as it is."

"That's an impressive barn." Josh pointed at the structure's ornate cupola as they made their way across the gravel drive. "It's in great condition; so many of them are losing ground against the weather and time."

"Horace's grandpa knew what he was doing. Same with the house."

Josh glanced over his shoulder and gave the white farmhouse an admiring glance. "I'd say so. I like those steep gables; they give the house so much character."

Melinda hid her smirk, as her home looked its best from a distance. Up close, it was impossible to overlook the faded paint and the wear that marred its dark-green shingles.

"I'd love to give it a fresh coat, and the gray trim around the windows, too. But that's going to be a significant investment, and I'll need to find someone reliable to do it."

"I had my house painted, just after I moved in. A neighbor recommended the guy, he did great work."

"Great, I'll keep that in mind. It's on my list for next year."

"I bet that list is endless."

"You're right about that."

"But that comes with having a farm," Josh said wistfully as he reached for the barn door's iron handle. "I grew up on one, and I miss it."

"So, that's why you're here!" She raised an eyebrow. "You're homesick?"

Josh laughed. "Part of it, I suppose."

The barn was dim and empty, its only visible occupants the motes of dust that danced in the small-paned windows' sunbeams. Melinda's appearance in the main aisle was usually met by an enthusiastic rush of cream wool and impatient "baaas," but not this time. And she knew why.

All eight of her girls had been strolling the front pasture when the unfamiliar truck came up the lane. This stranger needed to be evaluated, but from outside the open pasture door.

"There they are." Josh tipped his knit cap to a few black noses visible near the entrance. "Are they always this skittish?"

"Depends. They love Ed and Mabel, who live just north of here. The Bauers did chores the week between Horace's departure and my arrival, and they still like to bring down potato peelings and carrot ends." She reached for the rope halters that waited on a nail next to the feed area's gate. "Now, John Olson? They like John, but he's a serious sheep farmer. When he comes over, it usually means there's going to be some sort of rodeo."

"Like today?" Josh set his metal box on a nearby straw bale, careful not to make too much racket as he unsnapped the latches.

"Exactly." With a halter slung over one shoulder, she pried the lid off the bin of shelled corn. "Let me get them all in here, and we can get started."

The promise of the corn bucket soon outweighed the ewes' skepticism. As Melinda latched the bottom half of the pasture door behind the last sheep, she made a few introductions.

"Girls, this is our friend, Josh. I know you miss Karen, but she'll come another day." With the last of the shelled corn tossed in the trough, Melinda patted one of the two smallest sheep on the head. "Josh, this is Clover, one of my spring lambs. The other youngster is Lilac, her sister. That ewe on the far right? She had triplets last winter, popped them out like it was the easiest thing ever."

An indignant bellow sounded from the middle of the pack, and Melinda hurried over to dole out an affectionate pet. "And this one's Miss Annie. She was a bottle lamb back in the day, and Horace and Wilbur spoiled her. She's as stubborn as they come."

"That would have been my guess," Josh said wryly, but he seemed to be enjoying himself. Karen and Doc had many horror stories from their often-unpredictable farm calls; but Melinda could imagine Josh's usual routine, while rewarding, was probably much-less exciting.

He pulled out the bottle of dewormer with a wide grin. "Well, halter up the one you want to tackle first."

"I wish I could master this on my own." She reached for one of the older ewes. "But even when they're tied up, I can't get them to stay still long enough to get it done. I tell them I'm just giving them a big hug, but somehow, they know I'm really trying to put them in a headlock."

"They're smarter than people think. Besides, two sets of hands are always better than one."

The main barn door had been propped open to let in the afternoon's refreshing breeze, and there soon was an excited bark at the entrance. Hobo dashed down the aisle, pausing only long enough to sniff the contents of Josh's open vet kit.

Melinda was relieved to see his white feet were still clean, and his brown coat looked almost as smooth as when she'd brushed it out a few hours ago. It was a sign that, for the time being, he hadn't been getting into trouble.

Josh and Melinda moved on to the half-grown lambs while Hobo kept watch from the other side of the wide-board aisle fence. Lilac and Clover's damaged pride bounced back quickly, but some of the older sheep weren't so easily soothed. Just when Melinda thought she had the next patient in perfect position, the rattled ewe tacked to the right and stomped on Josh's boot. He didn't make a sound, but Melinda saw the pain flash across his face.

"Oh, no! How bad is it?"

"It'll be fine." But the set of his jaw told her the real deal. "That's what I get for wearing these. They're sturdy enough, but I'd meant to bring my old steel-toed pair along. Left the house in a hurry this morning, and didn't take the time to run back and get them. Lesson learned."

When the last of the doses were handed out, the ewes regained their freedom. Hobo gave Josh a sniff-over in the barn aisle, then ran ahead as Melinda and their guest started toward the house. Josh was favoring his stomped-on foot just a bit, and he noticed that she'd noticed.

"Don't worry, it's not that bad. I'll look it over when I get back, pop some ice on it if I have to. Next time, I'll be more prepared."

"Next time? Unless you're going to start a drive-through lane for farm critters, I don't think you'll need steel-toed boots to stay a step ahead of your patients."

Josh latched the tailgate of his truck and leaned against the dust-coated bumper. "So, can you keep something under your hat?"

She jerked down the brim of her orange knit cap, which was flecked with bits of straw. "Consider it covered."

He glanced around the yard. There was no one else within listening distance other than Hobo, who had found a sun-warmed patch of browned grass along the edge of the drive.

"I've been talking with Doc and Karen about some sort of partnership. Nothing's settled yet. I had clearance to tell you," he added quickly. "But ..."

"Say no more." She held up a gloved hand. "I promise not to add fuel to the fire. As Auggie likes to say, 'news travels fast around here, and gossip moves at the speed of light.'"

Josh laughed. "I bet he does. And, from what I hear, his co-op is the central switchboard. It's just something we're kicking around. I did large-animal work at my last practice, in addition to clinic appointments. There's two other vets based in Swanton that have the farm market mostly sewn up, and Doc and Karen's business is booming. They could use a hand."

Melinda nodded. "I know their coverage area is pretty impressive. The closest vet, going in the other direction, is over in Eagle River. Ten miles, at least."

Sunny appeared around the corner of the enclosed back porch, and rubbed his orange cheek on the last surviving pot of fall mums before wandering off in Hobo's direction. Josh's presence merited only a quick appraisal.

"I don't think Sunny remembers me." Josh pulled off his gloves and stuffed them in a pocket of his coveralls. "And maybe it's just as well."

"I can't thank you enough for helping him that night." Melinda blinked away a few happy tears as Sunny flopped down next to his canine buddy and stretched out his paws. "Doc was gone, Karen was on a call, and with both emergency clinics forty minutes' away, I don't know what I would have done."

"I was glad to help. I know how much he means to you." Josh's brown eyes filled with understanding. "Actually, I should be thanking you. Or rather, thanking Sunny. See, that's what gave us the idea of working together."

"Really?"

"Yep."

The coffee pot was on inside, and there were plenty of oatmeal-raisin cookies in the canister on the counter. A visit from Karen would have ended with two friends enjoying a snack in the kitchen. Why should this one be any different?

"I'm sure you need to get back," she found herself saying, "but there's coffee and cookies if you have time. I was expecting Karen, so ..."

Josh shook his head as he checked his phone. "Wish I could. But I have to get back to town and change." He glanced down at his dusty coveralls and grinned. "Extra laundry today, you know."

"Oh, I do. I'm sure it's endless."

"Tell you what." Josh paused at the truck's door. "How about we do coffee some other time? There's that cool shop in Swanton, on the town square. You can update me on everything going on out here at the farm." He gave the yard one last admiring glance. "I bet every day out here's a little different than the last."

Melinda was taken by surprise. This wasn't what she'd expected but, now that he'd mentioned it, she tried to keep her enthusiasm in check.

"Sure, sounds good."

"Great." He hopped in the cab. "See you next week, at the clinic? It's the last one of the season."

Hobo was now at her side, and she reached for his collar and guided him away from the truck. "I'll be there. Miriam can spare me long enough to help with check-in and pick-up."

She waved him off, then watched the truck disappear up the road toward the blacktop.

"Well," she said to Hobo as they continued toward the house. "What do you think about that?" He gave a happy whimper and wagged his tail.

"Oh, so you like Josh? That's funny, because I do, too."

* 3 *

When Melinda stepped into Prosper's future community center, it was clear the former bank would get a chilly reception from the steering committee.

The high-ceilinged front room was only marginally warmer than the chill outside. Uncle Frank was perched on the edge of a dusty, discarded office desk, still wearing his winter coat and a fleece-lined wool cap.

"Keep your gloves on," he warned his niece. "The furnace has been running just enough to keep the pipes from freezing. Jerry's down there now, cranking it a bit. Fingers crossed it works."

A rotund middle-aged man who had been studying the side wall's soaring windows offered Melinda his hand. "Emmett Beck; you must be Melinda. If we hear any ominous rumbles, Jerry made us promise to clear out before we call 9-1-1."

"A gallant offer, but I doubt it'll be needed." A white-haired woman with humor in her blue eyes patted Melinda on the arm. "I'm Patricia, Emmett's better half." She tipped her head toward Frank. "We've heard so much about you." Her smile indicated the talk had been positive.

"When Frank said you'd agreed to be on the committee, I was so glad; we need the young people in the area to have some say in the project."

Melinda held back a laugh. At forty, she didn't really consider herself one of the "young people" these days. But then, many of Prosper's residents were older. "I love historical buildings. They have so much character, and this place is certainly packed with it. With a good cleaning and some fresh paint, I think we can make a significant difference in a short amount of time."

"That kitchen is in sorry shape." Patricia shook her head. "Makes me want to get out the sponges and buckets and get to work. But I don't think we'll get that far tonight, since this is only our first meeting."

She turned to her husband. "Honey, promise me you won't talk about this at the shop, unless Jerry says it's okay to spread it around. People are going to be very interested in what's going on in here, I'm sure."

"Where do you work?" Melinda asked Emmett.

"I'm the proud owner of Beck's Barber Shop, over on Swanton's town square." He swiped off his brown knit cap, and laughed. "I went bald early, it runs in the family; but I can still snip with the best of them."

"Emmett used to be on the council," Frank explained as he scuffed the wood floor with the sole of one shoe. "You know, the boards don't look so bad, under all that dust. We'll probably need to refinish them, though."

"Well, you're in charge." Emmett slapped Frank on the back.

"I guess." Frank rolled his eyes. "I'm as excited about this as everyone else in town, but I didn't volunteer to be in charge. Jerry wanted a council member to do it, and he kept after me until I finally agreed. I have to say, though, I think our choices will be determined by their costs, and what the council as a group is willing to endorse."

"That's true." Patricia studied the plaster ceiling far above their heads. "Not too many cracks, but I think it could use a skim coat before it's painted. Those light fixtures look like they're from the eighties; I hope we can find some new ones with a vintage feel."

"Edison bulbs are very popular these days," Melinda offered. "Seeded glass is, too. There must be something that'll fit the budget."

Frank sighed. "It's a good thing Delores' deadline was only about picking a location, not when the center will open. There's a million things to decide between now and then."

"You're right about that." Emmett replaced his cap. "Well, we got the money, and the property transfer went through easy as pie. It's the best start we could hope for, I guess."

Delores Eklund, a retired teacher, shocked everyone when she offered two-hundred-thousand dollars to jump-start the community center project. The only catch was leaders had to choose a site before November's municipal election. After nearly two months of debate, both in the council chambers and around dinner tables across town, the former bank had been selected from among several empty storefronts and vacant lots within the city's modest boundaries.

A door creaked open, and Jerry emerged from the enclosed stairwell. "I set it to go all the way to sixty-five, we'll see how long it takes. Seems to be kicking in just fine. But I'm glad I asked Rich to swing by the other day and give it a look."

"Who's that?" Melinda leaned toward Patricia. "Just when I think I've met everyone in town ..."

"Oh, Richard Everton? He owns a construction company with his two grown sons; it's based at his acreage, just south of town. It was quite a win for us when he agreed to join the committee, given his obvious skills. When it comes to carpentry, I can hang a picture and that's about it. Oh, good, looks like everyone else is here."

As the other members filed in, wiping their shoes on the faded mat and exclaiming over their eagerness to get started, Patricia gave Melinda the rundown. And, as in most small towns, everyone seemed to wear more than one hat.

Betsy Carmichael, who looked to be a bit younger than Melinda, worked in the office at Eagle River's auction barn and was president of the Prosper Lutheran Church's women's club. Next was Bruce Scrivener, a retired farmer who was also a part-time janitor at Prosper's elementary school. Richard, who was tall and lean, was deep in conversation with Nancy. Her dark bob had been tossed about by the wind, and she rummaged in her always-packed tote for a soft cloth to wipe the fog from her glasses.

Patricia studied Nancy and Richard, then raised an eyebrow at Melinda. "Did I mention Richard is divorced?" she said sweetly.

"Oh, is he?" Melinda gave a noncommittal nod. "How interesting."

"Well, just thought I would point that out. I still work part-time in the school office, you know, and the younger ladies are always talking about how hard it is to meet anyone interesting around here. Or at least, anyone that's truly available." She lowered her voice. "But that's a conversation for another time."

There was movement in the vestibule, and Jake Newcastle burst into the room. "Hey, sorry I'm late. Practice ran over, then I had to stop at the house ..."

"What's he doing here?" Frank whispered to Jerry.

"Lucas called yesterday, said he has an online pharmacy class that has to be completed by the end of the year." Jerry kept his voice low, and Melinda could barely hear him under Jake's boisterous greetings to the other volunteers. "We needed another council member, and you know Jake loves to be in the middle of everything."

"Yeah, that's for sure." Frank sighed. "Fine, if you think the two of you can get along."

Jake, a high-school teacher and wrestling coach, had challenged Jerry for the mayoral seat. While he'd come up short, his push to build a brand-new community center had attracted its share of supporters.

"That's where you come in, old friend." Jerry clapped Frank on the shoulder. "I trust you to keep the train on the tracks."

Frank gave a quick recap of the inspection report as Nancy passed out copies. "I know you've all seen this before, but I think our first task will be prioritizing this list. And it's a long one. I suggest we start with ..."

Someone else was out front. Betsy's jaw dropped, but she quickly regained her composure and held one of the ornate interior doors open so Delores could focus on maneuvering her cane. Nancy widened her eyes at Melinda, then stepped forward with a smile.

"Delores! This is ... such a wonderful surprise. How good of you to stop by for a little peek before the work begins."

"Wednesdays at six-thirty, right?" Delores began to unfasten the vinyl bonnet that protected her white curls, then thought better of it. "Goodness, it's freezing in here. Well, I've got the time blocked out on my calendar. When you're my age there's not much going on, but everything takes longer than you think."

Frank and Jerry exchanged worried looks. Jerry, his shoulders already slumped in defeat, gave only the slightest shake of his head.

"I've had a busy day, too," Jake piped up. "This afternoon, right before my last class ..."

Delores paid him no mind. "Mayor Simmons, I trust our little group will not meet the weeks of Christmas and New Year's? I'm sure we all have many obligations during that time, and I don't believe it would be appropriate."

"Yes. Yes, of course."

Richard fetched a sturdy chair from behind a partition, and Jerry handed Delores a copy of the report once she was settled. She held the paper close to her glasses and, with her brow furrowed and her mouth set in a firm line, gave the inspection's findings her full attention.

Everyone else stared at the vestibule. Would there be any more surprises? When a few uneventful seconds passed, Frank went back to his talking points.

"As you know, there's an issue with bats on the second floor. Of course, that's for a much-later phase, but they'll need to be properly removed. We're getting some estimates from wildlife organizations, since they're an endangered species."

"I'm sorry to say this." Richard rubbed the gray stubble on his chin. "But when I stopped by the other day to check the furnace, I swear there was something fluttering around the basement when I flipped the lights on."

Delores suddenly let out a bark-like laugh. "Sounds like we have more bats than just what's in the belfry."

"Add it to the list," Jerry said wearily. Nancy was already taking notes.

Jake crossed his arms. "I noticed two of the front steps are cracking. We'll need a licensed mason for that. I hope it's just that the concrete's old, not a sign of structural damage."

"The foundation's been evaluated." Frank bit off his words. "No issues there."

Patricia tried to bridge the tense silence that followed. "Delores, you didn't walk over here, did you? Emmett and I are just down the street, we could have offered you a lift."

"Thank you dear, but no. I still drive at night." She held her chin high. "But we're going to need at least one official handicapped space, and it should be out front, not at the side entrance." Her appraising gaze swept over the group. "Makes it tough for an old broad like myself to get around when someone takes the spot closest to the door."

No one was about to own up to that. Delores didn't seem to expect them to, as she was reaching into her purse. "I started a little list of the other things we'll need to do. But before I begin, let me say I'm pleased to see so many ladies among us. No reason we can't be as involved as the men."

"She was one of the founding members of the local teacher's union," Nancy whispered to Melinda as Delores outlined her priorities. "I guess we should have known she wouldn't just hand us a check and walk away."

"Nancy," Delores called in her direction, "I think the floors need to be refinished. Maybe a bit darker on the stain, it would stand up to lots of use."

"I think that would be lovely."

Delores offered her an approving nod and moved on. The kitchen needed an overhaul, but most of the money should go to new appliances. A light neutral color would be best on all the walls; it would provide a simple backdrop for any decorations groups renting out the space might want to use. And it would be best to install a built-in coat rack, not one of those flimsy metal things on wheels ...

"I think we have our hands full," Nancy told Melinda. "And the bats are going to be the easy part."

* * *

Aunt Miriam set her box of extension cords on the counter, and ran a hand through her cropped gray curls. "Frank says he never should have let Jerry talk him into leading that committee. But he figured the worst was over, after a site was finally chosen. How tough could it be to spruce the place up?"

"Any time people get together, there's bound to be differences of opinion." Melinda added one more box to the display of holiday cards. "I suppose we shouldn't be surprised Delores would want to put her oar in."

"True." Miriam raised an eyebrow at her niece. "But it sounds like she's determined to steer the boat. Let's just hope the whole thing doesn't capsize."

The store was cozy and quiet, with the opening rush already over and the lunch-time surge yet to come. The hum of a power saw echoed from behind the steel door that opened into the back of the building. Bill was in the wood shop, as busy as one of Santa's elves with several customers' Christmas crafts and gifts.

"I'm so glad we kept the lumber side of things going," Miriam called over her shoulder as she started for the home-improvement aisle. "So many people don't have the means to cut their own. We're on track to have a near-record month for that portion of the business."

"And Bill loves it, too. You should see what he's working on today. Pieces for a rocking horse, and a toy chest."

Miriam glanced at the "Prosper Feed Co." calendar tacked up next to the refrigerated case. "Thanksgiving's only a week away now. Yes, Bill's really in his element this time of year. But before you know it, the holidays will have blown past, and he'll be back to cutting stair treads and shelves. Then it'll be chicken-coop frames, spring fix-up projects ... no, it's never dull around here."

Melinda slipped off her dark-green apron and tossed it on a nail behind the counter, then reached for her coat and purse.

"Speaking of how time flies, I'm going to run next door for some holiday stamps before it gets busy again. My cards aren't going to be as exciting as I'd hoped, but I still need to get them in the mail."

Her annual greetings to friends and family would only be pre-packaged cards from Prosper Hardware's inventory. But not for a lack of effort on her part.

There had been a grand plan to pose with Hobo on the front steps of the farmhouse, complete with a plaid bow tie for him and a new red sweater for her. The concrete steps were scrubbed one sunny afternoon, then a festive wreath added to the storm door and two potted evergreens brought in to complete the scene. Angie Hensley, her neighbor, was eager to snap the pictures, and Hobo was also very excited about the photo shoot.

Too excited, it turned out. The taunting squirrel in the nearby maple tree had to be challenged, and then a strange truck rolled by on the gravel. Angie suggested a change of scenery, one with fewer distractions, but photos around the fireplace never quite panned out, either. Hobo was worn out by then, and quickly dozed off on the floral rug.

Melinda's former foster kittens showed no interest in sending holiday greetings. Grace, a regal, longhaired calico, wanted to be the center of attention but refused to pose for the camera. Hazel ran up from the basement when she was called, but her thick brown-tabby coat was dusted with cobwebs and she didn't want to be brushed.

Melinda and Angie finally admitted defeat, and adjourned to the kitchen for a cup of cocoa instead.

"It's the thought that counts," Melinda reminded herself as she turned down the sidewalk and started for the post office. "Better to have boring cards than none at all."

The one-story, cinderblock building, painted an institutional light gray, was separated from Prosper Hardware by just a narrow swath of ground. In addition to being the only federal building for miles, the post office had a prominent location on the corner of Main and Third streets. That meant that during the warmer months, postmaster Glenn Hanson took great pride in keeping the lot's lawn neat and trim. Melinda wondered who would take over the mowing once Glenn retired next summer. While Prosper's post office served an impressive number of rural square miles, along with the town's residents, its entire staff could be counted on one hand.

It was going to be a big change for Glenn, and he hadn't made his decision lightly. But he was old enough to dip into his generous pension, and the first grandbaby had arrived just a few months' ago. It was time to slow down, he told his friends and customers, and really enjoy life. Even so, this last holiday season would surely be bittersweet.

A woman came down the walk as Melinda neared the entrance. "Hey, Melinda, how's it going?"

Melinda couldn't quite place her, but that wasn't unusual. Being behind the counter of Prosper Hardware meant she was often recognized when she was out and about. She simply nodded and smiled. "Good. And how are you?"

"Oh, I'm doing fine, thanks." The woman leaned in and lowered her voice. "I don't know what's going on, but something's wrong with Glenn. He barely said three words to me while he weighed my package, and he seems really down. I thought he was so excited about retirement! We're sure going to miss him."

"Things won't be the same around here. Thanks for letting me know. I'll see if I can find a way to cheer him up."

Jolly holiday tunes greeted her when she entered the post office. But they played at a low volume, and the place was otherwise empty. Except for Glenn, who was studying something on the counter and barely looked up.

"Hey, Melinda." The woman was right. Glenn was as rotund as ever, but he was far from jolly.

"I like this garland." She pointed at the front of the counter, eager for something positive to say. "Those red and gold ornaments really set off the greenery."

"Yeah, it's nice." He looked away. "I hope everyone else appreciates it, too. And the lights in the window, all of it. Because this is the last time. The last holiday season."

"I'm sure retirement's going to be a big adjustment," she said gently as she put her purse on the counter. "But just think, next year you'll get to enjoy the holidays! I mean, really enjoy them. No more extended hours, lines of cranky people dragging in heavy boxes. You can be at home, with your grandson in your lap, watching movies and eating cookies."

Glenn's face had turned red. Was he crying?

She pushed through the gate and put a hand on his arm. "Hey, what's the matter? You seem really upset."

He elbowed a sheet of paper her way. "This! This is what's wrong. I can't believe it!"

The letter was from the regional postal center. She scanned its contents, and suddenly felt lightheaded. "Glenn, this can't be! Can they even do that?"

"You're damn right they can!" He wiped his face with the back of his hand. "The feds want to shut us down! They're on a rampage, trying to cut costs by closing post offices, especially in little towns like ours."

Melinda jumped when Glenn slammed one meaty fist on the counter. "They've been planning this for months ... years!" His eyes blazed with fury.

"Do you know what my regional supervisor told me this morning? His bosses admitted they were just waiting for me to file my retirement papers. Saves them having to lay me off, see? They knew I'd fight it, and they're right about that. They want to divide up the rest of my crew, have them work out of Eagle River and Swanton."

"What are they going to do with the building? I don't know who would want to buy it. And why would they run carriers all the way out here from other towns? The gas alone would be expensive."

"Doesn't make sense, does it? But that's the government for you. Overages, cost projections, blah, blah, blah. We're nothing to them, our little town. Nothing but some numbers on a spreadsheet."

He dropped into the stool-height chair behind the counter. "We're through! This is going to end us. Not just the post office, but the whole town!"

Glenn's gloom was contagious, and Melinda searched for any ray of hope she could find. "Wait! It's not final, not yet. Further down, the notice says this is a proposal. A *proposal*, Glenn."

Lost in grief and anger, she wasn't sure he'd heard what she'd said. "Did you see this? They're going to host public hearings. The first one will be sometime next month."

"It doesn't matter," Glenn said through gritted teeth. "That's all a show. If they say they want to do it, it's already done."

"There has to be something we can do!" Melinda's anger now nearly matched Glenn's. "This is the dumbest thing I've ever heard of!"

"All we can do is tack that letter on the bulletin board." He pointed to a frame of cork on the far wall, next to the brass-plated mailboxes. "It's an official notice, it has to be posted where the public can see it." His eyes were sad again, pleading. "I just can't do it."

Melinda slipped around the counter and, with shaking hands, snatched a spare tack from the board. There was room between the lost-and-found items and a notice for the Methodist Church's holiday dinner.

She took a step back, and stared at a simple sheet of white paper whose shocking news was buried between government jargon about "infrastructure" and "operating expenses" and "synergies."

Glenn had his head down on the counter. "It's going to be OK," she told him, trying to believe it herself. "I don't know how, but it will be."

He didn't answer. The holiday stamps now forgotten, Melinda grabbed her purse and dashed out the door, barely looking both ways before she ran across Main Street.

"Nancy?" She burst into the library, her heart pounding in her ears. "Nancy!"

"In here." Nancy was on the other side of the cased opening, at city hall's front desk. Oh, my God, what happened? Is someone hurt?"

"No, no. Where's Jerry?" Melinda was panting now, from exertion and also the weight of the news she carried. "We have to tell him, right now. And someone needs to help Glenn."

Nancy steered her into a chair. "Sit down, take a deep breath, and start at the beginning."

✳ 4 ✳

Jerry was Nancy's first call. Next was Frank, who hurried to the post office to sit with Glenn until one of the carriers could take over the counter. Melinda was pacing by city hall's front window when Mayor Simmons burst through the door. His face was pale and tense as he motioned for her to hand over her phone.

She'd had just enough composure to take a picture of the notice before she ran across the street. Jerry scanned it with wide eyes, dropped into the closest chair, and put a hand over his face.

"It's that bad, isn't it?" She swallowed hard.

"Yes. Yes, it is."

Nancy came out from behind the counter. "I've called the rest of the council members. And even the county supervisors' office. I don't know if they can do anything to help, but I thought it best if they knew as soon as possible."

Jerry didn't say a word, so Nancy hurried on.

"We've had tough times before. We'll get through this somehow. Jerry, remember when they moved all the secondary students to Swanton? Everyone said this town couldn't carry on without a high school, that it was the beginning of the end." She gestured out the window, where a brisk wind was driving the last of the dead leaves down Main Street. "But they were wrong. We're still here."

"That was a nightmare. It nearly tore this community apart. I was principal then," Jerry explained to Melinda. "The state had been pressuring us for years to merge due to declining population. On top of that, because of the cost, our district was struggling to offer all the new college-prep classes. It got to the point where we just couldn't put it off any longer. And now, it's going to happen all over again."

"But we can fight this, can't we?" Even as she asked, Melinda knew Glenn was right. If the postal service was to the point of making this process public, the train had already left the station.

"Well, we can try. That's a grueling process, though. With the school, it was months of meetings, parents shouting and crying. That was it for me, that's when I decided to take the retirement buyout and save my sanity. They'd offered me the assistant job in Swanton, which honestly paid more than what I'd made here. But my heart just wasn't in it anymore."

"I guess it's to our benefit that you're mayor now. You know how this could go, you have the experience to get us through this." She turned to Nancy. "Can you imagine if Jake was mayor? Last one out, turn off the lights."

"Oh, Lord," Nancy groaned. "No, I can't. Jerry, listen: I don't think it's some crazy coincidence you got re-elected, and then this happened. You are exactly what this town needs right now." She looked out the front window and shook her head. "Looks like the word is already out."

Several vehicles had pulled up in front of the post office. Residents were huddled in worried groups on the sidewalk, their arms flying with frustration as they discussed the situation. Others elbowed their way through the crowd, trying to get inside.

Jerry glanced at the clock. "That didn't take long. Would've been nice of the feds to give us a heads-up, rather than blindsiding poor Glenn. Nancy, we need to get ahead of this as much as we can."

"Sure thing." Nancy turned to her computer. "Melinda, can you send me that screenshot? I'll post something online."

"What can I do?" Melinda pleaded. "Please, give me something to do."

Jerry sighed. "I wish there was something." Then he looked up. "Actually, there is. You're going to get bombarded with comments and complaints at the store. Tell everyone this: Nothing is final. We need to find out more before we start to panic." He squared his shoulders. "That includes me."

"And we're going to fight this with everything we have." Nancy crossed her arms.

Jerry shrugged. "There you go."

The phone rang. "Prosper city hall, this is Nancy. Just a minute, please." She put the caller on hold. "Sharon at the Swanton newspaper wants a comment. Are you available?"

Jerry was already halfway to his desk. "I guess I am. Send her over."

***

Melinda's mood the next morning was as heavy as the dark clouds hanging over the horizon. The air was raw and damp, so much so that her hands glowed with cold when she pulled her gloves off after morning chores. Her head ached, and her eyes were scratchy from lack of sleep.

Yesterday's shocking developments had played on in her mind long into the wee hours of the night: Glenn's anguish, Jerry's worry, everyone's outrage, and her own fears about how just one decision could threaten the new life she'd worked so hard to build.

Main Street was deserted at this early hour, but she caught a glimpse of defiant holiday cheer when she rolled past Prosper Hardware. Auggie was inside, setting the chairs around the sideboard, and he'd already turned on the Christmas tree. It glowed merrily in the window, and the store's ceiling lights glinted off the sweeps of tinsel garland Melinda and Esther had draped over the synthetic branches just a week ago.

It had been such fun to set up the tree, drag the box down from the storeroom and position it in its place of honor. As the women draped the lights and added the ornaments, they'd looked ahead toward the best moments of the season to come: the cookies, the presents, the shopping and, most of all, the moments spent with family and friends.

"I'm afraid the holidays aren't going to be quite so merry now." Melinda braced herself for the slap of bitter wind that would greet her when she opened the car's door. "About all I can hope for is that today will be a little less terrible than yesterday."

Aunt Miriam had joined her at the counter to sack purchases as well as field customers' worries and complaints. Bill stayed in the wood shop the rest of the afternoon, trying to drown out the bad news with the roar of his table saw. Esther had kept herself busy restocking shelves, replenishing cans of soup and packages of nails between bouts of despondent tears.

Prosper Hardware was calmer and quieter this morning, and Melinda was relieved to find Auggie hadn't switched on the holiday tunes. Their incessant chirps about sleigh rides and firesides were, at least until she'd had some coffee, more than she could bear right now.

Auggie tipped his head toward the tree. "I know it won't make a damn bit of difference about this whole mess, but I went ahead and turned it on."

"Good idea. We need all the encouragement we can get. I'm afraid, though, that it's not going to be enough."

Doc arrived next, then Uncle Frank. Within minutes, all the regulars were in their usual seats, but barely a word passed between them as they glumly sipped their coffee. Jerry seemed to be struggling to stay awake, and Frank looked so worried that Melinda hoped this stress wouldn't bring on another health emergency. She waited for someone to say something, anything. And then, she couldn't take the silence any longer.

"Just tell us how bad it is," she said to Jerry.

He sighed and stretched out his legs. "First off, we're not going to do anything drastic right away. Business as usual.

The holiday festival goes on as planned. This could take months to get resolved, one way or another."

"Glenn's taking a few days off." Frank answered what was going to be Melinda's next question. "He's a mess, and no wonder. He has plenty of sick time built up, he might as well take it. Pete's going to watch the counter."

"He's taking all this hard," Doc added. "I think he blames himself, which isn't right."

"There's no way he could have seen this coming." George shook his head. "To think, the feds have been planning this all along, just biding their time until Glenn decided to retire."

"Nothing's final yet," Auggie interjected.

"You know it is." Bill rolled his eyes. "That's how these things work."

"Well, fine, they may have made up their minds." Anger flashed in Auggie's brown eyes. "But we're not down and out, not yet. The postal service is a business, like any other. Make no mistake about that. If we can show the feds it benefits them to keep the door open, they'll back off."

"And just how are we going to do that?" George wanted to know. "Run off to D.C. and set up a picket line?"

"Des Moines is closer," Doc pointed out. "There's a federal building down there."

"I'm too old for that. Ever since I hit my eighties, I've been keeping close to home."

"OK, just hear me out on this." Bill leaned forward. "I don't want the post office to close, either. But would that really put the whole town in danger of collapse? Public services are consolidating all the time, and it's not just the schools. The county's provided our snow removal and law enforcement for years already. What difference does it make where the mail's sorted? It still gets delivered. And I like Glenn as much as anyone, but how many people actually visit our post office on any one day?"

Melinda knew Bill had some valid points. Times were changing, the ways people communicated were evolving. But still ...

"I do see what you're saying," Doc admitted. "Prosper's known hard times before. The farm crisis of the 1980s, the Great Depression. This community's always found a way to keep going, even when other small towns have faltered. But losing our post office? That would be a real blow to Prosper's identity."

"We could lose our zip code." Frank got a refill. "Before you know it, people start thinking the town's washed up."

Jerry rubbed his chin. "Next thing you know, the school district uses that against us, and tries to take our elementary students away, too. That would remove one of the reasons people want to live here."

"And spend money here," Frank added mournfully.

"It's a slippery slope." Doc shook his head. "Then, we're back to talking about whether Prosper should unincorporate. I was on the council the last time it came up," he explained to Bill and Melinda. "Man, that got ugly. But we managed to hold the town together."

Auggie crossed his arms. "This could literally wipe us off the map, if we let it. That's why we have to fight back."

Melinda was exhausted, and her mind was foggy. But her years of marketing and public-relations experience had served her well in the past. There was a problem here that needed to be solved. She surely didn't have all the answers, but she wasn't about to give up.

"Prosper's fought off these sorts of threats before. What exactly worked those other times? How did you do it?"

The men looked at each other.

"Well," Jerry finally said, "as I remember it, everyone pulled together. When it came to the district merger, we lobbied hard to keep the elementary here. Our class sizes are wonderfully small, and being so far out worked in our favor. Busing kids to Swanton was going to cost a fortune."

Frank nodded slowly. "As for the incorporation drama, it seems like they had to raise taxes a bit, but the residents got behind the plan. And the city started outsourcing things it couldn't afford to do on its own anymore."

Melinda thought for a moment. "So, what I'm hearing is, being small has actually been to Prosper's benefit. Everyone knows everyone, so they're willing to compromise to keep the community together. And, in the instance of the school, the town's remoteness worked in its favor."

Auggie raised an eyebrow. "No reason it can't work this time, too."

Melinda found a notebook on one of the counter's back shelves, then pulled a pen from the flowerpot next to the register. "There are two ways to persuade people to see your side of a situation. One is statistics, the other is emotion. Given what I saw in here yesterday, the second one isn't going to be a problem."

Jerry's smile wasn't very wide, but it was real. "So, we need numbers, then. Prove that Prosper needs to keep its post office."

"One way is to show how many people are affected." Now that she had a blank page in front of her, Melinda was eager to fill it. "There's about two hundred people in town, but that's not everyone. Anyone know how big this zip code really is? I mean, are there as many rural residents as there are town residents?"

"Oh, there has to be more." Auggie drew a map in his mind. "Let's see, the zip code goes at least five miles west. No, six."

"My son lives eight miles south of town," George shared. "And their address is Prosper, too."

Doc nodded. "It has to be a good seven to the east. Pete drives that route, and I know he's the carrier for my friend Don and his family."

"It has to be at least a hundred square miles," Jerry said. "No, more like one-fifty, if not more. And if there's even an average of five people per square mile, and you know it's more than that ..."

Melinda's jaw dropped. "You're saying over seven hundred people out in the country get their mail from this post office? And then, with the town itself ..."

"A thousand." Frank took a moment to let that sink in. "We could be talking about one thousand people, easy, surely more. Think about how many letters that is in a day, or a week, how many packages."

"Glenn would have those stats." Jerry put down his mug, and rubbed his hands together. "That public hearing's going to be early next month. We need to rally folks and get as many of them there as possible."

"What if the weather turns?" George worried. "I mean, if there's a bad blizzard, they'd postpone, but what if it's just nasty enough people stay home?"

Auggie frowned. "Or they set it for a night when there's basketball, or holiday activities going on? This is a terrible time of year to have this kind of a meeting, and they know it. Don't think they haven't thought about that."

"Residents could call and protest," Doc suggested. "Email or, of course, write letters. But we need something with big impact, something that shows the scope of the situation."

"A petition!" Auggie pointed at Melinda's notebook. "Get it in writing, if you will. Every adult needs to sign it."

"I'd love to drop a hefty stack of paper on the table at that forum." Jerry raised a fist. "Bam! See what they think of that! Name after name, all down the page."

Bill looked around the circle. "It's a brilliant plan. Trouble is, how do you pull it off?"

The store would open in half an hour, so there wasn't much time. Melinda wrote as fast as she could as the guys brainstormed their way through the problem. Divide and conquer seemed to be their best bet.

Several volunteers would be needed to oversee a few blocks each in town, or a few square miles in their rural neighborhoods. The forms would have to pass from neighbor to neighbor, as they couldn't ask the postal carriers to ferry the petitions. They were federal employees, after all, and no one wanted them to put their jobs in jeopardy. The same went for Glenn. It wouldn't do for him to get fired before he had the chance to retire.

As for the post office's operational data, Jerry knew Nancy would be happy to pull that together. It was public record, so the postal service would have to comply with the request. Melinda suggested the petition drive be somehow made festive to encourage people to participate. What if it included a cookie exchange? The section leader might start it off with a dozen or two, and then everyone along the way could take a few and add some to the container.

Frank was excited, but still cautious. "Do we think people will really make the effort? I could see the town's residents being plugged in, but maybe out in the country ..."

"Of course they will." George pointed at himself. "This retired farmer can tell you, they'll get it done."

Auggie also gave his approval. "Absolutely. Harvest is over, the rush is past. And the worst of winter's weather usually holds off until January. There's just enough time to push this through. We have, what? Two weeks?"

"I'd say so." Jerry glanced at the calendar. "But not much more than that, would be my guess. Good news is, I think we'll know fairly soon when the meeting will be. The feds don't like to leave anything until the last minute."

"So we can't, either." Doc drained his mug, then stood up. "And Jerry, I agree. We need to stay the course around here, no matter what. The holiday festival needs to go on as planned." He grinned. "Besides, I have my critters all lined up for the live nativity."

"What about the community center?" George wondered. "Does that have to be put on hold?

Jerry thought for a moment. "We took possession of the building. And we already cashed Delores' check, although I sometimes wonder if we should have." That brought a round of wry laughter from the guys. "No, I think we push ahead. We'll pinch every penny, for sure, but we would have done that, anyway. The town wanted a gathering place, and they'll get one."

"It'd be a blow to morale to give up on that now," Frank said.

"Or anything else." Auggie raised his cup in salute. "I have to say, Vicki is right. We need to shine things up around here, make this the best holiday season Prosper has ever seen!"

Jerry reached for his coat. "The decoration exchange's going to be the Saturday after Thanksgiving. I wasn't sure the idea would take off, but I guess there's quite the buzz about it. Nothing energizes people more than getting stuff for free."

"Either way, that magazine crew is coming in a few weeks," Doc pointed out. "We need to put our best foot forward, no matter what."

The group's excitement dimmed for a moment. Melinda saw their worried glances and knew what they were thinking: The feature on Meadow Lane wouldn't be published until late next fall. What if the shop wasn't even in business by then? What if ...

"Well, let's get after it." Auggie downed the last of his coffee. "I need to get out to the garage when I get home tonight, sort out all those Christmas lights I don't use. You know, we just might be able to save this town, one string of garland at a time."

* 5 *

Hobo ran ahead, his tail wagging with excitement, while Melinda brought up the rear with the wheelbarrow.

"I wish this thing was big enough to haul two rolls of snow fence at once. But then, it'd be so heavy that I probably couldn't push it across the yard."

Her dad waited in the dormant grass between the north side of the garden and the windbreak. Roger grinned from ear to ear, despite the brisk cold and the hour of hard work to come. A former farm boy, he'd been nearly as excited as Melinda when she'd rented Horace's acreage.

"My acreage." She had to smile, even though installing snow fence was far from her favorite late-fall chore. The wooden pickets were ripe for splinters, and there was always a stray wire or two ready to rip a hole in a new pair of chore gloves.

"What's that grin for?" Roger looked up, his cropped gray hair hidden under an old green cap. Hobo now danced at his feet, eager for attention.

"Oh, I was just patting myself on the back for buying this place. Of course, I hate the thought of winter coming around again. Last year was rough, to say the least."

"This one's not supposed to be so bad." Roger reached for one end of the fence roll while she held the wheelbarrow steady. "You'll get through it."

Diane appeared around the row of bridal-wreath bushes, her canvas tote filled with pinecones from the windbreak. She patted her daughter on the arm. "Besides, spring wouldn't be so wonderful if we didn't have winter first."

"I know. Can you two get this roll spread out on your own? I'll bring another one up from the machine shed."

The chickens were busy inside their screened run, despite the chill in the air. Most of them seemed unruffled by the commotion beyond the garden, but Pansy eyed Melinda with a sharp tilt of her head when the wheelbarrow rolled past.

"Things are different around here today, huh? Unless you can help me put up snow fence, Miss Pansy, I think you'll have to wait it out. Stormy, what are you doing?"

Just as Melinda passed the corner of the chicken house, Stormy dashed out from behind the garage and, in one graceful leap, installed himself in the empty bed of the wheelbarrow. She laughed at the smug look on his face as they made their way to the machine shed.

"Captain of the ship, I see. Want a ride back, too?"

As soon as she dragged the fence roll out of the shed, Stormy took off for the pasture. "Nope, guess not."

Her parents had part of the first portion anchored to the galvanized fence by the time she returned. Leaving the next section in the wheelbarrow, she grasped a handful of short wires from the pile by the sleeping strawberry bed and moved down to the next stake.

"When I came to see the farm that day," she told her mom, "I wondered what this wire fence was for. Why would anyone want to mow around it, all year long? Horace explained it to me, of course, with much more patience than I probably deserved. It takes a regular fence to hold the snow fence in place, and you can't get through winter out here without one of those. I can about imagine what he was thinking."

"He's an easygoing guy." Roger gently nudged Hobo aside to attach a wire along the bottom of the fence. "Just think of all the years of wisdom he has rattling around in his head!

They don't make guys like him anymore. He's surely forgotten more than most of us ever hope to know."

Diane helped Melinda lift the rest of the roll off the ground. "Living out here his whole life, he had to be prepared for just about anything. But sometimes, things come out of nowhere, and there's nothing you can do about it." She suddenly turned away.

Roger put an arm around his wife's shoulders. "We can't lose hope, not yet. There'll be that meeting in a few weeks, to start with. The petitions will get signed, people are going to rally behind the town. And we all know the government takes it sweet time about everything."

Despite his comforting tone, there was worry in Roger's eyes when he looked to his daughter for support.

"Dad's right." Melinda made sure to sound more positive than she felt. "It's only been a few days since Glenn got the notice. We have to give it time."

Diane pulled off one knit glove and wiped her cheeks with the back of her hand. "But if Prosper loses the post office, things will go downhill for sure. It's impressive how Frank and Miriam have been able to keep the store afloat." She looked at Melinda. "And now, they have you to help, but ..."

A sob escaped Diane's throat, and Hobo hurried over to lean his head against her jeans in a show of solidarity.

"I keep thinking about Mom and Dad, and Grandma and Grandpa. They worked so hard, all of them, put everything they had into that business. Good years, lean years, wars, depressions ... and now, it could all come to an end. All because some bureaucrats in Washington can't make their spreadsheet balance. We don't mean anything to them."

"You're right." Melinda found a clean, folded tissue in her coat pocket, and handed it to her mom. "We don't. But that town means everything to the people living there, living all around here." She gestured across the sweeping fields. "And you're right about the store, too. Our family's owned it for over a hundred years, we've been through everything, like you said. We'll get through this, too."

Roger nodded silently in agreement, and Melinda wished she felt as optimistic as she claimed to be. The coffee group had adjourned that first morning in a flush of excitement and can-do spirit, but Melinda's elation over their plan had ebbed away almost as quickly as it had arrived.

Prosper's residents had a major mountain to climb. So much was at stake, and so much was out of their control. Enthusiasm, as wonderful as it was, wouldn't be enough on its own to carry them to the summit.

Diane dried her tears and reached down to give Hobo a pet. Sunny, who had been supervising from under the evergreens just north of the house, didn't want to be left out. He sauntered over, rubbed against Diane's other leg, and began to purr when she picked him up.

"He's really coming along, isn't he?" Roger smiled. "I can remember when those two were scared and skittish, taking off for the barn the moment you even looked at them sideways."

Melinda decided her mom needed another distraction to take her mind off her troubles. And late-November on a farm held plenty of tasks that needed to be done. "Why don't we let Dad finish the snow fence? I need to bring in the last of the potatoes and carrots, get them to the root cellar."

Sunny requested his freedom with an impatient meow and a flick of his tail. Diane let him have it, then squared her shoulders. "Sounds good. Digging in the dirt will be therapeutic, I think. Feels like a good day to get a hoe in my hand and take a whack at something, you know?"

"I'll be sure to stay back, then." Melinda laughed, relieved to see her mom's mood had improved. "There's a clean tote on the back porch, I'll grab it. Why don't you go into the garage and choose your weapon?"

The garden soil was icy and damp under the knees of Melinda's old jeans, but Diane was right: This might be a messy task, but it was certainly satisfying. They worked in companionable silence for several minutes, Diane attacking the hard ground with gusto and Melinda following behind, adding the unearthed root vegetables to the tote.

The growing season had started with her crawling on the ground, adding tender seedlings to the soil. It seemed fitting to end it the same way, gathering the last of the dirt-dusted carrots and potatoes before the weather changed for good.

It took both of them to balance the tote on the way to the back porch. With their loot split into two buckets, they passed through the cozy kitchen and down the basement stairs.

"I can't believe it's only a few days until Thanksgiving." Diane deposited her bucket of potatoes on the dusty concrete floor of the root cellar, which was in the northwest corner of the basement. Rough wooden shelves lined two of its walls, and there was only one tiny window. "I wish Mark could've found a flight for Wednesday, but everything was booked."

"He likes to fly by the seat of his pants." Melinda shrugged at her younger brother's easygoing nature and pulled out a wooden crate. "Which is fine, except when you want to go from Austin to Minneapolis during the holidays. He'll have to get up really early, but at least he should be to Frank and Miriam's by noon. Liz says she and Isaac and the boys want to get on the road first thing Wednesday morning. They should be here by the time I get home from the store."

"I'm so glad you have this house." Diane began to unload her pail. "I mean, for several reasons. But it's a great help to have the extra rooms when everyone comes home."

Mark would stay at Roger and Diane's house in Swanton, but Liz's family was going to bunk with Melinda at the farm.

"With all the upheaval over the post office, I haven't had the time or the attention span to do much cleaning," Melinda admitted. "So, what it is will have to do."

"And that's all you can do. Liz and Isaac won't mind. And I suspect Liam and Noah prefer it that way. Living in Milwaukee, they don't get the chance to run free the way they do out here."

"Oh, I wanted to show you what I found the other day." Melinda reached for a glass bottle waiting on one shelf. "It was in a box in the furnace room, I guess it got passed over when the Schermanns cleaned out."

Diane's eyes grew wide. "Oh, look at that! Hawk Hollow Creamery. I bet it wasn't this clean when you found it, right?"

Melinda laughed. "Yeah, it was so dirty, it was hard to make out the raised letters. But Horace said there might be a few here, and I've been poking around when I have the time."

Hawk Hollow, a small settlement a few miles southwest of Melinda's farm, had disappeared decades ago. A post office operated out of a large farmhouse there in the years around 1900, and a small store and creamery once sat across the road. The buildings were long gone. All that was left was an iron-frame bridge over the creek, and three recently discovered graves that township trustees planned to honor as a pioneer cemetery.

"Just look at that." Diane held the milk bottle with reverent hands. "A piece of local history. It makes you think, doesn't it? If Hawk Hollow had managed to survive, even thrive, how different things would be around here."

Melinda added the last of her potatoes to a wooden crate. "I know. And I think that's why the idea of the place has captured everyone's attention. But I suppose, Hawk Hollow never really had a chance. Once the post office closed, well, its days were numbered."

She stopped cold, the meaning of what she'd just said echoing through the chilly shadows of the root cellar. Her mom's eyes again brimmed with tears.

"It doesn't have to happen that way," Melinda added quickly. "Not this time. Prosper's far more established than Hawk Hollow ever hoped to be."

"I know." Diane swallowed hard and handed back the bottle. "It's not the same."

Melinda glanced out the small window, to where the afternoon was slipping away. "I'll run out and see if Dad needs an extra hand to finish the snow fence. Can you put on the coffee? I want to pay you in cookies, at least, before you head home."

A few minutes around the kitchen table with her parents raised Melinda's spirits just a bit, but they fell again as she waved them off from the back steps. It was too soon to admit defeat, of course, but her mom was right to be worried.

She was, too. Because Prosper wouldn't have to disappear off the map before her new life here would be changed, and not for the better.

A brisk wind kicked up from the northwest, and slipped around the collar of her old coat. With a sigh of resignation, she turned for the door. "Well, Hobo, you have a free hour or so until chore time. I need to get upstairs and tackle one more project I've been putting off for weeks."

Melinda rummaged in the porch closet and pulled out her tools. As she passed through the living room on the way to the stairs, Hazel looked up from her favorite corner of the couch and stretched one fluffy paw in Melinda's direction.

Grace didn't seem to have much interest until she noticed the toolbox. Its appearance meant Melinda was up to something, and she wasn't going to be left out. By the time Melinda reached the closed door of the front bedroom, which was only used for storage, both girls were mewing with impatience.

"I know, this is where all the secrets are kept, huh? Just be careful when you explore, it's always a mess."

She slid a crate to the side and wedged her way into the room, then sought a path through the boxes and left-behind furniture to reach the three windows in the wide east dormer. The dust made her sneeze, but neither cat even looked up. Hazel had already scampered off to the right, her tiny toenails clicking on the hardwood floors, and Grace was testing the closed flaps of a cardboard box just inside the door.

The room looked, and felt, as if time had stopped fifty years ago. Dingy cotton curtains with ruffled hems were still draped over the window frames, and the cracked-plaster walls were coated in a drab light-green paint that must have offered a bit of color before it faded.

Several of the Schermann girls shared the room years ago, but it had been mostly neglected once the last of them grew up and moved away.

Even though the floor registers were always closed, Melinda had sealed the dormer windows with plastic last fall. Luckily, the film was still intact, and she found a moment to gaze out over the front yard. "One less thing I have to do. But I don't think the other window's going to be so easy."

The lone opening in the north wall wasn't even visible, as its wood frame served mostly as an anchor for the sheet of bare plywood screwed over the panes. Horace had told her the old storm window was cracked, and she'd long ago verified that claim by squinting up at it from the ground. But her latest visual inspection indicated the bottom of the storm window's metal frame might be coming loose.

As soon as she opened her toolbox and reached for a screwdriver, Hazel bounded over to assist.

"Whatever's behind here, it's best to find out and get it over with." The first two fasteners popped out easily, but the next was stubborn. "Ugh, I bet there's stuff in the sill, too, like moldy old newspapers. I'm going to need a shower when I get done. Hazel, move over, in case it all comes at once."

Cold drafts reached for her hands before she had the last screw removed. With a creak and a groan, the plywood pulled away. Melinda took a quick step back to keep her balance, then leaned the panel against the wall.

"Oh, no. Look at this. What a mess!"

Rolls of now-rotten towels filled the sill between the window and the storm frame. They were not only covered in grime, but dotted with dead flies and the carcasses of little orange beetles.

The bottom windowpane squeaked in protest and finally moved, but slipped down as soon as she let it go. "Great. The pulleys are broken, it won't even stay up." But she'd come prepared, and the scrap of wood in the bottom of the toolbox propped the sash high enough that she could reach inside. Which she did, after she donned a pair of vinyl gloves.

The decomposed towels went into a plastic sack, which was tightly tied to keep the cats out of it. Under the mess were more causes for concern. The sill was rotting, and one of the cracks in the side frame had widened into a hole large enough to let water seep through.

Despite the window's poor condition, it was both strange and thrilling to see her yard from this unusual vantage point. Melinda felt as if she'd stumbled upon a secret portal in the front room of this old farmhouse. The north yard was brown and dull now, except for the two large evergreens that flanked the silver-painted propane tank. Beyond that was the windbreak, where the bare-limbed hardwood trees shifted in the rising wind.

Grace, her right ear already dark with dust, vaulted into the windowsill before Melinda could snatch her away. Not only was the space filthy, but any pressure on the cracked storm glass could cause it to break. Melinda deposited Grace on the floor and carefully lowered the interior window. By the time she sank to the worn oak boards herself, her mood was as dark as the clouds hurrying by outside.

"It's worse than I thought," she told Hazel, then settled the young cat in her lap. Grace, annoyed at being told what to do, had already moved on to another mysterious box. "I can stuff the window with something again, but that's it. I wish I knew how to fix it, but I don't. Sounds familiar, doesn't it?"

The problem with the post office wasn't something she had to solve alone, of course. Jerry and the council were already working through their plan, figuring out the best way to rally the community to fight the impending closure. But that didn't make the situation any less troubling, especially when so much was at stake.

If everyone's worst fears came true, and Prosper Hardware's days came to an end, what would she do? Diane and Roger were retired from their own careers and, although Frank and Miriam hated to dwell on it, their remaining years of full-time work could probably be counted on one hand. Melinda, however, had decades stretching ahead of her that she needed to fill, one way or another.

She'd worked so hard to build a new life here, between the farm and the store. Could the loss of one force the end of the other? What else could she find around here for work? Would it ever be enough to justify staying here?

As she sat there on the cold floor, Melinda tried her best to stare this problem down. Prosper's leaders weren't the only ones who needed a plan. If she was going to weather this storm, whatever it might bring, she had to be ready.

Job security had been the last thing on her mind when she'd agreed to help at the store for a few months after Frank's heart attack. Everything had been temporary, at the start. But as she'd put down roots here, then decided to stay, the store's enduring success had brought her comfort and bolstered her confidence in the future. Through every economic downturn, Prosper Hardware had remained a cornerstone of the community.

The possibility that community could wither away, however, was something she'd never considered.

Setting Hazel aside, she trudged down to the basement and retrieved a stack of old-but-clean towels from a shelf in the laundry room. As she wedged the battered window back open and blanketed the gap as best as she could, tears formed in her eyes. What she was doing was barely better than what was there before. The storm window needed to be replaced; the window itself should go, too. And then there was the aging roof, the worn clapboards, the old furnace grumbling in the basement ...

While her tears brought her a moment of solace, they wouldn't get this window recovered before dark. She got to her feet and repositioned the plywood. Nothing was level, nothing was square, but she lined the holes up as best as she could and pulled the first screw from her pocket. It finally caught in the frame, then gained a toehold that gave Melinda a little leverage with the screwdriver.

"Sometimes, the only way out is through." She reached for another screw, and attacked the next hole. She couldn't see what the future would hold, and it was just as well. Because she would stay, no matter what might happen. She'd already made her choice. Or rather, her heart had made it for her.

There had to be a way out of this mess. Not just for herself, but for the whole town.

Melinda looked around the room, at her boxes and totes mingled with what the Schermanns had left behind. This was her home now, and she had no intention of letting it go.

The containers that held her holiday decorations caught her eye. She popped the lid on the closest one, and sighed. Even after she decked out her farmhouse with understated elegance, there would still be stacks of decorations stuffed in these totes. Too many lights, too many knick-knacks, too much glitz and fuss.

The decoration swap was Saturday. It was time to let most of this stuff go. She didn't need it anymore, and if it would literally brighten someone else's holidays during this tough season, all the better.

"We'll give it away," she explained to Grace, who had tried her best to slip inside the tote for a better look. "It's my past, you see; the Ghosts of Christmases Past. I need to live in the now, and not look back."

* 6 *

"Prosper never changes, does it?" Liz took in the view outside the windshield, which showed a sunny Thanksgiving morning. Despite the bright skies, hints of frost still clung to the brown grass and the little town's sidewalks.

"I love Milwaukee, but it's a comfort to know that when I come home, things are mostly the way they were when I left."

Melinda gave her sister a smile. "I just hope that continues to be true."

Isaac and the boys had left the farm a few minutes earlier, and their SUV was already parked in front of Frank and Miriam's Victorian on Cherry Street. But Liz had opted to ride with Melinda and, for a few minutes, it was as if they were teenagers again.

"You know, it's all going to work out somehow." Liz squeezed Melinda's arm before they got out of the car. "It has to. This town will find a way to survive, like always. So will the store. I mean, what's Prosper without Prosper Hardware?"

"I know. We have to stay positive. But some days, that's harder than others." Melinda reached for the slow cooker of cheese dip bundled in a box on the floor of the back seat. "We have a major fight ahead of us, but we can't let it spoil our family's Thanksgiving."

Liz led the way up the cobblestone walk. "Mom said that public hearing is going to be a long night. When is it, again?"

"Two weeks from Monday."

"How are the petitions doing?"

"We're just getting started. They began making the rounds in town yesterday, and we'll start passing them in the country on Monday. The more people who participate, the stronger showing we can make at the hearing. Look, there's Mom and Dad!" Melinda waved as Roger and Diane drove around the corner.

Liz held the side-porch door for her sister. "Mark will be here soon, then we'll all be together!"

Melinda was also looking forward to having everyone under one roof, even if it was only for a day. But for one second, she felt a pang of regret. If she and Chase were still together, this would have been his first holiday dinner with her family.

"Oh, Liz, it's been so long!" Miriam threw her arms around her younger niece, and her infectious smile snapped Melinda out her reverie. "Last Christmas seems like years ago, doesn't it? And the boys are growing so fast!"

The high-ceilinged kitchen was filled with a range of wonderful aromas, from the turkey roasting in the range to the pumpkin pies cooling on the side counter. Liam and Noah were in the living room with the rest of the family, but ran through the doorway when they spotted their mom.

"So, I have a question," Miriam asked her great-nephews. "Who is going to help me mash the potatoes?"

"I am! I'm the strongest." Liam, who was seven, was quick to respond.

"But I'm faster, I know it," said his little brother. Noah was only five, but his boundless energy was hard to miss.

"OK, then, we'll decide it with a flip of a coin."

After Liam was declared the winner, Liz settled him at the counter with a handheld masher. So Noah wouldn't feel left out, she asked him to help her set the dining-room table.

"They're so much fun to have around," Miriam said, then turned to Melinda and lowered her voice. "This is a big change for you. How are you holding up?"

"I'm hanging in there. I forgot how much energy they have. My peace and quiet's gone out the window, but it's for a good reason. And it's only for a few days."

After Frank and Roger agreed upon which football game they would watch after dinner, Frank took all the "menfolk," which Liam and Noah were proud to be counted among, out to his garage shop to show off his latest weathervane designs. He'd picked up metalworking to pass the time, and his creations were now in demand at Vicki's gift shop.

Of course, that left the women to finish preparing the feast. But Melinda didn't mind; it was a rare opportunity for the four of them to be together. Liz mentioned that she wanted to bring the boys into Prosper Hardware before they started for home the next morning.

"They're getting old enough to really appreciate the store, and what it means to our family." She opened the oven so Miriam could baste the turkey. "I'd love for them to pick out something, even if it's just a pair of gloves, so they can go up to the counter and make a purchase."

Aunt Miriam smiled, but there was a sadness in her brown eyes. "Black Friday will be crazy, as always, but we would love to have you."

No one wanted to say it, but as Melinda looked around at her relatives, she knew what they were thinking: What if Prosper Hardware's holiday seasons were numbered?

"We just got our first shipment of store shirts in children's sizes," she said quickly, trying to keep the conversation on safer ground. "We'll make sure the boys each get one. The tees have been so popular, it's definitely time to expand the clothing line."

Diane rummaged in a cabinet. "I'll cover the cost of the shirts as an early Christmas gift. Miriam, where is Mom's wooden platter? I'll get it washed and ready for the rolls."

"Check the top shelf, there on the right."

"Uncle Mark is here!" Liam slammed the front door in his rush to share the news. Diane hurried after her grandson, the heirloom plate quickly forgotten.

Liz raised an eyebrow at her sister. "Mark's thirty-four, but he's still her baby."

"What's new with him, anyway?" Miriam wanted to know. "I'm not on social media much, so I'm hopelessly out of the loop. Anything in particular that will make good conversation at dinner?"

"There's a new day job." Melinda shrugged as she sliced the German-chocolate cake Diane had brought. "Some insurance thing. He's bored with it, as usual. But I think his band had a good gig the other night, I saw some great photos online."

"The girlfriend is new, too," Liz added. "But really, that's not anything ... new."

Mark's smile lit up the room when he came through the entryway, Liam firmly attached to his uncle's hand. Diane had her arm around her son, and Roger clapped him on the back. "How was your flight?"

"Great, actually. Crowded, but I had a window seat."

Liz hugged her brother, then Melinda took her turn.

"It's great to be back, and to see everyone." Mark's sandy-blond hair, so much like how their father's used to be, was artfully tousled, as usual. But there were smudges under his blue eyes, and Melinda wasn't sure if they were from catching an early-bird flight. Had those extra lines on his face been there when he was home over the summer?

There wasn't time for Melinda to study her brother more closely, as he'd turned away to greet the rest of the family. Besides, it was time to bring the food out of the kitchen and make sure everyone found a chair around the Langes' generous dining-room table. The house was still decorated with faux-leaf garlands and synthetic pumpkins, giving it a festive air. Miriam had carefully ironed her burgundy damask tablecloth, and a wicker basket of tiny gourds served as a Thanksgiving centerpiece.

The group settled into comfortable silence as platters were passed and plates were heaped with food. Conversation slowly returned after the first bites were savored, and

Melinda was relieved the post-office dilemma was ignored in favor of lighter topics. The boys did their part, eager to share what they were learning in school and their hopes for what would be under the tree on Christmas morning.

Miriam eventually brought out the cake, pies and coffee. As she returned to her seat, Melinda saw Frank give his wife a barely visible nod. Miriam squared her shoulders and raised her chin.

What now? Suddenly, Melinda wasn't sure she could manage a slice of pumpkin pie.

There were tears in Miriam's eyes, and she looked to Frank for support. "Before we dig in, we have something to tell all of you."

"Aunt Miriam, no!" Liz gasped. "You can't close the store! Not yet! I know there's all those concerns about the post office, and what it could mean for the town, but please ..."

"We're not giving up on the store," Frank said gently. "No, it's far from time for that." Postures quickly relaxed around the table, but Liam and Noah still surveyed their elders with wide, questioning eyes.

Miriam leaned forward. "But there is going to be a big change around here. Frank and I plan to sell this house."

"You're moving out?" Diane stared at her sister in shock. "This has been your home for, what, over thirty years?"

"Thirty-three." Frank rubbed his chin. "Back in August. We hate to leave, but Miriam thinks it's for the best."

"We've discussed this. Both of us." Miriam gave her husband a look. "But I will say, I was the one to bring it up. This place requires so much upkeep; two stories, a big attic, the basement. And, it's far from energy efficient." She looked out the picture window toward the iron fence that marched around the property. "There's just too much yard work to do."

"I'm getting old," Frank muttered. "Old and feeble."

"Honey, that's not ..."

Roger jumped in before the bickering could escalate. "Sounds like it might be time to downsize, then. I'm sure you won't have any trouble getting it sold, it's a beautiful house."

"Yeah." Frank sighed. "It sure is. But it's not just that the house is too much work. We need to cut back financially. That way, if things get rocky with the store ..."

Frank didn't have to finish his thought.

Roger reached for Diane's hand. "No matter what happens, our family is still very blessed. We have each other, our friends, this community. And Prosper Hardware. I'm not ready to count us out. Not yet."

The dessert plates began to make their way around. Mark eagerly accepted a slice of apple-crumb pie, but his fork stopped in mid-air. "If you are going to sell this place, are you sure you can find something else in Prosper? I can't imagine there's a booming real-estate market in a town this small."

"You're right; it's not Austin, that's for sure." Frank had regained some of his usual good cheer. "But we do have a solid lead. Some friends of ours have a nice ranch over on Fourth Street, and they've decided to move to Charles City in the spring."

"Well, sounds like you have it all figured out." Diane let out a small sigh. "I guess things can't stay the same forever, can they?"

Melinda wasn't sure if her mom's reaction was one of resignation, or relief, or both. Frank and Miriam's news, while surprising, wasn't as dire as it could have been.

Even so, Melinda felt wistful as she started on her pie. Diane and Roger would host the extended family for Christmas, which meant today was probably their last holiday gathering at this house. A one-story home would be more practical for her aging aunt and uncle, of course, but why did things have to change?

"We'll find a Realtor after the holidays," Frank was saying, "see if we can drum up some interest in this place. But for now, let's talk about something else. So, Mark, how long will you be home? I'm guessing you'll fly back Saturday, or maybe Sunday?"

"I'm not exactly sure," Mark mumbled as he focused on his pie.

"Flying standby? This time of year?" Roger was surprised. "I thought you'd be able to get something for Monday, at least, since the rush will be over by then. Of course, I know you got that last-minute deal on the rental car. Probably good for a whole week if you need it."

"Oh, to be young and free." Frank grinned at his nephew. "Besides, I'm sure you're saving serious cash by being flexible. Roger and Diane, you raised him right."

Liz caught Melinda's eye across the table. In truth, Mark had always found it hard to hold on to his money.

"I'm not sure when I'm going back," Mark finally said. "I only got a one-way ticket."

Isaac frowned. "Surely there was something, even if you had to wait around a few days. I would think Minneapolis would have plenty of connecting flights."

"I don't know when I'm going back, OK?" Mark's voice was suddenly sharp, and the rest of the family stared at him. "Or if I ever will."

"What did you say?" Diane was aghast.

Roger frowned. "You don't mean that ..."

"I sure do." Mark threw up his hands. "I hate my job! Or at least, I did. I quit last week. I got tired of all those stuffy, corporate types. The band's two gigs for next month fell through, so I'm free to do whatever I want."

Melinda put down her fork. "But what about your apartment, all your stuff? And Katie ..."

"Kaylee. Her name's Kaylee."

"So, what about Kaylee, then?"

"What does it matter?" Mark crossed his arms. "Look, I need to live my own life, do my own thing. I need a change. I've given this a lot of thought, you know." This last comment was aimed at his parents, who were speechless. "I paid a few months' advance on the rent, it was cheaper than hiring movers and putting everything in storage. Until I can figure out what I really want to do, it was the best way."

No one said a word.

"What? Why are you all staring at me like that?"

"It's just ... a surprise," Diane finally said. "What are your plans, then?"

"Well, it's the holidays, right? I mean, if I'd gone back, I would've just turned around in a few weeks and came home for Christmas, anyway."

That wasn't necessarily true, Melinda knew, as her brother didn't visit very often. He'd returned in August for a family reunion, so she hadn't expected him to be home for Thanksgiving. This news was a surprise, to say the least, but maybe it wasn't as shocking as it first seemed. Mark had complained to her about his life when he was home during the summer, and she'd tried her best to offer some sisterly advice. Running away from your problems, she'd told him, was never the answer.

Back then, her words had been met with derision and contempt. He was watching her now, from across the table, waiting for her reaction.

Irritation burned in her chest. Mark might be the baby of the family, but why did he have to act like one? Did he ever think about anyone other than himself?

"So, you mean to stay at Dad and Mom's, then?" She tried to keep her voice neutral, but failed. "That's a whole month. Your old room's been an office, for several years ..."

"Don't worry, I'm not asking to stay with you." Mark's tone made it clear that while he hadn't heeded her advice, he certainly hadn't forgotten their conversation. "I'm sure Mom and Dad won't mind."

Liz's eyes flashed with anger. "You didn't even ask Mom and Dad, did you?"

Roger and Diane exchanged wary looks.

"Honey," Diane said gently, "you know you're always welcome at home. You caught us off guard, that's all."

"What about the car?" Uncle Frank asked. "Don't you have to get it back?"

"I got an open-ended lease. Anyway, I'm sure you're slammed at the store during the holidays, right? Most places hire extra help, and ..."

"What?" Liz beat Melinda to it. "First, you just decide to move in on Mom and Dad. Now you want Frank and Miriam to give you a job?"

"Just for a few weeks, part-time." Mark gave Aunt Miriam his widest smile. "I mean, if you're hiring, anyway."

Her aunt and uncle looked so uncomfortable that Melinda felt she must speak. "Sorry, we're not needing anyone. Esther's taken on some extra hours, is all."

"What's this 'we' stuff?" Mark leaned over the table. "Last time I was here, Frank and Miriam were running the store. I think if something had changed, I would have heard about it."

"That's enough," Roger said sternly.

Melinda looked away, but she could feel Miriam's shoulders stiffen beside her. Just last week, she'd signed the papers to officially join the store's board of directors. Frank and Miriam had asked her to do it, if nothing else so they would always have a majority vote on issues regarding the business. As for what it might mean in the future, Melinda wasn't quite sure.

It hadn't seemed like a big deal at the time and, with all the upheaval over the post office, she and her parents had yet to share the news with Liz and Mark.

Her sister wouldn't mind. But Mark? That might be something else entirely.

"I just work there," was all she said. "I'm just saying, I don't think there's any extra hours to be had."

"Well, this is great." Mark crossed his arms. "I mean, you all took Melinda in when she was laid off last year."

Gasps echoed around the table. Isaac motioned for the boys to join him in the living room. "That football game's going to be on in a few minutes. We'd better get our seats before the best ones are taken."

"Took. Her. In." Miriam's tone was low and cold. "Mark, I'm sorry to say this, but you're way out of line. Frank was in the hospital. I was half out of my mind, trying to run back and forth. We didn't know if he'd live through the surgery. Or if he did, if he'd ever be able to work again."

"It was supposed to be temporary," Melinda reminded her brother. "I didn't plan to stay."

"But you did. And they kept you on, right? Benefits, everything ..."

"I had a place to live!" She couldn't believe what she was hearing. "I was on my own, I wasn't ..."

"I won't stay at Mom and Dad's forever, you know!"

"Frank's practically retired," Roger told his son. "No one gave your sister a job out of charity. I don't know what you thought was going on here, but ..."

"Oh, I see." Mark wasn't swayed. "Is that it? Because I've been so far away, for so long, I don't get to be involved in things?" No one said a word, and he suddenly seemed more hurt than angry.

"I'm a part of this family, too." He pushed back his chair and looked at Liz. "What about you? Nothing to say?"

The set of her jaw told Mark what he needed to know.

"Fine. I know when I'm not wanted." He marched into the parlor, where the guests had laid their coats, then skirted through the kitchen to the side porch, avoiding his family's stares of shock and surprise as he stormed out.

"I can't believe this!" Liz turned to her parents. "Are you going to let this go on? He's just going to stay with you until, when? Until he gets bored with that, too?"

"He's going to have to pay rent," Roger told Diane. She nodded, but seemed to still be in a daze. "And a share of the groceries, the utilities. I guess he could have Melinda's old room, since she doesn't need it."

"That's right." Frank nodded. "She doesn't need it. Never did. Melinda, don't let him get to you. You came back, but you did it the right way. Besides, you're made of far stronger stuff than Mark."

Diane flinched, but said nothing.

"He needs to make his own way," Miriam told her sister. "I'd set some firm ground rules, if I were you. But I know how you love to have your children around this time of the year. I'd say you're going to get your wish."

* 7 *

Melinda looked out a few minutes later, and saw Mark's rental car was gone. "He's an adult," Diane said as she rubbed her temples. "I'm not going to call him, try to convince him to come back and have a perfect Thanksgiving afternoon with the family."

"He has a key, he can get in the house." Roger crossed his arms. "We'll deal with him later. Frank, let's get into the living room; we're missing that game."

There was just enough daylight left when Melinda's guests returned to the farm for Isaac and the boys to play a little touch football, with Hobo serving as coach, cheerleader and referee. Liam and Noah were eager to help with evening chores, and proud of their efforts to "get all the animals ready for bed," as little Noah told Melinda when they started back across the yard.

Isaac, Liz and the boys were still asleep when Melinda made her rounds outside the next morning. Liz's family had breakfast with Roger and Diane and then, as promised, stopped at Prosper Hardware on their way home.

Uncle Frank proudly showed Isaac and the boys around the store, and Esther took the register so Melinda could spend a few more moments with Liz.

"Mark just sat there, sullen and distant, while we tried to make things cheerful," Liz reported with a frown. "He barely said two words to us the whole time. I don't know about Mom, but I suspect Mark and Dad got into it last night."

"So he's really staying, then?"

"I guess so, at least for now."

Liam ran over with a toy truck in his hands. "This is so cool! Can I get it?" He reached into his jeans' pocket. "I want to pay for it, myself."

"Of course, it's your money." Liz beamed proudly, then gave her sister a wry smile. "Too bad Mark's not here to take a few financial lessons, huh? Noah, what do you have?"

"Uncle Frank found my size!" The little boy held up a dark-green tee sporting the store's logo. "Can I wear it, right away?"

"Only if you can get it over your sweater, which I doubt you can." Liz ruffled her youngest son's hair. "It's too cold. But you can model it for us when you get home."

The boys got in line with the other customers, and their wide eyes took in the sights and sounds of the bustling store as they waited to place their purchases on the oak counter. Esther, who was wearing a Santa's hat and a red sweatshirt decorated with snowflakes, helped the boys aim the handheld scanner at their purchases.

"This brings back so many memories." Liz turned nostalgic. "I always felt like such a big, grown-up girl, handing Grandpa Shrader my candy bar or peanuts, and counting out my coins. Remember how we would roam the aisles for what seemed like hours? It was like we had the whole world, right here in this store. What else could we need?"

"Grandpa always gave us an extra dime or quarter after we helped him count out our change." Melinda picked up the memory. "He made such a show of it, pretended he was sneaking something past Grandma."

"As if she wasn't in on it. Oh, how I miss them! What is it about this store that makes it feel like that was only yesterday?"

"Maybe it's because the place has barely changed in a hundred years." Melinda glanced at the pressed-tin ceiling.

"Or maybe, we're just getting old."

"I'll vote for the former."

"Just think, Noah and Liam are the sixth generation to be part of this store." Melinda paused to return the warm greeting of one regular customer. "Could our ancestors have ever imagined it would last this long, or be this successful? I just hope that ..."

An unspoken thought passed between the sisters.

"Don't say it." Liz gripped Melinda's arm. "Don't. Not today. Let's just enjoy every minute we have."

"Jerry keeps saying the same thing. Says we're going to have the biggest and best Christmas this town has ever seen. The city's lights are up, and tomorrow's decoration swap promises to be a success. I dropped off a ton of stuff Wednesday; it felt so good to let it all go! And in a few days, I think this community's going to be aglow with holiday cheer."

"I wish we could get back to see it." Liz sighed and glanced at her phone. "I suppose we should get on the road. As you know, we're going to Isaac's parents' for Christmas this year. Be sure to post lots of pictures for us."

Aunt Miriam hurried over to give her a departing niece a final hug. "You'll be here in spirit, like always. Doesn't matter where any of us are, at any one time. This store is our home."

***

The next morning was even busier than the day before. Small Business Saturday brought crowds of shoppers to Prosper's Main Street, as regional residents were in the mood for a much-different experience after braving the crowds at the malls and big-box retailers. Just before noon, Melinda found a chance to sneak next door and check out the scene at Meadow Lane.

Vicki's gift shop was tricked out with what had to be thousands of clear lights. Burgundy-plaid ribbons cascaded over swags of greenery, and the fragrance of scented candles and fresh-brewed coffee greeted Melinda when she stepped through the door.

"I'd ask how your morning was," Melinda told Vicki as she stepped aside to allow a group of women to pass by, "but I can see that it's been a huge success."

"We had over a hundred visitors in just the first two hours!" Vicki clapped her hands with glee. "I just wish I'd hired an extra part-timer for the holidays. If it stays like this, I don't know if we'll be able to keep up. I guess it's not too late to spread the word."

"Well, I know someone looking for some extra cash." Melinda laughed as she imagined Mark dusting ceramic figurines and aligning rainbow-hued rows of candles. "But I'm not sure he's quite the help you need. Everything looks so beautiful! Are you going to do more decorating before that magazine crew arrives in a few weeks?"

Melinda couldn't imagine where Vicki might add more holiday cheer, but given her friend's penchant for going overboard, it was a fair question.

"Not sure, we'll see how much time I have. I'm thinking the left-side window could use a little more zing, don't you think?"

"Oh, I think it's lovely, just as it is." Liz's visit to Prosper Hardware was still fresh in Melinda's mind, and it had her thinking about the future as well as the past.

"I hate to say this, especially on a day like today, but have you talked to the editor about what's going on here in town? The feature isn't going to be out for almost a year, and ..."

"You're starting to sound like Arthur." Vicki waved it all away, but her smile was a little too bright. "Worry, worry, toil and trouble. All new businesses are a crapshoot, right? Besides, Jerry says we can beat this thing. We'll find a way forward, even if we lose the post office. I let myself have one sleepless night about the whole mess, then decided that was enough."

Something caught Vicki's eye, and she was eager to change the subject. "Oh, there's the editor of the Swanton paper." She patted her already-smooth hair and wove through the crowd, and Melinda followed.

"It's never too early for some good publicity," Vicki said over her shoulder. "And I figured, it's the perfect trial run for when the national media arrives. Sharon, my dear, I'm so glad to see you! Oh, yes, we've been swamped today, the response has been incredible ..."

Melinda let herself out, and was glad to take a gulp of the cold, clear air when she reached the sidewalk. Maybe things weren't as dire as they seemed. Vicki was obviously determined to stay on the sunny side of the street. Could she find the courage to do the same?

***

If the crowds swarming city hall late that afternoon were any indication of the town's mood, most residents were still determined to make the season merry and bright.

The start of the decoration swap had been delayed until two, to give people time to drop off the last of their leftovers that morning. By the time Melinda arrived just after four, shoppers were packed shoulder-to-shoulder in the council chambers and spilled into the kitchen, where more festive freebies were scattered on the metal table and across the worn counters.

"Can you believe all this loot?" Nancy's brown eyes were tired behind her glasses, but even the extra hours of sorting and arranging couldn't take the spring out of her step. "It's like Santa's workshop in here! Trees, garlands, lawn ornaments. Anything you want, I think we have it."

"That's going to be my problem." Melinda almost had to shout to be heard over the chatter echoing through the building, as well as the holiday tunes Jerry was blasting from the one set of speakers the city owned. "I really don't need to take anything home with me. I just wanted to stop in, see how it's going."

"Sure, you did." Nancy smirked. "See if you can resist. There's so many cute things up for grabs."

There was a commotion in the far corner, where two women each had one hand on an elaborate wreath festooned with purple and red ribbons. "You'd better step in," Melinda told Nancy. "Wouldn't be very festive if a brawl broke out."

Thanks to Vicki's vision, the decorations were arranged so attendees felt like they were strolling through a holiday boutique rather than crawling through someone's garage. Similar items were grouped together, and every piece was displayed to show off its unique features.

Synthetic Christmas trees were lined up by height along one long wall of the council chambers, and boxes of ornaments were organized by color on several tables.

Richard Everton, the contractor helping with the community center project, had installed dozens of nails in another wall to create a pleasing gallery from the wide selection of wreaths. The room was in desperate need of a paint job, Nancy had told Melinda, so the resulting holes would be spackled after the first of the year.

Light strings had been wound around lengths of cardboard, and Frank helped bargain-hunters plug into a power strip to ensure everything worked properly. Rolled-up garlands waited on another table, and every remaining flat surface was filled with ceramic villages, nativity sets, candles, snow globes and more.

Melinda was in the kitchen, trying to resist a miniature building that resembled the church down the road from her farm, when Auggie burst through the back door.

"Happy holidays!" He gave the end of his Santa hat a little flip. "See something you have to have?"

"I already told Nancy, I don't need anything." She pointed at the little white church. "But I could see this sitting on a shelf in Horace and Wilbur's apartment. I bet it would bring back good memories for them."

"Well, snatch it up. Quick, before someone beats you to it. Have you been out back yet?"

"Out back?" She clutched the collectible close. Auggie was right; a woman hovering nearby gave Melinda a disappointed look before she moved away.

"You mean, there's more?"

"Oh, yeah!" The little boy in Auggie could hardly contain his excitement. "Light-up reindeer, fake trees in porch pots, inflatable Santas, all kinds of stuff."

"Do Miriam a favor, then. Try to keep Frank from hauling anything home, OK? This place is dangerous. I'd better head out before I cave in again."

She stopped to chat with some people admiring the rows of mantel stockings, then spotted Father Perkins from the Catholic church eyeing the selection of nativity displays. Cardboard boxes had been set out for shoppers to cart away their loot, and the one in his arms was already half full.

"I guess I'm not surprised to see you over here." She pointed at the figurines. "Find any you like?"

"Oh, yes." Father Perkins' blue eyes twinkled. With his white hair and beard, he could almost be mistaken for Santa. "Found one to add to my collection at the rectory, and a second for my office. I know you love cats. Did you see that one over there?"

He pointed to the back row of displays, and her jaw dropped. "Wow, look at that!"

"A clowder of cats celebrating Christmas." Father Perkins leaned in. "Clowder means group, you know. I think it has your name on it."

She picked up one of the wise men, a gray tabby with a gilt-edged box in its tiny paws. A miniature orange kitten, wrapped in a white blanket, slept in the ceramic manger.

"I have never seen anything like this. I don't know, I don't need it. I already have a nativity set."

"Who cares?" Father Perkins chuckled. "That's half of the fun. Look, it even still has the box. Just clear off a shelf somewhere. The real Joseph and Mary weren't picky about where they stayed, remember? I can't imagine these will be, either."

Melinda grinned like a fool as she packed up her new treasure. The holiday spirit was certainly contagious in here. She added a few dollars to the donation box, whose proceeds would benefit the community center project, and found her

way to where Nancy, Bev Stewart and Sam Hayward were
visiting by city hall's front counter.

Sam owned the insurance office down the street, and Bev
and her husband farmed northeast of town. Both were
members of the library's book club, and the four friends soon
found themselves in a discussion of that month's selection.

"I think we'd better change the subject," Bev finally said
with a chuckle. "Nancy, isn't this against the rules?"

"Oh, I suppose it is. But there's just so much to discuss! I
can't wait until ..."

"Hey!" shouted one man standing by the front window.
"What's going on across the street?"

"Sheriff's car just pulled up!" Another man popped
through the front door, his ruddy face bright from more than
the cold air outside. Prosper didn't have a police department,
so the sight of any law enforcement in town was something of
note. Or, given the sudden interest shown by several people in
the room, at least a welcome distraction.

Melinda tried to get a better look, then stepped away. One
of the drawbacks to small-town life was the constant
surveillance conducted by those who had nothing much else
to do. She, at least, would try to keep her curiosity in check.

"I hope everything's OK." Nancy's brow furrowed as she
glanced toward the council chambers. Jerry hadn't suddenly
appeared, nor had any members of the town's volunteer
emergency crew.

"I don't see anyone rushing across the street to assist.
Maybe it's not too serious." Melinda couldn't help it; she
hurried to peek out at the scene. "Hey, I know the deputy.
That's Jen Fuller's husband." Jen had attended Swanton High
School with Melinda and now lived in Prosper, which meant
Steve often drew the assignments in this community.

"Well, I know he can't drink on the job," someone said
with a chuckle as Steve entered the Watering Hole. "Wonder
what all the fuss is about."

More residents gathered at the windows, and others
lingered on the sidewalk in front of city hall. A few appeared

to be involved in conversations, but Melinda sensed they all had one eye on the Watering Hole's front door.

When Steve reappeared a few minutes' later, he had an elderly man in custody. Gasps echoed around the room, and Melinda's was as sharp as the rest. "Hey, that's Bart Wildwood!"

Nancy leaned in to hear what Melinda was saying, as the room had erupted in jeers and shouts of speculation. "He's your neighbor, right? The one who ..."

"Yeah." Melinda crossed her arms. "That's him."

She'd met Bart last summer when Angie asked her to hand-deliver invites to the neighborhood church's women's luncheon. Bart and his wife lived in a rundown house south of Melinda's farm, a place as unwelcoming as the sneer on Bart's haggard face when he found Melinda on his kitchen stoop. Mabel later told her Bart had a drinking problem and a bad temper, and Melinda had since gone out of her way to not cross paths with him again.

Steve had allowed Bart to pull on his dirty coat and worn knit cap before placing him in handcuffs. Doug Kirkpatrick, the bar's owner, held the squad car's back door open as Steve tried to usher Bart inside.

"Why doesn't he just get in the car?" A man at the window shook his head. "Drunk and disorderly is bad enough; resisting arrest won't help his case."

With his prisoner finally secured in the back seat, Steve drove away. Nancy and Melinda exchanged looks of concern.

"Has this happened before?" Nancy frowned. "His poor wife. How does she deal with him?"

"I don't know." Melinda suddenly felt guilty. "Mabel says Marge has some memory problems, and neither of them is in the best of health. I've been avoiding them, I have to say. Maybe that hasn't been the right way to handle it."

Melinda walked slowly back to her car, the thrill of her newfound treasures momentarily forgotten and Nancy's question weighing on her mind. Marge surely could use some support. Bart, too, although he was probably too proud to admit it. In any case, Melinda was about to hear what had happened.

Jessie, Doug's wife, saved the scraps from the restaurant's salad bar for Melinda's sheep, and she needed to pick up the latest batch before she went home.

The Watering Hole was packed and noisy when she slipped inside. It was Saturday evening, after all. The tables were starting to fill with early dinner guests, and Bart's vacated stool at the bar had already been claimed.

The Kirkpatricks, who were only in their thirties, had taken over the place a few years ago after the previous owner passed away.

The restaurant's walls had been painted a brighter hue, and fresh curtains draped the window frames. While Doug had expanded the menu somewhat, it still tilted toward burger baskets and diner mainstays like fried chicken and hot-beef sandwiches.

Jessie was busing tables, her dark curls pulled up in a ponytail. As soon as Melinda caught her eye, she pointed toward the back.

"It's busy in here today," Melinda said once they were behind a closed door. "Sorry I didn't get over here earlier, we were swamped at the store. And I wanted to stop at the decoration swap before things were picked over."

She'd already decided not to bring up Bart. Especially since Jessie, true to her laid-back nature, seemed unfazed by whatever had happened.

"We had a record day Thursday for the catering!" Her brown eyes were bright with pride as she opened an industrial-sized refrigerator. "And it's been crazy-busy both yesterday and today. That means Annie and her friends are going to be really thankful for all the leftovers. There's two totes, this time."

"Oh, that's great! On both fronts."

"There's lettuce of course, and green-bean ends and, oh, pounds of potato and carrot peelings. Did you pull up out back? It'll save you some steps. Here, I'll get the door."

They took out one tote, then came back for the rest of the greens. "I know you live west of town," Jessie said as they brought out the last batch. "But are you to the north, or the south?"

"Oh, south of the blacktop."

"Do you know Bart Wildwood, by chance?"

Melinda blinked at this sudden turn in conversation. If Jessie needed to talk, she would listen. "Sort of. Bart is ... well, he's a little difficult to get to know."

"Yeah," Jessie said ruefully. "I'm sure everyone across the street saw the little commotion we had this afternoon. Doug hated to call the cops, but Bart grew belligerent when we cut him off, shouting and swearing. He'd been in here since eleven, when we opened. It's happened before." Jessie shook her head. "Other times, there was a friend around, one of the regulars who was sober enough to take Bart's keys and give him a ride home. But not today."

"I guess I'm glad he has a few friends to look out for him, at least."

"It's not just the drinking, although that's our biggest worry as the owners of this place." Jessie leaned against the car and zipped up her fleece jacket. "Bart seems ... really down. The holidays are here now, of course, and things seem to be getting worse, not better. Do they have any family around here, any kids? They'd be grown now, I'd guess."

"They're adults, yes, and I think there's grandchildren, but ... I don't know what's going on there. Some of our neighbors have tried to reach out to them, and people from our local church, too, but he just shoos everyone away."

"It's so sad." Jessie shook her head. "I guess it just goes to show, you never know what other people are dealing with. Especially this time of year."

* 8 *

Bart and Marge's troubles weighed on Melinda's mind as she marked the miles out of Prosper. Not just because of what had transpired that afternoon, but because of her evening plans.

She'd invited her closest neighbors over for supper, a simple potluck that would allow everyone one last chance to enjoy their leftovers from Thursday's Thanksgiving feasts. It would be a fun way to wrap up one holiday and look forward to the next, and there was also a bit of business to discuss.

Last year, the neighbors helped a local family that had fallen on hard times. The project had been as rewarding as it was unexpected, and there was talk about making this an annual effort. Melinda assumed several ideas would be batted about as the neighbors feasted on turkey and pie, and wondered what might be decided about this year's direction.

What if they tried to help Bart and Marge? But what, exactly, could they do?

Melinda decided to bring it up, at least, and get the group's feedback. One thing she didn't doubt: Word of Bart's arrest had surely spread around the township by now, so she wouldn't be feeding the flames of gossip by sharing what she'd witnessed.

Hobo ran out his doggie door to greet her, and she had to block him with one elbow to keep him from jumping into the back of the car. The totes of vegetable scraps had his nose working overtime.

"Sorry, those are for the sheep. Jessie's really spoiling them, this time. I guess they are getting their Thanksgiving feast two days' late, right?"

Her critters now expected a bucket of these snacks once or twice a week, and the greens were especially welcome now that the ground was frozen and the grass had turned brown.

The ewes charged to their troughs when they saw the first tote appear in the main aisle of the barn, and Stormy and Sunny were circling it by the time Melinda returned with the second. To keep the cats out of the way, she tossed them a few pieces of lettuce. Which they promptly rejected.

"See, I knew you wouldn't like it. Annie, just a minute! There are more potato peelings in here somewhere. Let the others get a few, at least."

Part of the last bin was saved for the chickens, who clucked with excitement as they pecked at their treats. As she started back for the house, the collar of her chore coat raised against the cold, Melinda pondered how her plans for this evening's celebration had changed in the past few weeks. She first had the idea back in October, when the glossy hearth-and-home magazines in her mailbox began to dedicate their pages to picture-perfect holiday parties.

Initially, she'd planned to purchase new table linens and candles, and create an elaborate menu filled with fresh takes on seasonal dishes. And then, there were the place cards, and the centerpiece ...

The post-office debacle put all of that on the back burner. Times were already hard, and the uncertainty that now cloaked her little community deemed such an elaborate party unnecessary at best and tone-deaf at worst.

Instead, she went in the opposite direction: A potluck of leftovers washed down with coffee and hot chocolate, served on a brown-and-white checked tablecloth left behind in one of the built-in buffet's drawers. The Schermann ladies had carefully parceled out the family's heirloom pieces, but left the work-a-day ones at the farm. And Melinda, with a grateful heart and a love of history, used them any chance she could.

Her neighbors had eagerly agreed to this meal plan. Mabel cooked a larger-than-usual turkey for her family on Thursday with tonight's party in mind. A container of cranberry-and-orange salad waited in Melinda's refrigerator, along with half of the apple-crumb pie from Miriam's feast. Other attendees pledged to bring more salads and desserts, two kinds of potatoes, hot vegetables, and lots of gravy.

"We are going to have a serious spread, because it's the last day any of it will be safe to eat," she explained to Hazel and Grace as they followed her into the downstairs bedroom. That space had been mostly turned over to Hobo and the cats, so its closet door was rarely opened for inspection. But Melinda needed the extra leaves for the dining-room table, and the girls were eager to scoot around her shoes and sniff the dusty corners.

"All of you kitties and Hobo will get your own turkey feast at the end of the night," she told Grace and Hazel, who howled in protest when their closet access was taken away so soon. "You can have as much as you like, since no one will want to take their leftovers home."

Expanding the table was easier with two people but, like many singles, Melinda had devised a way to do it herself. She moved two chairs to one of the short sides and pushed them tight against the table's edge, which gained her just enough force to slide the other end across with ease.

There wasn't much else to do to get ready. The tablecloth had already been washed, and its tumble in the dryer had smoothed most of the wrinkles. She swept the worst of the muddy paw tracks off the back porch's painted floor, and removed her coats from the hooks inside the door. Fresh towels were added to the small downstairs bathroom, and the kitchen counters got one last swipe.

Melinda changed her shirt, started a fire in the hearth, and then cleared a space for the cat nativity on top of the right-hand bookcase.

Hobo had to sniff each character before it was added to the scene, and Grace jumped from the back of Melinda's reading chair to reach the display. Every piece was evaluated and apparently approved, as Grace's enthusiastic cheek rubs nearly sent Mary and the shepherd flying to the floor.

"OK, maybe they aren't going to live there the entire season." Melinda shook her head. "They might have to move inside the bookcase to survive. We'll leave them out for the party, at least."

Ed and Mabel were the first to arrive. Mabel's white curls were all in place, and she sported a wine-colored top that neatly matched her lipstick. A crisp plaid shirt was Ed's one attempt to dress up his lanky frame. "Mabel said I ought to change my shoes," he told Melinda as he fussed over Hobo, who was waiting inside the kitchen door to greet his guests. "But I couldn't find the dress socks that go with them."

"Never mind, those are clean enough. But you can kick them into the corner if you like, just as you would at home. Here, Mabel, I'll take that pan. The oven is hot. Does the turkey need more water before it goes in?"

"There's plenty of pan juices in there, but maybe add a bit to make sure things don't dry out. Everything's in slices and chunks, it shouldn't take long. I have more stuff in the car. Oh, there's Angie and Nathan and the kids!"

The Hensleys lived just around the mile section, north and east of Melinda's farm. Three small children and a large farming operation kept the young couple on their toes. Angie had also started a small bakery business, and was thrilled when Vicki asked her to provide the sweet treats offered at Meadow Lane's coffee bar.

Melinda had the honor of holding Blake, who was just four months old, while his parents unloaded their car. Emma and Allison rushed through their greetings so they could run upstairs to find Grace and Hazel. The young cats were sometimes shy around visitors, and had likely decamped to the safe space under Melinda's bed, but they secretly adored the two little girls that lived just up the road.

"This was such a great idea." Angie handed Mabel half of a pecan pie. "There's some salads in the cooler, too. I hope everyone is starving, since I don't want to take even one spoonful home. I need my refrigerator back."

John and Linda Olson soon arrived with Dylan, their only son who still lived at home. Will and Helen Emmerson, an elderly couple who lived up on the blacktop, weren't far behind. Melinda's farmhouse was soon filled with chatter and laughter. The buffet was set out on the kitchen counters, and everyone gathered around the dining-room table with full plates and contented smiles.

They ate in silence for several minutes. Melinda was eager to try some of the less-traditional dishes, which included a spinach-blue cheese salad and a corn casserole. There were two kinds of stuffing, too, and other sides both hot and cold. The kitchen table was loaded down with parts of pies and stray pieces of cake.

Will finally pushed back from the table. "More coffee? I'll bring the pot around."

"I better slow down." John set his fork aside for a moment. "Need to save room for some of that pie. Mabel, was that one of your famous coconut cakes I saw out there?"

"The last three slices. The kids and grandkids nearly polished it off."

"Well, there's really four," Ed admitted. "But one's at home in the fridge, for later." He grinned at his wife. "What? It'll be a few weeks before you make another one, and then I might have to wait for months."

Helen accepted a coffee refill from her husband, then smiled at her neighbors. "So, while we're stuffing ourselves, should we talk about who could use our help this holiday season?"

"Last year's project was so rewarding." Mabel scooped up the last spoonful of green-bean casserole. "I'd love to do it again. Any ideas?"

Several options were shared. The closest food pantry was in Swanton, and it was always looking for donations. But

John, who was a member of the local Kiwanis Club, reported that group already had a significant food drive under way. All the local churches were doing something, as usual, whether it was a clothing collection or a toy-donation program.

"Should we wait until after the holidays?" Angie wondered. "There's always a need, and this is the time of year when many people do more than usual."

Ed nodded slowly. "I hate to say it, but if this post office deal goes through, next year's likely to be worse around here, not better. The drought is over, but not before it affected so many people's pocketbooks."

Mabel shared her husband's concerns. "I'm afraid you're right, dear. Those petitions are going around, and the response is encouraging so far, but it may not be enough to save the post office."

"I say we do as much as we can, as often as we can," Linda suggested. "Giving doesn't have to happen only at the holidays."

"There's always a need for monetary donations." Nathan started on a piece of cranberry dessert. "But that's something we can all do, on our own. It would be nice to find someone around here who is often overlooked, someone who maybe wouldn't have much of a Christmas otherwise, and make it special for them."

Mabel nodded. "I agree. The trouble is, some people are too proud to ask for help. They don't want charity. Melinda, any ideas? You see so many people at the store, day-in and day-out."

Emma and Allison were listening intently, as was Dylan. He might already be aware of Bart and Marge's troubles, but the little girls didn't need to know.

"Hmm, I'm not sure, right off hand," was all Melinda said. "But I'll ask Frank and Miriam. And Auggie."

Will chuckled. "Auggie's got a bead on just about everyone around here, whether they know it or not. There might be someone who's down on their luck; or just lonely, if they don't have family nearby."

Angie gave her girls permission to leave the table, and Emma and Allison dutifully carried their plates into the kitchen before running back upstairs to play with Grace and Hazel. Once they were out of earshot, Melinda knew it was time to speak. "Well, I don't know if this would backfire on us, but there is someone I've been thinking about."

News of Bart's arrest had already spread around the neighborhood. Apparently, one of Will's longtime friends had been out in front of city hall when the incident happened. "It's a terrible shame. But I guess it's not the first time he's caused trouble in there."

"Doug and Jessie were right to call the sheriff, no matter how embarrassing it must have been for Bart," Angie commented. "You'd like to think this might show him he has a problem."

"That's not likely, I'm sorry to say." John shook his head. "He and Marge need help, that's for sure, but I doubt this will change anything. I try to stop by once in a while, just to say hello. My dad used to do the same, and then when he and Mom moved to town, it just seemed like the thing to do. Bart's a crusty old bear; and poor Marge, I don't know how good her memory is these days."

"How she puts up with him is beyond me," Mabel said sadly. "Neither of their kids have much to do with them, anymore. I can't imagine their holidays are going to be very happy this year. Or any year, for that matter."

Ed leaned back in his chair. "So, the question is: How do you help people who don't want help?"

Helen sighed. "Oh, if someone could just come up with a good answer for that one. But I don't think it's ever going to happen."

"I really wish we could do something for Bart and Marge," Melinda added, "but I have a feeling he'd just chase us off."

Nathan crossed his arms. "And maybe with a shotgun, if he's on a bender."

"He's done that before?" Melinda raised her eyebrows. "Seriously?"

"Not me, but another neighbor, once, a few years back. I hate to be cynical, but I don't think Bart's going to want any Christmas cheer unless it comes in a bottle."

The group fell silent again. As Melinda studied the kind faces of her neighbors, she sensed they also felt the storm of emotions present in her heart: Gratitude for her many blessings, compassion for those who were struggling, and a yearning to make things better, if they could.

Finally, Ed let out a long sigh. "Well, I don't think we'll solve all the world's problems tonight. I guess I'll just get myself a slice of pumpkin pie."

"Might as well bring the whole thing in here." Angie patted her stomach. "I mean, both halves, or whatever is left. We'll finish it off, one way or another."

With plans for their charity effort abandoned, talk turned to everyone's holiday plans. There was so much to look forward to in the coming weeks, and the mood around the table soon improved.

The neighborhood ladies would gather a week from Monday to bake cookies, and there was Prosper's holiday festival to look forward to. Angie, who was on the Sunday school committee at the Lutheran church down the road, was once again in charge of the children's Christmas program. As she described her efforts to craft angel wings that might stay aloft through an entire service, Melinda's thoughts turned back to Bart and Marge.

Any big overture of charity would be met with discomfort and disdain, but was there something else she could do? Dropping off a plate of cookies, or even just mailing them a holiday card, had a better chance of being accepted.

Maybe the obvious answer wasn't the only one. There had to be some other way to brighten someone's holiday. But for now, she'd just enjoy this time with her friends. Mabel soon urged Melinda to take the last slice of coconut cake, and she wasn't about to turn it down.

* 9 *

Melinda checked her phone again, then set it aside and took a deep breath.

"This is not a date," she whispered. Then she ran one hand over her hair, which had received more attention this morning than it had in several weeks. "We need to talk about the clinic grants, and Karen is coming, too. Nope, not a date."

But was that actually the problem? That Melinda wished this meeting with Josh was more than a friendly lunch? If so, what was she going to do about that?

The bells chimed above the coffee shop's door, and there he was. Josh pushed back the hood of his parka, and pulled off his knit cap. The place was mostly full and within seconds, the eyes of nearly every woman in the room turned toward the handsome man who'd just appeared in their midst. Melinda could even feel their collective swoon.

Or was that just her own emotions? No, really, she didn't feel anything. Anything at all.

And then, one by one, the women's gazes shifted toward Melinda. Because Josh had spotted her, and was moving her way with a warm smile. Arrows of curiosity and jealousy were now aimed at her from across the room, and her stomach flipped over as she pretended to study the menu.

Where. Is. Karen? If she would just get here, the stares might stop.

"Hey there." Josh dropped into the other side of the booth and unzipped his coat. "Sorry I'm late. This morning's surgery ran over, and then a parakeet came in."

"A parakeet?"

"Yeah." Josh's brown eyes sparkled with humor. "Big Bird hasn't been eating well lately, and his owner's worried. I'm trying to save her a trip to the specialist in Ames. Ran blood work, we'll know soon if there's anything going on there."

Melinda's phone beeped. At last, a text from Karen. Whether it was good news, though, Melinda wasn't sure. *Farm visit's running over. Can't make it. Whatever the two of you want to do is fine.*

"Karen won't be coming. She's stuck on a call."

"Oh, that's too bad." Josh didn't seem the slightest bit concerned. "I think we can sort things out on our own, right?"

"Sure." She returned his smile. "I think she's out by Eagle River. Maybe it's just as well, that's quite a drive and the snow's really starting to come down."

"We can run through these grants quick, if you want. Don't want you to have trouble getting back to the store."

"Oh, I'm in no hurry," Melinda said, a little too quickly, then made herself take a pause. "I'm off today, so I'll just be heading home after I run a few errands."

"Good, then we don't have to rush." Josh picked up the other menu from the rack. "I've lived in Swanton for almost nine months now, and I don't come in here as often as I should. I'm starving. What do you recommend?"

They took turns at the counter so their table wouldn't be snatched away. As soon as they were both settled back in their booth, Melinda pulled a stack of papers from her tote and they began to review more than a dozen grant programs that could benefit the cat clinics. The events had been halted until spring, due to the unpredictable winter weather, so there was plenty of time to find financial support.

"All of these look promising." Josh paused to take the first bite from his chicken club sandwich. "But the national organizations seem to offer the largest grants."

Melinda hid a smirk behind her turkey panini, as the waitress had given her a "way to go" raised eyebrow when she delivered their sandwiches. Maybe Patricia Beck was right; maybe the "acceptable man" shortage around here was worse than Melinda thought. But then, Josh had that perfect mix of smarts, charm, and good looks. His hair looked a little different today, maybe shorter? No, he had just put some product in it. Why would he make such an effort? Especially since this wasn't ...

He was staring at her, waiting for her to respond to ... something. She had to focus on the conversation at hand. She wasn't an airhead; now wasn't the time to start acting like one. "Oh, sorry. What?"

"The grants." He tapped the stack of documents. "Which ones do you prefer?"

"Hmm." She reached for a potato chip to gain a few more seconds. "We won't know for a few weeks yet if that first application will be approved. Let's just pretend we haven't tried for it, at least for now. I don't think it's a good idea to get our hopes up."

That could also apply to the rest of her life right now, but she let that thought pass.

"As for these, I think we should go for a good mix. The national pet food company's program is very competitive, but it has the biggest payout. Besides, it sounds like if you get one, you're more likely to get a second, and a third."

"Great! That one's a yes." He set the form aside.

She wiped her hands on her paper napkin and reached for another document. "This state nonprofit is a big advocate of programs like ours, especially new ones. Our chances are good. But we need to pick some grassroots groups, too."

"That's what I was thinking." Josh shuffled the pile. "It would be an insult if we don't request funds from the ones in this region. Their grants don't amount to much, but we're practically a lock. We should be building relationships with those organizations, anyway, to expand our network of partners. Who knows where it all might lead?"

The question hung in the air between them for a second.

I'm wondering about more than just the grants, Melinda thought. *Maybe I shouldn't, but I am.*

"Well, I think we have a good start on this," was all she said. "I'll fill Karen in, pull the stats we need, and draft the cover letters. Some of these are due in January; I'd like to get them all firmed up before Christmas."

"It's a busy time of year. Is that too much for you to take on? Let me know what I can do to help."

"Thanks, but I think I can manage." She sighed. "Actually, this might be a good way to get my mind off everything else. I'm not sure the holidays are going to be as wonderful as they were last year."

Melinda had been looking everywhere for a reliable source of holiday cheer. But on most days, it seemed to elude her. She caught glimpses of it in the glossy catalogs that appeared in her mailbox, and in the saccharine-sweet movies that had dominated the airwaves for weeks. But those moments were fleeting, and too hollow for a season that was shaping up to be less than merry.

"That trouble with the post office sure puts a damper on things, doesn't it?" Josh's eyes filled with concern. "Everyone's talking about it, even here in Swanton. I bet it has you really thinking about the future, huh?"

"I try not to, actually." She looked away and out the window, to where the flakes were falling faster now. "But it's not just the post office problem. My family's sort of in upheaval these days, and not only because of our worries about the store."

Why was she telling Josh this? But he was listening, and she felt compelled to continue.

"My brother ... actually, my baby brother," she added with a wry lift of one eyebrow, "came home from Austin for Thanksgiving and announced he's planning to stay. He's camped out at our parents', streaming shows half the night and sleeping until noon. My dad roused him enough yesterday to help hang Christmas lights for a few of the elderly neighbors, but other than that, he's just couch-surfing. Mom's upset, but she's too kind-hearted to make him pull himself together."

"And it's the holidays ..."

"Right. He's thirty-four, for goodness' sake. And he barely speaks to me, the few times I've seen him since he came back." Melinda recounted their fight from the summer, and Josh let out a low whistle.

"Well, a little tough love's sometimes the right way to go. Sounds like he needed to hear it from someone. Good for you for stepping up and setting him straight."

"I don't care about gifts this year." Melinda looked down at her half-eaten sandwich. She wasn't hungry enough to finish it. "I mean, not that I normally do that much, anyway. I have plenty of sweaters, my house is overflowing with furniture, I don't need any more stuff. Hobo and the cats are all healthy, as are the chickens and the sheep. I just ... I wish everyone was getting along better, I guess."

"I know what you mean." Josh picked at the last of his fries. "I'm from Elkton, two hours' away. This is the first Christmas I'll be so far from my son."

Melinda almost choked on a potato chip. Josh had a son?

Karen hadn't mentioned it, but why would she? Josh was only two years younger than Melinda; she shouldn't be shocked by this bit of news. She managed to make a small noise of interest, and he was so focused on his thoughts that he didn't notice her surprise.

"Amber and I were divorced by this time last year, but at least I was right there in town. It was awkward, but we made it work. This time, it's going to be different. Harder."

He looked so sad, Melinda quickly set her own feelings aside. "I'm sure that spending time with his dad is all he wants, no matter what day it is, or where."

Josh nodded, as if trying to convince himself it was true. "Well, Aiden's five now, so he's getting to where he notices everything." There was a fleeting smile. "And Amber's dating someone, so he's full of questions."

"Oh, I see. Yes, that's going to complicate things for him."
Melinda wondered if that development was troubling for Josh
as well, but didn't dare ask. "Do you have a photo of him? I'd
like to see it."

Josh reached for his phone. "Now, this one was taken at
Halloween. He wanted to go as a superhero, and ..."

They spent several minutes going through pictures. Along
with dozens of shots of Aiden, Josh also shared snaps of
Charlie, his rescue dog. Melinda scrolled through her albums,
too, offering bits of her life in return, and her worries about
the coming weeks were soon forgotten.

"I should get back," Josh finally said. "Too bad Karen
couldn't join us but, well, that's how it goes."

"I'll get rolling on these applications as soon as I can."

"Oh, there's one other thing." Josh was about to reach for
his coat. "I've been thinking about the community cat
program, about how it's too bad we can't keep it going all year
long. I know you're busy, we all are. But I have an idea for a
little project we could do in the meantime."

"A project? Like what?"

Josh suggested they create shelters for strays and barn
cats out of plastic totes, insulation panels and straw. The huts
were easy and inexpensive to make, so even a small group of
volunteers could knock out several dozen in a matter of
hours. "We're taking care of their medical needs," he said,
"but what about adequate shelter? Winter's coming on fast."

Melinda thought of the barns and sheds that dotted the
countryside. Some were snug, but many were falling into
disrepair. And colony cats had it even harder. Gertrude's
group on the edge of Prosper had only a meager selection of
wooden crates and a few plastic carriers draped with tarps.

"I love that idea! Not only would it help the animals, but
it's a great way to keep up awareness for the clinics between
now and spring. We don't want to lose all the momentum we
already have."

"I thought you'd be on board. As usual, we'll need to
scrape up some cash, materials and manpower." He glanced

at the clock. "Wow, I really need to go. But think it over, OK? I'm open to any and all suggestions."

Melinda's mind was churning before she even reached her car. She'd been searching for a way to help others. Maybe this year, her focus wasn't supposed to be on people. Josh was right: there was a need in their community, and they should find a way to meet it.

The snow stopped as quickly as it had started, and Melinda reached for a broom and shovel as soon as she got home. She cleared the picnic table first, which provided Sunny and Stormy the perfect perch to supervise the rest of the cleanup.

Hobo was out of the way, for once, running figure-eights in the few inches of white fluff behind the garage. He loved snow, as long as it wasn't too deep, and his barks of glee carried across the still air of the farmyard.

"If only I could gin up half of his excitement." She adjusted her knit cap and tackled the back sidewalk. "Maybe this project for the community cats will make the holidays more meaningful."

Helping critters in need would certainly warm her heart. But that wasn't all. The chance to spend more time with Josh was just as appealing. She turned her focus toward dusting off the potted evergreens that flanked the front steps. Sunny had followed her around the house, and now waited just out of range of the broom's cloud of displaced snow.

"Josh Vogel could be really distracting, if I let him," Melinda admitted to Sunny, who only blinked his golden eyes in response. "What, you have nothing to say about that?"

Several of the ewes had gathered at the front pasture's fence to watch her work. One of them now let out an indignant bellow, and Melinda set the broom aside.

"Let's get some treats for the girls," she told Sunny as they started for the back porch. "That'll take my mind off things, right?"

When she returned with her hands full of carrots from the root cellar, the ewes' demands grew louder.

"Here, there's some for everyone." Melinda snapped the snacks in half and pushed them through the fence. Out of the corner of her eye, she saw another wooly face in the open pasture door. "Clover, get out here before they're gone!"

The rest of the flock was quick to join the group. Annie, of course, wasn't afraid to budge in line. If she could snatch a carrot fast enough, she could have a whole one for herself.

"Stop that!" Melinda scolded her, but laughed. "You girls are spoiled, but it's fun. We do as we please around here, don't we? At least, most of the time." She sighed wistfully. "Not all farm critters have it as good as my group does."

Stormy had joined Sunny and Melinda at the fence, and now rubbed his cheek against the leg of her insulated coveralls. His meow meant only one thing: he wanted to be held. Right now.

"I can't cuddle you and hand out carrots at the same time. Just wait a second! It still amazes me how you and your brother can brave the cold as well as you do. I guess when you have a heated hideout in the barn, it makes things much easier, huh?"

She passed out the last chunk of carrot and lifted Stormy into her arms. He leaned in for a nose rub and started to purr.

"Some kitties don't have a nice barn to live in, like you boys do. But I think there's something we can do about that. I'm sure we can rustle up some volunteers to help out, and the materials won't be hard to find."

Despite her rising spirits, she let out a small sigh. "That leaves the thing that's usually the toughest to get. We need money." She started back toward the house, Stormy still in her arms and Sunny trailing behind. "People like to help, especially during the holidays, but times are hard this year."

As she reached the picnic table, Melinda had an idea. She gently set Stormy on its boards, then crossed her arms.

"What we really need is a corporate sponsor. If I can catch him in a good mood, I think I know who might step up."

***

"Oh, no! What is that?" Melinda hit the brakes harder than usual as she turned into Prosper Feed Co.'s lot. There, just off Main Street, sat a red-lettered sign painted on what looked to be a full sheet of white plywood: "Fight the Feds ... Save our Post Office!"

"That wasn't there this morning." She eased into a parking spot and cut the engine. "He didn't say a word during coffee hour, and he's been rather quiet lately, especially concerning the post office. I should have known something was brewing in that brain of his. At least the other new display has a holiday theme."

The south lot of the co-op was now dominated by almost-life-sized wooden cutouts of Santa, his sleigh, and the usual reindeer with Rudolph in the lead. It had been the largest item by far at the decoration exchange, and there was much discussion among the men in the alley over who should take it home. A sort-of-auction was decided upon, and Auggie's generous donation toward the community center bested his three rivals for the prize.

Jerry told Melinda that Auggie's wife wasn't so thrilled about his win, and insisted he not stake the oversized display on their lawn. The co-op's lot, however, would allow more people to enjoy its oversized seasonal spirit.

This Santa and his reindeer had an interesting backstory. A local farmer known for his outrageous holiday displays cut it out of plywood almost forty years ago, and he and his children painted the characters in bright colors and set them up along their gravel road.

And there they appeared, year after year, until the farmer passed away about a decade ago. One of the sons kept the tradition going for a few holiday seasons, but the pieces were eventually shelved in a dusty barn. The family didn't have the time to restore the cutouts, but hadn't the heart to throw them on the scrap pile.

When the decoration exchange was announced, they saw their best chance of finding their father's special project a new home.

And now, the jolly old elf waved his greetings to everyone entering and exiting town. There wasn't time to repaint the display before this Christmas, but Auggie promised to get that done next year. In the meantime, he had gone overboard with the rest of his decorations.

Strings of multi-colored bulbs threatened to suffocate the single-story, beige-sided building that served as the co-op's retail store and office, and green-tinsel wreaths glinted in all the windows. Classic holiday tunes blasted forth when Melinda opened the door, and she tried to keep a straight face when she saw pinecone garlands draped along the paneling in the coffee pot's corner.

"Welcome to the North Pole," one grizzled farmer said wryly as she wiped her feet on the mat. "If you're looking for Santa, you'll find him in his workshop ... er, office."

"It's rather festive in here." Dozens of cutout-paper snowflakes twirled just below the ceiling. "But when Auggie decides to do something, he goes all out."

"That's for sure," another man grumbled as he studied a newspaper. "I like the holidays as much as anyone else, but this is too much. Three more weeks, and things will get back to normal in here."

"Four." A woman popped out of the supplement aisle. "Auggie says it all stays up until New Year's."

Melinda left the groaning farmers behind and started for the counter, where Dan, the assistant manager, was simultaneously ringing up an order and chatting on the phone.

"Sure thing, Bob." Dan gave his Santa hat a dramatic flip and rolled his eyes at Melinda. He was a large man with a coppery beard, and his too-small holiday cap was about to slip off his head. "We'll get those bags ready for you, they'll be on the loading dock. Yep, we're here until six."

He sighed after he ended the call. "I'm supposed to greet you with a belly laugh and wish you 'happy holidays.' But it's been a long day. How about I just ask if you need help with anything?"

Melinda leaned on the counter and greeted Mr. Checkers, a sizable buff-and-white tomcat, with a friendly scratch under the chin. He'd left his roaming days behind, thanks to Karen and Josh, and then used his feline powers of persuasion to pressure Auggie into also adopting his lady friend, Pebbles.

"I'm looking for Auggie. Is he around?"

Dan pointed toward the partially open office door.

Auggie was at his computer, so intent on the screen that his dark-framed glasses were about to slip down his nose. "Hey, kid." He barely looked up. "What's goin' on? Getting grub for those spoiled sheep of yours?"

"They aren't spoiled." Melinda took the padded chair on the other side of Auggie's desk. Its past life had likely been in a doctor's office, and the blue-vinyl cover was cracked and faded. "Well, only a little."

"Fresh veggie scraps and lettuce this time of year." He gave her a knowing look. "I'd say they have it pretty good."

Melinda gave him the side eye in return. "I'm not sure what you mean."

"Oh, come on." Auggie leaned over his desk, smirking. "I've seen you going in the back door of the Watering Hole one-too-many times. And then I got into Bill's shop fridge one morning, and I saw the buckets of veggie snacks."

"You'd better not tell anyone!" Good thing she had already shut the office door. The co-op's regular customers seemed to have supersonic hearing when it came to local gossip. "Bill's kept it quiet, and I promised Jessie not to spread it around, or other people will want some for their critters, too."

She stared at him. "Wait, why were you snooping in Bill's fridge? When did you figure this out?"

"Oh, maybe a month ago. Don't worry, I'm not going to spill the beans."

She waited for him to answer her other question, but it was soon clear that wasn't going to happen. Auggie had worked at Prosper Hardware during high school and, even though he'd had his own business for decades, still was very emotionally involved in the store. Frank usually let his friend's comments roll off, but Miriam and Auggie had battled about his too-honest opinions more than once.

"Anyway, that's not why I'm here. I have an idea."

Auggie groaned. "How much work is this going to be?"

"Not much. Nowhere near as much as that sign! What do you think you're doing? Does Jerry know about it? The city probably has a sign ordinance, you know, and if it's planted in the highway easement, the county ..."

"Oh, pipe down." Auggie frowned, but there was a glint of triumph in his eyes. "No one's going to arrest me for it. They can't! I'm just exercising my First Amendment rights. Other people have signs up, too."

"Yeah, but not ones the size of a whole sheet of plywood!"

"Well, I like to do things big." Then he grinned. "Anyway, it's bigger than that; it's six-by-twelve."

"Well, no matter the size, it's sure to stir things up." Of course, that was exactly what Auggie wanted, so she tried to change tactics.

"That's a pretty strong message, you know. Maybe a bit much during the holiday season."

He snorted. "Peace and goodwill have their place, but this is our chance to fight back! It can't wait until after New Year's." He lowered his voice. "Besides, I could have picked a different 'F' word for the sign, you know."

Her jaw dropped. "You wouldn't ..."

"Yep, gave it some thought." He chuckled. "Oh, that would've livened things up around here!"

"For sure. And it would have gotten you arrested, too. The magazine crew will be in town in a few weeks, remember? That sign doesn't fit Vicki's vision for her store's big break. It seems like *someone*," she pointed at him, "mentioned this was our big chance to put this little community on the map. For the right reasons."

"Hmph," was all he said, then slid his glasses back up his nose. "So, what did you want to talk to me about. I mean, beyond a lecture about my sign?"

"Oh, yes." She sat up straighter. "See, Josh and I had lunch the other day, and ..."

This bit of news made Auggie's bushy eyebrows shoot straight for the ceiling. Melinda's cheeks began to burn, and she hurried on.

"No, not like that. Karen was stuck on a call and, well, we're trying to get a new project going to help the community cats, now that winter is coming." She took a breath. "And it would be wonderful to have a corporate sponsor."

"A sponsor, huh? By which you mean me."

"Look." She leaned over the desk. "The clinics are a huge success, but that's only part of the equation. These cats need shelter, too. Barns and sheds on their own are fine for most of the year, but when it gets really cold, they need small spaces to curl up inside, conserve their body heat. And just think of the kitties like Gertrude's, who don't have a barn at all. She has some old carriers and wooden boxes on the porch, but it's not much."

Melinda had one more card to play. "You know, if it hadn't been for your big heart, Mr. Checkers and Pebbles would still be over there. Don't you want their friends to be warm, too?"

"So, I take it you'd like to make houses out of plastic tubs and insulation. Give them away."

"Exactly!" She blinked. "How did you know about those?"

Auggie's gaze briefly dropped to the floor. Melinda peeked under the desk and saw Chaplin, the co-op's newest feline employee, curled in a padded basket near Auggie's feet. The cat's long, black-and-white coat was now soft and glossy, and he bore no hints of the bedraggled animal who'd appeared in the back lot's shed two months ago.

Chaplin's markings were strikingly similar to those of several cats Auggie had loved and lost as a boy, but their connection hadn't been strong at first. It took several weeks of food and patience before they developed a bond.

"He comes inside now, and I'm glad." By the look on Auggie's face, Melinda knew that was the understatement of the year. "Started doing it last week. Took some coaxing, for sure. That old shed wasn't much of a haunt once the weather started to turn, and I didn't know what to do. I'd started searching online, and I saw those tote things. But now, I don't have to get crafty. He's happy in here."

"They aren't expensive to make, as you know. We aren't going to do a big push, since there's not much time, just some donation boxes around town and a press release. But a corporate sponsor would really put things over the top. And it'd be good publicity for your business. I know you carry quite a few lines of cat food."

"And I'm going to get more. I'm floored by what people will pay for a bag. Saves them a drive to a bigger town, I guess."

Auggie now had a soft spot for the strays, but the businessman in him had to run the numbers. Melinda waited while he mulled it over, and hoped sympathy would win in the end.

"Why not?" He shrugged. "We're already all decked out for Christmas. A charitable program fits right in." He rubbed his hands together. "Now, let's see. How about I kick in a couple hundred?"

Melinda's mouth fell open. "That would be wonderful! I didn't expect that much."

"Nonsense." Auggie waved it away. "I'll take it out of the advertising budget. Just put 'Prosper Feed Co.' in bold type on everything, and we're good." He stuck out his hand. "Make that *all caps*, and bold. Do we have a deal?"

People needing cat shelters would be asked to call the vet clinic. Some of the huts would be set aside for Gertrude's colony, and the rest would be distributed before Christmas. Auggie suggested a drawing for several heated water bowls, which he always had in stock, as a way to build buzz in the community.

The more they talked, the lighter Melinda felt. It was the season of giving, after all. And now, she had something tangible to give.

Before she left, she crouched down and extended a gentle hand to Chaplin. "He's such a sweet boy. I'm so glad he found his way here. It wasn't by accident, it was meant to be." Chaplin stared at her for a moment, but then graciously allowed her to touch his fur. "It's great that he gets along with Mr. Checkers and Pebbles."

"Oh, I wouldn't say that." Auggie shook his head. "Mr. C tolerates him most of the time, but Pebbles? She can't stand to be in the same room with him. You should have heard the howling and hissing when he tried to follow me up to the weather lab the other day. Pebbles rules that roost. He didn't put up much of a fight, though, just came in here and curled up in his bed."

"He has a warm place to live, and that's all he cares about." Melinda reached for her coat. "And now? All these other cats are going to have one, too."

* 10 *

Melinda had her best coat folded over a kitchen chair as she waited for her ride. "They'll be here any minute. Hobo, no, please don't put your nose on my skirt." She took the lint roller off the counter and gave her outfit one more going-over, then adjusted the ruffled sleeves on her fine-knit burgundy sweater and smoothed a hand over her styled hair.

The Hartland County Historical Society's carols and desserts celebration was the highlight of Swanton's limited social season, and a rare opportunity to wear something other than sweatshirts and jeans. Melinda was eager to spend a few hours with Miriam, Karen, and Diane, but that wasn't why she had a case of the butterflies. Josh had texted just a few hours ago to see if she would be at the party.

It'll be great to see you. And then, he'd added with his usual wit: *Besides, I won't know very many people there.*

"I can't wait to see him, either. I wish it didn't matter, but it does." She took another peek out the kitchen windows, but there was still no sign of Miriam's car. Hobo had turned his attention to his bowl of kibble, and Melinda was too restless to take a seat, so she wandered into the dining room to admire the hundreds of clear, glowing lights on her tree.

Her farmhouse was charming all year long, but it really shined during the holidays. A swag of faux evergreen crowned the cased opening into the living room, where a matching piece was draped over the fireplace mantel. She'd kept the holiday hues simple this year, with lots of silver and blue to harmonize with the soft-gray living room walls and the matching shades in her rugs. The effect was simple, a little rustic, and ...

"Grace, again? Really?"

Grace was perched on top of the right-side bookcase, curled up next to the cat nativity. Her fluffy paws were wrapped around the far-end wiseman, whose orange-tabby coat was still visible under its ceramic robe. Grace's green eyes only opened when Melinda gently pried the unfortunate character out of her grasp.

"I don't know if you're trying to protect them, or attack them, or what." She put the feline wiseman in its proper place. "I really should move everyone out, but they look so good, right where they are. It's no use to tell you to get down, since you'll climb back up the minute I leave. Oh, good, they're here!"

She shut off most of the lights and grabbed her wool topper. Or at least, she tried to. A sleepy Hazel blinked up at her when she pulled out the chair. "Oh, baby, that's my good coat! How is it possible for you to shed that much?"

Miriam pulled up by the garage, and Hobo rushed out to greet his guests. Karen soon appeared in the kitchen, but Melinda hardly recognized her friend. "Hey, look at you!"

Karen laughed and gave a little twirl. "This coat hasn't seen the light of day in years. Not exactly work wear, given my profession." She unbuttoned it enough to show off her paisley-patterned dress, then pointed at Melinda's outfit. "And I love that sweater! So festive!"

"Well, my skirt has an elastic waist, so I'm ready to stuff myself with desserts." Melinda reached for the lint roller again. "I was ready, but then I laid my coat on the chair."

Karen rubbed Hazel's ears. "I know. I told Doc, we should buy stock in the company that makes those things. We have to be two of their best customers." She gave Melinda a sly smile. "Speaking of veterinarians, is Josh going to be there?"

"Yes, he is." Melinda pointed at her friend. "And that's it. He's going to be there, and so am I. End of story."

"Mhmm," was all Karen said, then she reached into her purse. "Here. It's from Pumpkin."

"Oh, you didn't have to." Melinda took the gaily wrapped package and hid it in a top cabinet, away from sensitive noses. Karen's collie was Hobo's favorite playmate, other than his cat friends. "Hobo didn't get her anything for Christmas. If we can find a day when the weather is decent and we both have the time, you'll need to bring her out for a run."

Hobo was soaking up attention from Miriam, but quickly left her side when he spied the biscuits in Melinda's hand. "Here's your bribe to stay on the back steps until we're down the lane." She and Karen piled into the backseat, and Melinda texted her mom to let her know they were on their way.

"Girls, I'm feeling rather festive today." Miriam's curls were more polished than usual, and she sported a flattering shade of lipstick.

"It's not very often that I get the chance to dress up. Had to stop and think where my best nylons were hiding."

Karen and Melinda exchanged looks of surprise. *Nylons?*

"I don't think I have even one pair, not anymore," Melinda said. "I'm glad I still have these dress boots, although I rarely wear them. It's certainly cold today. Oh, aren't we taking the blacktop?" Miriam had turned south at the end of the drive. "I mean, you'll eventually hit the state highway, but it's the long way around."

"I know." Miriam smiled at her niece in the rearview mirror. "But we have a stop to make. Or at least, somewhere I've been eager to see for myself. Now, which corner should I take to reach Hawk Hollow?"

"I'm liking this plan." Karen leaned forward expectantly. "Haven't had a chance to drive by it, been meaning to before winter gets any worse."

"Well, then, let's go." Melinda smiled. "We have enough time. Take a right at the first crossroads, it's two miles. Then back south again."

Melinda's festive mood was momentarily dampened by the sight of the Wildwoods' battered mailbox slumped on the side of the gravel road. Karen noticed it, too. "Hey, is this Bart's place?" She peered up the rutted lane as they rolled past. "I see what you mean, it's pretty rundown. Doc was out here a few times, way back before they sold their cows, but I haven't had a reason to."

"And that's just as well." Miriam frowned. "You heard how he practically ran Melinda off last summer. It's just sad, that's what it is. I saw him going into the Watering Hole the other day, like nothing ever happened. Just goes to show, you never know what people are dealing with, on the inside."

Melinda sighed. "I know. I wish there was something someone could do, but they refuse any offers of help, always have. Mabel was over there the other day, she's the coordinator for the post-office petition in our neighborhood. Bart was as sullen as ever, but she sensed he was a bit embarrassed, too. So many people saw the deputy hauling him out of the Watering Hole last week."

"Maybe that will be a good thing, in the end." Karen tried to sound hopeful. "Show him he needs help."

"I don't know. Marge seemed eager to accept some of the cookies from the container, Mabel thought she was having one of her better days and understood what was going on. She didn't have any treats to contribute to the swap, but Mabel hadn't expected she would. Instead, Mabel added a few extra to their plate before she left."

"Did they sign the petition?" Miriam wanted to know.

"Oh, yes." Melinda laughed. "That was the highlight of her visit. Bart, as you can imagine, was rather eager to participate in anything that smacked of giving the government the finger. He was still ranting about the injustice of it all when Mabel was finally able to get away. Well, here's Hawk Hollow."

There wasn't much to see, especially this time of year. The gravel dipped down from the north on a grade that wasn't exactly steep, but still counted as a hill compared to the relative flatness of the fields around it. The metal gate that offered access to the pioneer cemetery was not only closed, but now sported three chained padlocks instead of one. Hawk Hollow was now back on some residents' radars, but the discovery of the bodies had also drawn too many nosy people eager to explore.

The driveway across the road, where the general store and creamery once stood, now opened only into a sleeping cornfield. But the iron-frame bridge stood tall and strong over the creek, and the water below it still flowed freely despite the change in the weather.

"Wait a sec." Miriam stopped the car once they crossed the bridge. "Where's the cemetery? I know they don't have signs up yet, but I thought it was on that side of the creek."

"It is." Melinda pointed behind them. "But it's far down from the road, and so close to the creek that the trees make it hard to see. The township trustees squared the plot with stakes, once the bodies were reburied, and added some cattle panels for a makeshift fence. That's it, so far."

"Now I see why the historical society earmarked this afternoon's proceeds for this project," Karen said. "There's so much work to be done."

Adelaide Beaufort, who lived just up the road, had asked Melinda to join the cemetery committee, and she hadn't been able to say no. "We need a real fence, headstones, historical markers. I think I'm most excited about the landscaping, if you want to call it that. We hope to plant the entire cemetery plot with native prairie grasses, make it the way it used to be."

After a few more miles of snow-dusted gravel, they reached the state highway and turned west. With around ten-thousand residents, Swanton was the largest community in Hartland County as well as the county seat. Its long history meant there were a few streets lined with gracious homes built by the town's most-prosperous early settlers. One of those, a grand two-story brick residence, was now owned by the historical society and served as its museum.

The side streets around the mansion were already lined with cars, so they had to walk a few blocks to reach the entrance. The structure's tall windows were festooned in yards of evergreen boughs, and more greenery graced the grand columns on every porch. Electric lights glowed behind the panes, despite the early-afternoon sunshine.

"This looks like something out of a movie," Karen said with awe as they walked up the cobblestone drive. "I half expect a butler in polished shoes and a frock coat to answer our knock at the door."

"Pretty close," Miriam said over her shoulder as a man in a top hat appeared to greet the next batch of guests. "I don't know about the rest of you, but I'm ready to set my troubles aside for an hour or two and step back in time."

The receiving room was filled with twinkling lights and the delightful scents of fresh evergreen, cinnamon and citrus. More boughs covered the fireplace mantel and swooped over the doorways. An impressive live Christmas tree held court in one corner, its crown still a foot short of the grand home's high ceilings.

"Am I glad I busted out this skirt," Melinda told Miriam, who was smoothing her short gray curls after their walk. "I don't know the last time I've seen people around here this dressed up. Oh, there's Mom, through the archway."

The formal dining room's oversized mahogany table had been slid to one side and draped with an olive-green damask cloth. Silver pyramid trays of cookies, candies and miniature cakes filled its surface, and the hand-carved console on the adjoining wall offered a buffet of flavored coffees, tea, and hot chocolate. A donation box waited on a nearby table, next to an easel explaining the Hawk Hollow pioneer cemetery project.

A gaily dressed woman in her fifties soon approached them, and Melinda gasped with delight. "Adelaide! It's you, right?"

"Don't recognize me without my coveralls?" Her gray hair was swept into a soft bun, rather than its usual set of braids, and her teal sweater set was highlighted by a glittering snowflake pin. "I had to dig deep into the closet, I'll admit, but I guess I can shine it up when the cause calls for it."

"And it's a good one, for sure." Melinda tried to peek through the donation box's slot, but it was too small. "I'm not going to shake it, but you know I'd love to. I can't wait to see how much is raised this afternoon."

"I'm hoping it's enough for the fence and the signs. We can always add the grave markers later." Adelaide lifted her china cup for a sip of tea, and Melinda noticed her low-maintenance friend had recently received a professional manicure.

"You know, during our pre-retirement life in Madison, I worked for the state and Mason was an engineer for a development firm. Because of our jobs, we used to go to more of these social events than we liked. But this one feels much different. This project is really special to us, and it's the holidays, after all."

Mason appeared at his wife's side, wearing a turtleneck in a festive shade of dark green. "My sweater's clean, I'm proud to say. And I think I got all the dog hair removed. The goats snuck out of their pasture again this morning, but at least they did it early enough that I still had time to change."

"Well, you look like a true community leader." Melinda raised her china cup in salute, and both of the Beauforts laughed. Mason was on the Fulton Township board of trustees, which normally didn't have much business to conduct. But since cemeteries fell under its jurisdiction, the discovery at Hawk Hollow had provided the panel with a project to tackle.

Mason rubbed his wife's shoulder. "There's a guy over there I know. Since you ladies outnumber us at least five to one, I'd better keep him company."

Volunteers bustled through the butler's pantry that connected to the kitchen, where they refilled dessert trays and beverage dispensers. Even that hardworking space was decked with ribbons and garlands.

The main parlor, whose pocket doors were pushed wide to accommodate all the guests, held two additional Christmas trees and more swags of lush greenery. A row of antique nutcrackers stood at attention by the generous hearth, and a vintage grand piano waited in one corner.

Adelaide was called away, but the small space Melinda's group had found was still too close for comfort. There seemed to be a bit of room by the bay window, so they started in that direction. The parlor was so packed, Melinda had to turn sideways to follow her mom through the crowd.

"I can't believe the turnout," Diane called over her shoulder. "This is always a popular event, but look at all these people! That dusting of snow yesterday put everyone in the holiday spirit, but it's not cold enough to keep folks at home."

Melinda tried to balance her plate of treats and cup of coffee and, although she hated to admit it, scan the room for any sign of Josh at the same time.

There he was, over by the piano, talking to a group of people she didn't recognize. His olive sweater perfectly set off his brown eyes and hair, and her spirits soared when he caught her eye across the crowded room.

Really, she needed to pull herself together. She might be attending a holiday tea at a Victorian mansion, but she didn't have to swoon the second a handsome man looked her way.

Karen quickly pulled her back to the present.

"Just look at those girls." She tipped her head toward a group of ladies by the staircase. Karen wasn't one to refer to other women in a condescending manner, but apparently felt it was warranted. "Some of them must be in their late thirties, even, but they're giggling over Josh like he's the captain of the football team."

"He was, actually. But in a small town, somebody has to do it."

"Oh, was he now? Hmm, I didn't know that. Perhaps you need to find out more about him." She gave Melinda a playful elbow. "Now would be as good of a time as any."

"Come with me," Melinda pleaded. "If nothing else, there's strength in numbers. Maybe it'll keep me from getting my eyes scratched out. Those girls look like they are waiting to pounce."

Part of the group gathered around Josh began to drift away, but one woman didn't seem in a hurry to step aside. Her long hair was glossy and very blond, and she tipped her chin attentively when Josh spoke to her. When she laughed and put a possessive hand on his arm, the two cookies Melinda had already inhaled turned to lead in her stomach.

Oh, jealousy. She hadn't felt it in a very long time. And she wasn't sure if its sudden return was a good thing.

"Who is that?" she whispered to Karen.

"Don't know. Maybe she's just a client. Seems like the type to have a little lap dog. You know, fluffy-white fur with a polka-dot bow." Karen smirked, then narrowed her eyes at Melinda. "You seem ... distracted. Did something happen when you and Josh had lunch? Anything I need to know?"

"No." Melinda was a little too quick to answer. Karen crossed her arms and waited. "No, not really. Look, I'll tell you later, it's ..."

Josh waved them over, and it was too late to escape. Before they could even say hello to Josh, the woman coolly offered her hand to both women. It was obvious she wasn't about to be left out.

"This is Gretchen Cumberland, she's an attorney here in town," Josh said. Melinda felt Gretchen's piercing gaze land on her, slide away, then snap back with lightning speed. Because as she studied Melinda, she realized Josh was, too.

"So, Gretchen, does Doctor Vogel look after your dog?" Karen's voice was a shade too sweet.

"Why, yes, he does. Cupcake just loves him." She tilted her head at Karen. "That's amazing. How did you know I have a dog?"

"I'm a veterinarian, too. We get pretty good at that, after a while." She gave Melinda a side glance. *See, I told you so.*

"Well, Josh is more than a wonderful caregiver for my baby." Gretchen put her hand on his arm again, as if to reinforce they were on a first-name basis. "He lives just down the street from me. And he's also going to be the newest member of the chamber of commerce's board of directors."

"Well, I don't know if I ..." Josh looked embarrassed, but Melinda couldn't tell if it was because he didn't want to take on another commitment, or because Gretchen seemed unable to keep her hands off him.

"Oh, nonsense, you'll be wonderful," Gretchen trilled, then turned to Karen and Melinda. "We need more men on the board, and in other leadership roles in the community, too. There's too many of us hens in the chicken house, if you know what I mean."

"I can see how that becomes a problem." Melinda couldn't stay quiet one more minute. "Hens love to fight over scraps. And they're not afraid to peck each other to get what they want. Josh, I think you'd better say yes."

Gretchen gave his arm one more squeeze. "We'll talk later this week, OK?" Before he could respond, she lifted her teacup from a nearby table and sailed away.

Josh watched her go with a smile on his face. One that Melinda couldn't quite read. She needed to steer the conversation to safer ground, and fast. "Well, I have good news. I found us a sponsor for the cat shelters."

"Really?" Karen quickly took the bait. "Auggie actually said yes? I saw that crazy sign he put up the other day. We're all worried about the post office, but I don't know if taunting the feds is the way to handle it."

"The sign sure has people talking." Josh shook his head. "I guess it's one way to raise awareness about the issue." He raised an eyebrow at Melinda. "If he's as angry as everyone says he is, I'm impressed you were able to get him to back our little gesture of goodwill."

"Auggie's more of a softie than he seems. Besides, I don't think I can take all the credit. Chaplin was there, curled up in his basket under Auggie's desk."

"That cat has his heart, for sure." Karen took a sip of her coffee. "You should have seen Auggie the other day. Chaplin had sneezed twice that morning, and he called the clinic and begged us to work them in. Chaplin's fine, I told Auggie it was probably just dust. He lives at a co-op, after all."

Josh laughed. "Poor Chaplin, he's not used to being smothered with affection. Who knows, he might wish he'd stayed out in that shed." He turned quiet for a moment. "He was alone, sure, but at least he could do as he pleased."

Melinda saw him glance in Gretchen's direction. She had only made it as far as the gaggle of women by the piano, and there was no doubt what the ladies were discussing with so much interest.

A middle-aged man by the fireplace raised a hand in greeting, and Josh made his goodbyes and moved on. Diane soon appeared out of the crowd.

"Sorry to pull you away." She almost had to shout to be heard over the din.

"Melinda, Adelaide asked me to track you down. Some of the historical society members want to meet you."

As they started toward the dining room, Diane leaned in. "You know I pride myself on staying out of my children's personal lives," she said in a low voice. "But, honey, I have to say it: He's a catch."

Melinda sighed. "You sound like Karen."

"Well, Karen is one of the smartest women I know." Diane waved away her daughter's eye roll.

"You don't have to throw yourself at him. But give it a chance, at least. I think he likes you."

"He likes animals, and anything that helps animals. That's where we intersect. And it's the only place we do, as far as I know."

"Oh, you might have more in common than you think. And, since my two minutes of meddling are nearly up, I'll say this, too: I never thought you and Chase were all that compatible."

"You're right; we aren't." Melinda felt a sudden sting in her heart. It came less and less these days, and it didn't hurt like it used to, but ...

"I mean," she tried again, "we *weren't*. But that doesn't mean Josh and I will ever be more than friends, does it? Wait. Don't answer that. I know what you're going to say."

Fortunately, Adelaide saw them coming. She stepped in and guided Melinda toward the society's board members. "I know the carolers are about to start, so there's not much time to chat. But everyone, this is Melinda Foster."

There were warm nods and handshakes all around, but Melinda had to choke back her laughter. Gretchen was right about one thing: the ladies did rule the roost in this town. Every single board member was a woman. And one of them, she already knew.

"I'm so glad you could join us," Patricia Beck said. "Now that this holiday party is almost in the books, I'm ready to go all-in on the community center. Sounds like we're going to look over some paint samples this week?"

"I believe so. Jerry says we might even tear out the half-wall partitions up front, so wear your safety goggles." The idea of demolishing something sounded wonderful to Melinda just now. The air was warm and close, and the backs of her knees were starting to sweat.

"I'll bring my sledgehammer, then." Patricia's eyes twinkled. "The more work we do ourselves, the more money we can save. I can't wait to get that nasty countertop out of the kitchen. But we probably won't get to that until after the holidays."

Miriam joined the group. "Patricia, I didn't know you were part of the historical society. How did you get involved?"

"Oh, one of my great-grandfathers was an early settler, and my neighbor talked me into it." She turned to one of the other women. "Marjorie, this is Melinda."

"Yes, good to meet you at last! My dear, I'm so sorry to hear about the Prosper post office closing. What a terrible blow it will be to the town."

"Nothing is settled yet." Melinda quickly set the record straight. "There's a public forum next week, and we're bombarding the regional office with calls and emails. Then there's the petition ..."

The older woman shook her head and sighed. "If you can pull off a Christmas miracle, I'd love to see it happen. Glenn is taking this hard, but it's not his fault. Oh, the carolers are here!"

Eight singers dressed in hoop skirts and frock coats descended the grand staircase to a smattering of applause. They arranged themselves around the piano, and one of the women took a seat on its bench. The countless conversations throughout the mansion ebbed away, and the visitors turned toward the choir with smiles of anticipation. Except for Marjorie.

"How hard it must be for Prosper to be down on its luck at this time of the year," she whispered to Melinda. "It's a shame the community center is only getting started. Why, a celebration like this might have been the one chance to raise everyone's spirits."

"We're managing the best we can." Aunt Miriam smiled, but she bit off the ends of her words.

"That's all anyone can do. Community center or not, Prosper's residents are determined to be grateful for all of our blessings this season."

"That's right," Patricia added. "Maybe we're a day late, but at least we're not a dollar short. Delores has seen to that. Sure, it would have been wonderful to have the doors open for the holidays. But we can look forward to that next year."

The opening chords of "Jingle Bells" brought the antique piano to life. The carolers launched into the first lines with enthusiasm, and their voices rose in cheerful harmony. Melinda took a deep breath and surveyed the scene: the fresh pine scent in the air, the rousing holiday music, the guests dressed in their holiday finery. It only took a moment for her troubles to melt away.

Diane and Karen were engrossed in the concert, but Aunt Miriam seemed preoccupied.

"Is anything wrong?" Melinda whispered.

A slow smile spread across Miriam's face. "No, I'd say not. Not anymore."

***

"You mean, a big bash?" Auggie blinked as he tried to process Miriam's proposal. "Streamers, midnight countdown, the whole bit?"

If the guys hadn't been fully awake when they arrived at Prosper Hardware Tuesday morning, they certainly were by the time Miriam finished sharing her proposal.

"New Year's is only three weeks away." George consulted the calendar by the sideboard. "Can you really get it done that fast? Isn't the community center still a wreck?"

"Yes, it is." Miriam held up a hand. "I'm not saying it has to be polished and perfect. We have the space we need, and that's what matters."

Doc leaned forward in his chair. "It's a nice idea, but are the restrooms in decent shape? What about the electrical system, is it up to code? Can the place handle such a crowd, and this soon?"

Miriam looked to Frank for support. "We think it can," he told his friends. "Sure, it'll be rough, but the mechanicals have all been checked out. We'd have to shift our focus to scrubbing the place from top to bottom, put any repairs on hold until after the holidays. But I think we can pull it off."

"There's not much happening around here for New Year's Eve," Melinda added. "Not only would it be fun, but it'd be a great way for everyone to see what the building looks like now, what we're up against. Delores' donation is certainly generous, but we may need more money to cover any unexpected expenses."

"And those are sure to show up." Uncle Frank sighed. "The building is over a hundred years old. Who knows what we might find?"

The fifteen-minute drive from the historical society to Melinda's farm had been enough time for Miriam's plan to take shape. A simple open house was her first idea, but the weekends leading up to Christmas were already packed with community events and family celebrations. New Year's Eve, however, was the perfect opportunity to bring everyone together.

Vicki, Melinda and Nancy had already draped lights inside the former bank's windows to make it festive enough for the magazine crew's visit. More decorations waited in storage at city hall, as Nancy hadn't found time yet to haul the holiday-exchange leftovers to a second-hand store.

And the idea had snowballed from there. Bill had rigged the speaker system at Prosper Hardware. What if he did the same up the street, so they could have a dance? What if the Watering Hole catered a meal? Would Angie want to create desserts for the event? Where could they get sparkly streamers and party hats on the cheap? Could tables be brought in from city hall?

Frank had been momentarily stunned by his wife's idea, but quickly got on board. He and Jerry discussed the possibilities yesterday, and Jerry promised to check with the council and the rest of the community center committee before he arrived at the store this morning.

Miriam was at the window now, her palms pressed together. "Here comes Jerry! Oh, I hope he has good news."

Everyone waited while the mayor removed his knit cap and unzipped his parka.

"Good morning." Jerry's smile was wider than Melinda had seen it in weeks, but she had to be sure.

"Well? Is there a consensus? Are we good?"

"I called everyone, and it's a go!" The store erupted with applause and cheers.

Now that her plan had been approved, Miriam was ready to put it into motion. "All it needs is a good scrubbing, a few more decorations ..."

"But, this is the busiest time of the year," Auggie interjected. "No, I'm not a Scrooge; I think it's a fine idea. It's just that there's so much going on, with the holidays and this post office thing. We can't lose sight of our real goal, we can't let the feds beat us."

"You don't have to lift a finger." Miriam's tone implied she was fine with Auggie staying out of the way. "We have it all planned out. We just have to get it done."

"Set up a few workdays," Doc suggested. "People will show up. Who doesn't love a party? Besides, whether they will admit it or not, most of them are dying to see what's going on in there." He gave Auggie a pointed look.

Karen had seen Auggie in front of the community center just the other day, his face pressed to the entryway's windows, trying his best to get a sneak peek.

"What? I was just walking by." He crossed his arms. "It's a public building now, it's not like I was trespassing. Fine. I don't mind getting my hands dirty. Put me down."

"I'll work with Nancy to draft a press release today," Melinda offered. This good news was even more stimulating than Auggie's strong coffee. "We'll send it out once the details are finalized. But there's more to do than just get the space ready. We'll need to figure out the food. And what about alcohol?"

"Oh, no." Frank rubbed his chin. "I hadn't thought about the booze. We'll need a temporary permit for that."

"You have to have it!" George insisted. "Wouldn't be New Year's Eve without it. Mary and I have been known to have a nip when the clock chimes. Of course, we celebrate early these days. Can't stay up late like we used to."

"Neither can I," Doc admitted. "Years of starting my rounds by six cured me of that a long time ago. But I think I can make an exception, for one night."

"It'll be worth it." Jerry rubbed his hands together. "Why, if we do it up right, this could be one of the biggest nights in the history of this town. We might even start a new tradition! Unless ..."

"Don't say it." Frank pointed at each of his friends in turn. "Don't say this could be the town's last big bash. We have to stay positive; it's our best chance to get through this."

* 11 *

Melinda handed Mark a Santa hat. "Look, you have to wear it. Miriam says so."

"Who cares? It's dumb."

They were in Prosper Hardware's upstairs office, getting ready for the holiday open house. Or actually, the rest of the family was preparing for the onslaught of shoppers. Mark was too busy trying to duck his duties. Melinda wasn't sure why, as this was one of the few times he'd left their parents' house in the past week.

He rolled his eyes when she forced the cap into his hands. "Fine. But these hats are like something out of a kids' movie." His eyes lit up with sarcasm. "Hey, where's Rudolph? When's he going to get here?"

"You're not exactly a jolly elf tonight." Melinda gave up and reached for her chore coat and heavy gloves. Having Mark around meant she was free to join the live nativity this year. "There are no reindeer, OK? There aren't too many around this part of the world. The few specialty farms that have any were booked a long time ago."

"Guess it's a good thing Doc found some better goats than the ones he had last year." Mark pushed back his chair. "I don't know if I remember goats being at the stable in Bethlehem, though. Does he have a cow, at least? Isn't there supposed to be a cow?"

"No cow. But Gus the donkey is making an encore appearance. John Olson's bringing his sheep again, and I have high hopes that Adelaide and Mason's goats will be more tolerant of crowds than the last bunch."

Some of the human faces in the nativity were new as well. Doc had bowed out of his wiseman role, claiming the change would let him keep a better eye on the critters, and Karen had drafted Melinda to take his place. There was also the issue of the Holy Family to consider. John's son Tyler, who portrayed Joseph last year, was now at college. Dylan had agreed to step in, but the former Mary wanted no part of it this time around. Lauren was now Tyler's ex-girlfriend, and the split had been full of teenage angst. Nancy's daughter, Kim, was drafted to fill the role.

In addition to the live nativity and extended hours at Prosper's handful of businesses, the festival also included a soup supper at the elementary school, hot sandwiches and warm cinnamon doughnuts from the Watering Hole, and strolling carolers. The evening would be capped off with a short program in front of city hall, where Jerry would announce the winners of the holiday lights contest.

When Mark realized his sister wasn't going to offer any sympathy, he slapped the Santa cap on his head. "There. Happy?"

"It's not so bad. Everyone else is wearing one, so you can all look silly together." She started for the stairs, and Mark finally followed. "Look at it like you're in character, as you would be when you sing a song. The hat will get you in the right headspace. Of course, if you're worried about there not being reindeer, I could have Nancy check the costume bin in the library's children's department."

"No, that's fine." Mark was suddenly on board. "This is way better than felt antlers and a fake nose."

The mood downstairs was certainly more festive. A cheerful area rug was arranged by one front window, and on it waited a rocking chair that would be Santa Claus' seat of honor. George was resuming his role, and Mary would again play Mrs. Claus. Diane and Miriam were setting out the cookies on the sideboard, and arranging the drink dispensers on a small table nearby. Mark's current task seemed to be distracting Esther, who was trying to buff the oak showcase to a shine before the festival officially started at five o'clock.

"Why don't you see if Dad and Frank need help?" Melinda motioned for Mark to stop chatting and start helping. "They are checking the seasonal items one last time. Third row."

She started for the clothing area, where Bill was stuffing the wall hooks with more hats and gloves. One good thing that might come from this evening, she decided, was that Mark was sure to quickly tire of helping at Prosper Hardware.

Maybe a few hours on his feet would show him how much work it took to keep the family's store running, and he'd quit moping about not being offered a seasonal spot on the payroll.

Bill only offered a curt nod in response to Melinda's greeting, and turned back to his bin of new inventory.

"What's the matter?" Melinda reached for a three-pack of chore gloves and added them to the display. "You're never this gloomy. You're almost as bad as Mark."

Bill sighed as he rummaged for knit caps. His Santa hat drooped at a dejected angle. "I don't see how you can be so cheerful. What are we going to do if this town goes down, and the store goes with it?"

Melinda was too surprised to answer. Was Bill really that worried? Come to think of it, he'd been rather quiet the past few days. She'd just assumed he felt the pinch of the holiday rush, like everyone else. He and his wife had two little kids at home, and Christmas was approaching fast.

"Miriam and Frank could always retire." Bill shoved the caps on an empty hook. "They don't want to, I know, but they're getting close enough, age-wise. Esther's only part-time and already retired. But you and me? We're screwed."

"Look." She lowered her voice. "I've lost some sleep over this, too. Working here was the one thing I could rely on when I moved back. It made everything else possible. The farm, my animals ..." She squared her shoulders against the past. And the uncertainty of the future.

"I've already thought this through. I'm all-in, just like you. I can't survive on freelancing, and there aren't many jobs around here where my professional skills would be in demand."

"I don't want to drive to Mason City every day, get a job in one of those home-improvement superstores. No way." Bill shook his head. "Where else would I have this kind of creative freedom? Doing custom woodwork isn't enough to make a living on, not around here, and I've been out of the corporate world for too long." He took in the sight of Prosper Hardware in all its holiday glory. "I was thrilled to land a job here. I don't know how I could give it up."

Melinda had to get to the vet clinic, but this conversation couldn't wait.

"We can't panic. Not yet. Who knows what might happen? Worst-case scenario, if Frank and Miriam decide they can't make a go of it anymore, I'll find a way to keep this place open. I might have to tweak things a bit, do something that would widen our customer base. But I think I could pull it off. Or at least, I hope so."

Bill stared at her. "So you have it all worked out, huh?"

"Not really, and I hope I don't have to."

"I guess I didn't realize plans were already being made." His tone had turned icy. "What if I had some ideas, too?"

"Well, sure, I'm open to whatever."

"That is just my point." A rousing holiday tune began to blast from the speakers, and Bill's cheeks flushed from irritation. "I'm glad this has all worked out for you, that you decided to stay on. But I've been thinking about the future of the store, too, and doing it long before you came back. Post office or no post office, Frank and Miriam will have to retire, one day. Did it ever occur to you who might take over if you weren't around?"

Melinda was taken aback. "I didn't know you were interested in that."

"Well, I am." Bill's eyes flashed with disappointment. "Or should I say, I was."

"I'm sorry." She looked at the floor. "I hadn't thought about that." There wasn't anything else she could say. At least, not right now. Because Bill had already turned his back and returned to the task at hand.

Melinda looked around the store, at the rest of her family rushing to complete their last-minute chores, and suddenly felt foolish and useless. There wasn't anything left for her to do here, not tonight, and her phone was beeping. It was Karen, wondering where she was. She hurried for the front door, taking care to keep her head down so no one could see her sudden tears.

Despite her worries, Melinda was pleased with the turnout as well as Vicki's idea to set every storefront aglow with lights. Little Prosper had never looked so beautiful.

The sun had already set, and the dark was the perfect backdrop for the already-lit snowflakes and trees that danced under the light poles along Main Street. The gentle flurries were just enough to create a winter wonderland without hampering the celebration. A cluster of children oohed and aahed over the model train in the wide front window of Sam's insurance office.

More lights, entwined in heavy garland, now adorned the grand entrance of the future community center. Every one of its tall windows blazed with color. Even the vacant properties, their rundown edges softened by the dark and the glow of holiday lights, had taken on an unexpected dose of good cheer. They were as festive as the rest of the buildings ... as long as you didn't look too closely.

Melinda decided it was the same for the town as well. Everyone around her was smiling and laughing, even singing, as if they didn't have a care in the world. But she thought again of Bill, and the post office, and how uncertain the future seemed to be.

Monday night was the first public forum, their best chance to take a stand against the federal officials' plan. As she pulled her hood up against the chill, Melinda could only hope their efforts would somehow be enough. A decision wasn't expected for months, but this meeting would surely show residents whether they had any chance at all.

As for Bill ... well, everything she needed to know was right in front of her. While the animals were certainly the stars of the live nativity, her friend's handiwork was all over the wood-plank backdrop.

Last year, he'd crafted the scene-setting display out of recycled pallets and reclaimed lumber, then cleverly constructed it in sections that allowed for easy storage. Its back wall was a full twelve feet wide, and rose to a peak with a short section of roof for a three-dimensional effect. Bill and Doc had reassembled the scene just a few days ago, and thatched the roof with fresh shocks of hay.

Working at some big-box retailer would be a waste of Bill's impressive skills. He belonged at Prosper Hardware, just as Melinda did. But she'd been so busy with her own worries, so consumed with trying to carry the weight of Prosper Hardware's future alone, that she'd never stopped to consider how Bill fit into all of this.

Frank had told Bill she'd joined the store's board of directors. Bill never said anything to her about it, but she'd been wrong to assume he had no objections. She had to mend fences with her friend. Not just for now, but the future. Because he was right; someday, things would change. And she'd need his help to keep Prosper Hardware afloat.

"Hey, what happened to you?" Karen's grin dimmed when Melinda finally made it through the crowd assembling at Fourth and Main. Doc, who was adjusting one of the spotlights near the clinic's entrance, gave her a wave of greeting.

"Oh, it's nothing, I'll tell you later." She pulled off one of her gloves and rubbed the stray tears from her cheeks. No one was likely to notice, anyway, as the menagerie forming on the clinic's lawn looked to once again be the highlight of the festivities.

"Why don't you let Pumpkin give you a hug?" Karen abruptly handed Melinda the end of the collie's leash. "She's bound and determined to make Gus stay in his corner, even though he shows no signs of wanting to roam."

The donkey, already in place on the left side of the scene, divided his attention between the oats bucket at his feet and the tufts of still-green hay dangling from the display's eaves. Karen reached behind the backdrop for Melinda's oversized velour robe, which was trimmed with wide, sparkly ribbon from a Mason City craft store, and helped her pull it over her chore coat.

Doc soon welcomed everyone to the nativity and, after a quick round of applause, a loose line formed in front of the display. Karen had brought out the clinic's donation box for the cat shelters, and cleverly placed it on a table next to one of the spotlights.

Thankfully, the animals adjusted quickly to the swarm of admirers. John's trio of ewes apparently felt safe inside their makeshift pen, and even allowed a few children to touch their curly wool.

The Beauforts' goats were also well-behaved, helped by Mason's constant supply of snacks. Gus, who brayed with almost-comic timing when he wasn't trying to eat the barn backdrop's roof, patiently posed for photos with visitors.

At first, Melinda had hesitated to help with the nativity, worried she would be needed at the store. But she was glad Karen talked her into it. Sure, it was cold, and the robe was bulky and awkward over her coat, but her post on the vet clinic's lawn allowed her to fully experience the holiday festival's charm. Many local visitors recognized her, despite her costume, and she didn't have to squeeze in her holiday greetings between ringing up purchases.

"Hey, there's Josh!" Karen pointed into the crowd. "He said he was going to try to make it."

Melinda made sure her foil-covered crown was still secure. "Looks like he found Eric. Quite a feat, in this crowd of people." While Melinda's personal life was up in the air,

Karen's new relationship with an elementary-school teacher was progressing nicely.

"Oh, no, I told Eric to text him. Josh doesn't know many people, I thought they could hang out together." She turned toward the guys. "How's it going?"

Eric held up a small brown sack. "We got some of the last of Jessie's doughnuts, they're going fast. I'll be sure to save you one."

"That settles it," Melinda whispered to Karen. "He's a keeper."

"Yes, he is," Karen whispered back. "So, Josh, what do you think of our little festival?"

"Eric said there'd be a crowd, but I never expected this." He studied the packed sidewalks. "This is an impressive event for a town this small."

"Well, you can thank Melinda for helping us kick it up a notch last year. Even more impressive, I think she's the only wiseman on record who's volunteered to help look after the goats."

Mason had offered her the sack of treats, and Melinda had been quick to oblige. It gave her something to do, as she suddenly felt shy. Talking to Josh at the coffee shop had been one thing, but this was different.

And after she'd seen him with Gretchen at the historical society's open house, she wasn't sure where she stood. This wasn't the time to say anything that might catch the ears of anyone nearby.

Did it even matter? What would she say if she could? This was all so ...

"Did you see the donation box?" she blurted out. "Karen brought it out. We'll be able to provide housing for every stray in the county if people keep dropping in cash at the rate they have so far."

"The more, the better." Josh beamed. "A week from Sunday, right? I have the whole afternoon blocked out. Let me know if you need another truck to haul supplies from Mason City."

"I think we can get it," Karen said. "But I'll let you know if that changes. Just tell everyone to be at Prosper Hardware around one."

More visitors were angling to get closer to the nativity, and Josh and Eric gave a final wave and moved on.

Karen was about to say something, but Melinda held up a hand. "Don't. Besides, we need to focus on our duties." She fluffed her robe. "We've traveled hundreds of miles through the desert, by camel, no less, to reach this stable. We should be like Pumpkin, and focus on the Baby Jesus."

The collie had finally settled down, and planted herself in front of the manger. The doll wrapped in a white towel didn't seem keen on escaping, but Pumpkin remained on guard.

Once the nativity wrapped up, Melinda started back toward Prosper Hardware. The carolers from the Catholic church were now in front of city hall, conferring with Jerry and Nancy, and a crowd was forming in the blocked-off street. Diane and Miriam met Melinda in front of the store, and Vicki soon appeared out of Meadow Lane.

"Amanda's finishing up our last purchases. I won't run the numbers until tomorrow, but everything exceeded my expectations." Vicki rubbed her hands together. "Which is saying something, as you know how high they were."

"That idea to share a coupon among the businesses was brilliant," Miriam told Vicki. "I can't tell you how many people had one in their hand. It benefitted all of us."

"Well, I have more good news! You can tell Frank I sold two more of his weathervanes tonight. And Diane, they cleaned out every one of your scarves. When can you have more ready?"

"How about Saturday? I have three that are almost done."

Melinda turned to her mom. "So, how did the rest of the night go?"

The store had been packed, of course, and Santa's arrival brought squeals of delight from the children. But the best part, Diane reported, was that Mark's mood seemed to improve as the evening went on. Several people recognized him, even in his Santa hat, and the well wishes from old neighbors and former classmates made him smile.

"A few hours of productive activity did wonders for him," Aunt Miriam added. "Makes you wonder, how much of his bad attitude is from not having a clear purpose in life?"

"Does that mean you're going to hire him?" Melinda asked.

Miriam laughed. "I wouldn't go that far. We're doing fine this holiday season, but the money just isn't there."

"He needs to find his own way." Diane took a deep breath. "And he needs to earn it, whatever he decides to do. Melinda, you should see the donations that came in for the cat shelters. But that wasn't the most noteworthy part of the night."

Aunt Miriam leaned over. "One guy asked me about the post office plan. He's not from the local area, so he can't sign the petition, but he was sympathetic to our plight. He wanted to know how to donate to our legal fund to fight the closure."

"Legal fund?" Melinda's jaw dropped. "I didn't know there was one."

"Exactly. Makes me wonder, though, if there should be." Miriam sighed. "Who knows where this will end?"

"It's too soon to tell." Diane clasped her hands together. "Oh, looks like Jerry's about to speak. I know he hates to talk in public like this, but he seems to be in a good mood, at least."

Jerry grinned as a smattering of applause rippled through the crowd. Nancy handed him a microphone, and he adjusted the burgundy-plaid scarf draped around his black coat. "Hello everyone, thanks for coming out tonight. Doesn't our little town look wonderful?"

The clapping intensified and was now accompanied by whoops and cheers.

"At most events like this, I'd be throwing the switch on a massive Christmas tree. But here in little Prosper, we like to keep things simple. The evergreens in our city park aren't very tall yet, anyway." Jerry gestured up and down Main Street. "Have you noticed all the lovely lights in our store windows? I think we used every spare string in Hartland County. And speaking of decorations, it's time to announce the winners of our holiday-lighting contest."

The top three vote-getters approached city hall's steps to accept their gift certificates, which were good at any of Prosper's businesses. Once the winners were absorbed back into the crowd, Jerry turned more serious.

"And now, I want to talk about something else. For those of you who don't know, the federal government is considering a plan to close our post office."

This was met with gasps and boos, and Melinda looked to where Auggie stood with his wife on the edge of the crowd. His mouth was set in a hard line, but he thankfully stayed silent.

"Many of you have approached me tonight to express your concern and support," Jerry went on, "and I can't tell you how much I appreciate that. We are going to fight this thing with everything we have!"

Cheers and shouts erupted in the street. Jerry urged everyone to contact the post office to speak out against the plan, and reminded local residents of Saturday's deadline to sign the petition.

"And then, and this is very important, I need each and every one of you to be at Prosper Elementary School by seven on Monday night. The feds are holding an official public hearing on this awful idea. We want to bombard them with questions, give speeches about how much this town means to all of us, how important it is to keep our small communities strong. Don't feel comfortable speaking in front of a crowd? Well, join the club."

This admission was met with a round of laughter.

"But it has to be done. Even if you don't approach the panel, your very presence will tell them what they need to know: Prosper is still a vibrant community, and we have your support."

There came a rousing round of applause, and more cheers. Once those subsided, Jerry held up a hand.

"Oh, and there's one more thing. Prosper is going to host its first-ever New Year's Eve party in just a few weeks. Details will be available tomorrow morning, in the usual places. It'll be at the future community center, just up the street from here, and all money raised will support that project."

Jerry turned toward the carolers, who had gathered under the nearest light pole. "And now, some of our talented singers from the Catholic church's choir will close out the evening with some special music. Goodnight, everyone, and happy holidays!"

The tallest man in the group took the microphone. "We're going to sing something that's near and dear to many of us during this holiday season."

He looked out over the crowd. "German immigrants settled this area in the middle of the nineteenth century. We have them to thank for so many of the holiday traditions we enjoy, and that includes this song. Many of you know the words, but you're used to singing them in English. We're going to share it in its native tongue, the way it was first performed two hundred years ago. If you are able to join us, please do so."

Miriam grabbed her sister's arm. "I hope it's what I think it is! Remember when Grandpa Shrader used to sing it in his fine baritone?"

"Oh, it was beautiful! And tears of joy would stream down Grandma's face when he sang."

The quartet gathered around the microphone, the pitch was played on a harmonica, and the lyrics of the beloved hymn spread through the still, cold air.

"*Stille nacht, heilige nacht ...*"

Melinda saw a few older people around them try to pick up the tune. They sang quietly, as if hoping to recall the next line just in time to put it into words. Her mom and aunt knew every line, and Melinda's heart swelled with love and hope.

She turned to stare at their family's store, and felt a lump in her throat. Prosper Hardware didn't boast the grand ornamentation of city hall. But it offered simple charm and a warm welcome, from its dark-green awning and wide windows to the reproduction sign that jutted out from the second floor.

The inside glowed with light, and the last of the shoppers were gathering up their sacks and saying their goodbyes. Frank leaned on the counter, lost in conversation with an old friend. Santa and Mrs. Claus were by the sideboard, laughing over some secret joke, and Santa suddenly reached out to give his lovely wife a little spin.

The post office was still open, and there was a cluster of visitors just outside its door. Melinda picked Glenn out of the crowd. He was singing with all of his might, and when she nodded her approval, a grin broke out on his weary face.

She smiled back, and wrapped her scarf a little closer against the chill. Maybe she didn't know the words in their original language. But she knew the tune, and the hope it held, and followed along in her heart.

✳ 12 ✳

"Look at this crowd," Melinda told Miriam as she glanced around the gymnasium. "I guess Jerry's a better public speaker than he thinks."

"That editorial in the Swanton paper on Friday surely helped. Auggie threw another match on the fire, for sure." Miriam eyed her niece with a mixture of humor and skepticism. "Are you sure you didn't know about it?"

"I had no idea." That was the truth, too. "I'd already told him the sign was too much, so I guess he figured he was on his own with that letter. Of course, it's always possible that Jane helped him with it, or even Dan. You know Auggie can't keep his opinions to himself, no matter how trivial they often are. And now, when so much is at stake ..."

"Oh, that sign." Miriam laughed and shook her head. "And that photo of him out in front of it, with his arms crossed and scowling like that. Then there's Santa and the reindeer lifting off in the background, as cheerful as you please! Seriously, though, he's going to end up on an FBI watch list if he doesn't tone it down."

Then she sighed. "But if I wasn't concerned about coming off as crazy, I might get up and say some of those very same things tonight."

"Are you?" Melinda sat up straighter in her metal folding chair. "Going to speak, at least?"

"Oh, we'll see. I keep thinking, what would Dad do, if he were here? Or Grandpa? They'd raise hell, that's what. They loved that store, and this town." Miriam looked around the gymnasium, then back toward the raised stage recessed into one end. "This place hasn't changed much since I graduated forty-five years ago."

"Jerry says the district's been wanting to shine it up, get new bleachers, at least. Of course, there's only elementary kids here now, so it's no longer a priority." Melinda shook her head. "But maybe it's just as well they haven't."

"I can't face that, not right now. Oh, there's your mom and dad. I'm glad we saved them seats. Diane, over here!"

Uncle Frank was in the front row, with the rest of the council. Jerry was next to him, nervously shuffling a stack of paper as he reviewed his notes. There was no formal queue to address the federal officials, as interested speakers would simply line up along one side wall, but Uncle Frank told Melinda that Prosper's leaders had discussed the best way to kick off the comments. Jake offered to be the lead batter and, for once, Jerry was eager to let his most-vocal council member hog the spotlight.

"We saw the post-office officials on the way in." Roger dropped into his seat and removed his coat. The racks in the hallway had been filled to capacity half an hour ago. "They look like a tough-nosed group."

"I have to say, I feel a bit sorry for them." Diane put her purse under her chair. "Their only role is to listen and take notes. Any decisions will be made by people far above their pay grade. Besides, it's the holidays. I'm sure they all have other, better things they'd rather be doing tonight, instead of driving up from Des Moines in the snow to listen to people complain."

"We're not complaining." Roger crossed his arms. "We're speaking up for what's right."

"I know. I'm just saying, this isn't their fault. I hope people treat them with respect, at least. Bullying them won't help our cause."

Melinda scanned the rows of occupied chairs that filled the floor of the gymnasium. More attendees spilled into the bleachers, latecomers content to sit on the sidelines. Tonight was shaping up to be a turning point in Prosper's history, for better or worse, and people from all around the region wanted to experience it first-hand.

"Quite the crowd," Aunt Miriam was saying. "Look at this show of support. Makes you feel good, you know?"

"Yeah." Melinda spotted Josh, there in the bleachers with a large group of people she didn't recognize. Except one. Gretchen was leaning in, laughing about something, and Melinda felt an uneasy weight settle in her stomach.

Miriam grabbed her arm. "Hey, they're here! Oh, dear, they do look like a take-no-prisoners gang. I'm afraid we're in for a long night."

Three stone-faced men and one barely smiling woman, all in dark suits, marched into the gymnasium and took their seats at the table in front of the stage. Someone had tacked a garland across the table's front in a half-hearted bid to add a little holiday cheer to this grim gathering. The chatter that echoed through the gym had died down as soon as the officials appeared, but now returned as an ominous buzz.

"I just hope this doesn't get too ugly," Diane whispered. "Everyone's on edge, emotions are running high. Oh, there's Pastor Paul. Wow, is that the petition? Look at that stack!"

Paul Westberg was the pastor at the Lutheran church in Melinda's rural neighborhood. He and his wife, Amy, lived in Prosper, and she taught at this school. Jerry and the council, with input from Glenn, had asked Paul to present the petition. He was a community leader, and well-respected, but didn't have direct ties to either the post office or Prosper's city government.

"Nancy carefully combed through the petition," Miriam confirmed. "Made sure there were no duplicate pages, or doubled-up names. It's airtight. Over eight hundred people! When you consider only adults could sign it, that's darn near just about everyone in this zip code."

Diane shook her head. "I just hope it's enough."

Principal David Johnson soon stepped to the podium, which was off to the right of the table, and asked everyone to take their seats. He raised concerns about high emotions at tonight's forum, and urged speakers to take a deep breath before they approached the panel.

"This is our democratic process." Principal Johnson looked down, possibly to avoid the skeptical stares of the crowd as well as to check his notes. "These officials are here to listen to what we have to say. Please give them the courtesy of keeping your remarks on-point and as brief as possible."

"Not when they're trying to wreck our town!" one man shouted from the back of the room. A round of defiant applause swept through the gym.

"Here we go," Diane said. "Five minutes, and it's already going off the rails."

The principal squared his shoulders. "Jeff, I need you to take your seat, or remove yourself from the premises. We are determined to conduct this meeting in an orderly fashion." He looked around the rest of the room. "Anyone who doesn't want to comply should leave right now. If there are any more outbursts, we have law enforcement here to take care of the situation."

Melinda noticed two sheriff's deputies leaning against the wall in the far corner of the gym. "Wow, I guess they are prepared."

"Jerry insisted on it," Miriam said. "You weren't here a few years back when the district decided to send the middle- and high-school students to Swanton, but those meetings got really nasty. He's hoping to avoid that, this time around."

Principal Hobson turned to the panel, gave a small shrug, and held out the microphone. The oldest of the three men pushed back his chair and came to the podium.

He introduced himself and the other representatives of the postal service, then turned the floor over to the woman, who gave a five-minute speech about budget constraints, efficiency studies and departmental consolidation efforts. Her rundown was met with icy glares, random whispers and shuffling feet, but the crowd otherwise stayed silent. When she finished, no one moved. Her colleague rose again, and announced the start of the public-comment session.

Jake was already out of his chair. He snatched the microphone away and launched into his speech before the moderator could even get back to his seat.

"I'm Jake Newcastle, a member of the Prosper city council and a teacher in this fine school district," he told the federal officials, who stared at him with stony expressions. With introductions made, Jake turned back to face the crowd. "And I bet most of you already know who I am."

Miriam put a hand over her face. "Oh, he's on a roll."

Jake, however, managed to keep his comments on point.

"Maybe he learned something after that run for the mayor's seat," Melinda told her mom as Jake continued his passionate plea.

"Well, he's certainly fired up. I wonder if Jerry's next?"

Prosper's mayor, however, remained in his chair. Frank said something to him, and Jerry shook his head. Instead, Frank went forward, and motioned for Paul to follow.

"What's going on?" Roger was concerned. "Does Jerry have stage fright?"

"I don't know, but he might." Melinda sighed. Jerry was flipping through his notes again, a deep frown on his forehead. "He has to speak! How bad will it look if he doesn't?"

Uncle Frank echoed Jake's concerns in his usual calm way, then handed the microphone to Paul. The pastor talked about the outlying locations supported by Prosper's post office, which included his church, and how that service linked the rural residents to those in town. He shared an impressive list of statistics highlighting the depth and breadth of the post office's role in the area, and Melinda was pleased to see he had the federal employees' full attention.

"Way to go, Paul." Roger nodded. "He's showing them we mean business."

"Nancy pulled all that data together," Melinda told her dad. "It gives serious weight to what he's going to share next."

"I know my time is almost up." Paul's tone was calm and respectful. "But I have one other number for you to consider." He lifted the thick pile of papers off the podium, and walked over to the table.

"Eight-hundred-and-twenty-three   people,   from   all around this zip code, signed this petition in protest of the plan." Paul put the stack in front of the lead official, who seemed to shrink back into his chair. "I think this shows how much local residents value the Prosper post office, and how the area would be negatively impacted if it closed."

"That's a nice way to put it," Miriam muttered.

"Thank you for your submission." The official reached for the stack of paper and held it for a moment, as if marveling over its weight. "I'm sure we'll take it into consideration." The woman's eyes widened as he passed her the petition. One of the other men now stared at the floor, as if afraid to meet the piercing eyes of the crowd, and the fourth member glanced around nervously. The balance of power in the room had started to shift.

"Bet this makes it harder, huh?" Roger rubbed his hands together. "All those names. And all these people, staring you down. I wanted to see them squirm and, well, they are now."

"Be quiet." Diane slapped his knee. "Promise me you aren't going to make a scene."

"There's enough other people willing to do it," Melinda told her dad. "Look at the line that's forming."

The other council members stated their objections. As a newer resident and the owner of Prosper's latest commercial venture, Vicki gave a thoughtful, enthusiastic overview of the town's vitality and community spirit.

Auggie was next. He recited his flaming letter to the editor with great gusto, and punctuated it with several sharp stares and a few rounds of raised eyebrows. When he finished, the gym erupted with cheers and whistles, and he raised his fist in triumph.

"I bet Jake is jealous," Melinda said to Miriam. "Auggie's not exactly tactful, but he knows how to get a crowd on his side."

After that performance, the session became more heated. Thunderous applause echoed through the gym after every speaker, and sometimes during the middle of a speech. There were whistles, too, especially when anyone made a snide jab at the postal service's plan. Farmers talked about how they'd had the same rural carriers for decades, and relied on them for package deliveries as well as their mail.

Prosper residents offered similar stories, and spoke about how the post office was a gathering place in the community. The officials remained rooted behind the table, their jaws tense and their faces pale, as person after person challenged the government's plan.

Glenn's years of service were referenced several times, and each mention incited another round of applause. He was near the front of the crowd, on the end of the third row, but had told Jerry he had no intention of speaking that night.

As for Jerry himself, he had yet to leave his chair.

"What is he waiting for?" Diane asked as the crowd rose to its feet again, stomping and cheering as another resident finished his remarks. The forum was well into its second hour, and the line of people waiting to speak was shorter than before. "Everyone wants to hear what he has to say."

Uncle Frank turned in his chair. He pointed at Melinda, and then at Jerry.

She ducked through the rest of her row and hustled down the aisle. "Come on." She tapped Jerry on the shoulder, and motioned to the closest corner of the gym.

"I just don't know if I can do it," Jerry admitted once they were out of the fray. The roar in the gym was deafening now, as one young man had the crowd whipped into an emotional frenzy. "Look at him." Jerry pointed at the speaker. "How am I going to follow that?"

"He has them fired up, for sure. But shouting at the top of his lungs? Not really needed. Look, it's not just the residents that are hanging on his every word." She tipped her head toward the sheriff's deputies, who studied the speaker with eagle-eyed interest. "I think you can get your point across without risking arrest."

"I just have so many things to say." Jerry shuffled the papers in his hands. "And you know I hate to talk to crowds."

"You certainly knocked it out of the park the night of the festival. Keep it short and focused, that's all you have to do." Melinda pulled a pen from her purse.

"Here, this part is really good! And this here." She circled a few more paragraphs. "Oh, and this. There. A minute maybe, tops."

Frank had joined them, and put a hand on his friend's shoulder. "You're the designated hitter. Batter up! We'll hit the Watering Hole when this is over. I'll buy."

"Well, then." Jerry sighed, but then he shrugged. "Guess I better get going."

The hoots and hollers were just starting to subside when Jerry took the podium. A wave of respectful applause began in the back, and soon swept the room. Jerry was smiling by the time he picked up the microphone. "Sorry to keep you all waiting."

The room settled into respectful silence as he began his remarks. He gained confidence with every sentence, buoyed by the nods of understanding offered by the audience. His wife was in the second row, wearing a proud smile.

"There's something you need to know about our little town," Jerry told the panel. "Prosper may be small in size, but it has a big heart." He pointed out into the crowd. "And every single one of the people in this gym tonight is a part of that."

As the latest round of applause began to subside, Jerry grinned and flipped to another page of his notes.

"So, I guess I have one more thing to add. Prosper is strong, Prosper is proud, and we aren't about to give up. To paraphrase one of the Midwest's greatest writers, I'll just close with this: Word of Prosper's demise has been greatly exaggerated."

Hoots and claps rose from the crowd. Jake, who was still in the front row, ran to the podium and took the microphone out of Jerry's hand.

"Let's hear it for our mayor!" he shouted. "Let's hear it for Prosper!"

The crowd was on its feet, cheering and shouting. Even Auggie, there in the second row, had a gleeful grin on his face. The government officials stared at each other. What now? They had clearly lost control of the room.

The moderator finally shrugged and stood up, and the others soon followed. They gathered their binders and notepads, and the woman tucked the petition into a file folder. By the time they left the gym, no one seemed to even notice.

Jake was really warmed up now, and leading the crowd in a chant of "Prosper's number one! Prosper's number one!" that was accompanied by a series of claps and hand motions.

"Is that an official cheer?" Melinda asked Frank as they stood off to the side, taking it all in. "Or did he just make it up on the fly?"

"Back when we had a high school, it was a staple of every game. Seems like everyone remembers the rhythm. Look how fired up they are."

"You know, maybe Jake's not so bad."

Uncle Frank sighed. "Depends on the day." Then he smiled. "But with this much community spirit in our corner, maybe we still have a chance."

* 13 *

Emotions were still high the following morning, but the guys quickly turned their attention to the sideboard when Melinda deposited a covered tray on the counter.

"What'cha got?" Auggie was only a step behind. "Looks like bread."

"Just a little flat," Jerry said. "But I'm sure it's still tasty."

Bill reached for the paper plates kept in the upper cabinet. "I'd guess this is some sort of cinnamon-roll thing."

"None of you are quite right, but none of you are wrong." Melinda removed the tent of foil, careful not to smudge the icing drizzled on top of the loaf. "It's a holiday tradition. German, I believe. I found it in the binder of Schermann family recipes."

Ada had taken her mother's recipe box home to Mason City long ago, but she fulfilled her promise to photocopy its contents for Melinda. The rest of the guys seemed more interested in tasting the treat than learning its history, but George sported a smug grin.

"I think I know what this is. Anyone want to take a stab at it before I spill the beans?"

"I will." Auggie volunteered. "Take a stab at it, I mean." He reached for the serrated knife and sawed away at the loaf. "Nuts, raisins, dried fruit and frosting; man, this is just what I needed today."

Melinda hadn't slept well, and was content to simply pour her coffee and let the guys dish out the treats. Between the crowd's roller coaster of emotions at the public hearing, and the sight of Josh sitting with Gretchen, she'd tossed and turned half the night.

George nodded his thanks as Bill passed him a plate. "Melinda, correct me if I'm wrong, but I'd say this is stollen."

"You're right." Her love of baking and cooking had only expanded since she'd moved to the country, but working with yeast was something she was still trying to master. Between the blending and the resting and the kneading, it was a good thing Monday has been the second half of her weekend. The effort had consumed most of yesterday afternoon, and she'd had to hurry to drizzle on the icing before she left for the public forum.

"How'd you guess that one?" Doc asked George, then took a hearty bite.

"My mother made them every Christmas. And I'm a Freitag; you don't get much more German than that."

Auggie took a gulp of coffee. "My grandma made them, too. Oh, this brings back memories! We always gathered at Grandma and Grandpa's farm at noon on the big day. We'd have a huge dinner, then there was sledding on the hill out behind the barn, and hot chocolate."

"Was this around here?" Bill asked. "Or on a Hallmark card?"

"Easy, kid," George chuckled. "Let us geezers get sentimental if we want. Half the time, the old days are easier to remember than what we had for dinner last night." He fished a scrap of paper from his cardigan's pocket. "Oh, that reminds me. Mary needs two bags of mixed chocolates, three of nuts, and one of those with the dried cranberry things."

"Oh, those darn craisins." Doc sighed. "I had to buy some of those once. I was at the superstore in Swanton when Anne called and said she wanted them for a party mix. Walked around everywhere in that store, I swear."

"Didn't you just ask a clerk?" Auggie frowned.

"Yeah, I did. Some high-school kid, but he didn't even know what they were. And one woman, she knew, but wasn't sure where they were stocked."

"Well?" Frank couldn't take the suspense. "What if there's a craisin emergency, and we're fresh out here?"

"Juice aisle." Doc nodded sagely as the guys mentally filed away that bit of trivia. "The raisins are there, too. Just so you know."

Melinda went into the grocery aisle and pulled George's requests off the shelf. Prosper Hardware's selection of sweets and baking ingredients was basic at best, but Miriam stocked a wider variety this time of year. The seasonal items were in high demand, so Melinda hid George's stash behind the counter. The guys weren't likely to wrap up their discussion before the store opened, and she wanted to be sure Mary got what she needed.

His stomach now full of stollen, Auggie stared out at the flurries dancing along Main Street. "We always had snow at Christmas." He sounded far away. "High drifts, sometimes. It really made the season special."

"The snow is pretty," Doc admitted. "But it'll be better for travel if we don't have a big storm right around Christmas. What are the odds this year?"

"About even, as it looks now. It's a little early to say for sure, the long-range models aren't the greatest." Auggie turned back to his friends. "Hey, I have an idea. Why don't we draw names for gifts? Play Secret Santa, just among us guys. Nothing fancy, little stuff."

"Nope." Jerry shut that one down fast. "I hate to shop. It's hard enough to find the right thing for Candace, even though she always says she's not picky."

Doc shook his head in the negative.

So did Bill. "I'm out. No time for that." Bill's usual good humor had returned after the night of the holiday open house, but Melinda still tried to give him a wide berth. They needed to talk more, but she had no idea when the right time might be. Or what to say.

Frank tried to ease Auggie's disappointment. "Sorry, Santa. I guess our friendship will have to be enough. Besides, the season's not supposed to be about material stuff."

"Bah humbug, then. I just thought it would be fun, liven things up around here."

"Well, if you want lively," George said, "I think there's an easy way to accomplish that. Last night's meeting really got me thinking. I know we have a long way to go until this post-office thing gets resolved, but it's going to be important to keep that momentum going. People are fired up, and we need them to stay that way."

"What are you thinking?" Jerry was curious. "I'm open to suggestions, but I'd say we don't need any more letters to the editor."

"What?" Auggie crossed his arms. "Got a right to my opinions."

"Yeah, you do. Just share them in a more-appropriate way, OK? I mean, you already have that sign."

Melinda sensed a fight brewing. "George, what do you have in mind?"

"We need something that'll draw people to the post office, remind them we're all in this together. The holidays are always Glenn's busiest time of year, we should make the most of it. I think a stamp-in would be perfect."

"A stamp-in?" Frank frowned. "What's that?"

"See, everyone is sending out holiday cards." George was really warmed up now. "We pick a day, spread the word, and people show up to buy those books of seasonal stamps. It boosts the post office's revenue, which is good for the cause. But it also makes a great photo op for the local paper. Can you just imagine it?"

He pointed out the window. "Dozens of people ... no, hundreds of people, lined up out there on the sidewalk, just waiting to get in next door."

Auggie nodded slowly, thinking it through. "Show the feds that the Prosper post office, by which I mean the building itself, is a vital part of the community. This isn't only about keeping our carriers local, although that's important. We have to show how the physical site generates foot traffic."

"What about inventory?" Melinda wanted to know. "I'm sure Glenn can request more stamps to have on hand, but how will he know how many booklets to get?"

"Oh, word spreads fast in this town." Doc grinned. "And people don't promise to get behind something unless they have every intention of following through. He should be able to get a sort-of-estimate on how many he might need."

Auggie had an idea. "We could cast a wider net this time. You don't have to be a resident of Prosper's zip code to buy stamps at the counter. Anyone can do it."

"Wait a second." Jerry held up a hand. "I'm all for supporting the cause, but won't this slide into ... oh, what's the word I'm looking for?"

"Misrepresentation?" Auggie smirked.

"Cheating." The mayor looked around at his friends. "That's what I mean."

"People do come to Prosper to shop." Frank shrugged. "And eat at the Watering Hole, take part in activities at the school. We always say this town may be tiny, but it's still a hub for people from miles around. That's what has kept Prosper on the map this long."

"And it can work in our favor, again." Auggie nodded. "I say, let's give it a go."

Jerry sighed. "Well, I guess it might work. Personally, I'm happy to participate. Professionally, though, I think Mayor Simmons is going to pretend this conversation never happened in his presence." He reached for his coat. "Besides, the mayor has paperwork that needs his attention. Time for him to get across the street."

George called Glenn, the event was set for Saturday, and the plan was the talk of the town by late afternoon. There was just enough time for the post office to request an extra allotment of holiday stamps.

"I'm already overstocked," Glenn told Melinda that afternoon when he stopped in for ice melt and a pair of insulated boots. "But they won't question it, since we're supposed to keep extras on hand this time of year. Besides, it would be even better if we ran out. So many customers, so much demand, Prosper's little post office can't even keep up!"

Glenn had been pale and quiet lately, but this scheme put the spring back in his step. "Make people think something's scarce, or special, and they want it even more, right? I mean, that's what you always say."

Melinda could only shake her head. "Yeah, you've got me there. That's marketing 101. I didn't realize you all were listening that closely when I talk about advertising and promotions. But I see now, I've created a monster."

Glenn grinned as he shouldered his bag of ice melt. "No, not really. You've just given us the tools we need to keep fighting."

***

"Oh, come on." Sam lifted his cup of cider and raised an eyebrow at Nancy. "A little civil disobedience never hurt anyone."

"I want to save the post office, too. I just hope this doesn't backfire on us in some way. If nothing else, we need to make sure Glenn isn't implicated in this little stunt."

Nancy paused long enough to accept the tray of Christmas cookies Amy was passing around the table in the library's meeting room. The book club had decided to give Dickens' classic a fresh read for this month's meeting, but there were more-pressing matters to discuss first.

"It would be wonderful to see so many people at the post office at once," Nancy added, "and it would make a great media moment. But it seems a little ... manufactured."

Melinda hid a smirk as she added her seven-layer dip to the growing spread of appetizers on the side table. She shared Nancy's concerns, but knew there wasn't much difference between George's stamp-in and Vicki's push to make Prosper picture-perfect for the magazine crew's visit next week. Sometimes, it was all about the presentation.

Sam was thinking the same. "Well, it wouldn't be the first time folks around here stretched the truth a little for a good cause." He tipped his head toward Main Street. "There's enough lights strung up around this town to guide Santa's route from the North Pole and back."

"OK, you're right." Nancy laughed. "I'm just glad the stamp-in is Saturday, so it'll be over and done with before the photo shoot. One stunt at a time."

"I've been meaning to tell you," Melinda said to Nancy as she took her seat. "The tree looks so pretty, and I'm glad nearly all the children's tags have been taken. I keep forgetting to bring my gift; maybe I'll get it over here tomorrow."

The city owned only one artificial spruce, and it was set up in the library since that door saw more traffic than the adjacent entry into city hall. It was also the center of the giving-tree program, a long-standing effort organized by the library and the elementary school. The wrapped gifts were due next week, and would be distributed just before winter break.

"I have a whole section of the storage room cleared out to hold the packages," Nancy said. "Five more were dropped off this afternoon. The school office's secretary is going to make sure the last of the requests get filled." She studied Melinda's plate. "Amy, are those your meatballs? I'll have to try them, maybe several times."

More club members came through the library. Bev nodded her thanks as Melinda hurried to take the slow cooker from her hands. "Thank you, dear. Couldn't decide what to bring, so I thought, why choose at all? That's cheesy potatoes, and there's peanut clusters in this tote."

"You'll have to roll me out of here." Karen took off her coat. "I'm starving. Hardly had time for lunch, then three farm calls in a row this afternoon. One thing after another. The critters are all up to something; you'd think a storm was coming."

"Is it?" Nancy glanced toward the library's front window.

"Auggie says no," Melinda replied. "At least, not until this weekend. Just lots of wind."

"Well, that gives me comfort," Bev said sarcastically. "Count on Auggie to give us the latest. Whether he's right or not, well, that's part of the fun."

Because the library was closed most evenings, the club had the place to themselves. Shelby Dunlap, the elementary school's music teacher, soon arrived, but Vicki texted Nancy that she was running late. The other members settled in for tasty snacks and good conversation while they waited.

"So, how is the cat fundraiser going?" Shelby asked Melinda and Karen. "How many of those little condos are you going to make?"

"At least thirty, and that's just a start," Melinda said proudly. "We'll get those together, and then can make extras as more donations come in. Of course, we'd never have so many upfront without Auggie's sponsorship." She turned to Karen. "Oh, I meant to tell you; Bill wants to help. He'll be there."

Melinda had been pleased by Bill's interest in the effort. She wasn't sure if he was trying to make amends for his cutting comments at the open house, or if the lure of a new project was something he couldn't ignore. Either way, she was grateful to accept another set of hands.

"How are those grant applications coming?" Amy asked. "My parents brought three of their barn kitties to the clinics this fall. Now that the girls are done, they want to get the toms fixed in the spring."

"I'm finishing the last of them this week." Melinda got up to pile more snacks on her plate. "And the very first one we applied for, a few months ago, we should hopefully hear about before the end of the year."

"I can't believe that's only a few weeks away." Nancy sighed. "Where does the time go?"

"That's one of life's great mysteries," Sam replied, "and I don't think we'll solve it tonight." A round of barks and yips echoed through the library. "Oh, great, she brought the dog."

"Now, be nice." Bev elbowed Sam and lowered her voice. "Francesca's an emotional support animal, she has the right to be here. I'd suppose the holiday rush has Vicki going six ways from Sunday, and Francesca's a calming influence."

"I know," Sam muttered. "But does she have to dress her like that?"

The brown Pomeranian's sweater was especially festive tonight. This pullover was bright red, with colorful ornaments knitted on the front and three petite bells stitched along the neckline.

"Oh, Sam, would you be a dear?" Vicki waved the end of the leash under his nose, and Sam obliged. Truth be told, he was as besotted with Francesca as everyone else. Who could ignore that sweet little face?

"I feel terrible about being so late." Vicki seemed flustered as she added her vegetable tray to the buffet. "It took longer than usual to close up the store, we were so busy today with that sale going on. I'd asked Arthur to start dinner, but he had a late board meeting, and ..."

"No worries," Nancy said gently. "We've just been visiting. Here, let me take your coat."

"And that's not all. I wish there was better news about the New Year's Eve party." Vicki wasn't on the steering committee for the community center's renovations, but had eagerly volunteered to help plan the big bash.

Melinda put down her fork. "I thought everything was on track? I mean, the Watering Hole is going to handle the sandwiches and the chili, then everyone else is bringing chips and snacks."

"Is there a problem with the liquor permit?" Nancy's eyes widened. "Are Jessie and Doug not able to ..."

"No, it's not that." Vicki dropped into a chair, and Francesca took over her lap. "But the place is still a mess. Oh, we're making progress," she added quickly, "I don't mean to imply people aren't working hard. But there's still so much to do! Even if everything is scrubbed until it shines, the walls are still that blah color, the floors haven't been refinished ..."

Melinda knew what Vicki meant. The building had been vacant for about ten years but it might as well have been fifty, given the dirt and dust accumulated inside. "All of that can come later. Actually, this is a great way to show how much work still needs to be done."

"And inspire people to support the rest of the project," Nancy reminded Vicki, "either with money or donated materials or labor. It doesn't need to be perfect, right out of the gate."

Shelby leaned down the table. "Speaking of cheap labor, the juniors and seniors get credit for volunteer hours. And school's out that whole week, between Christmas and New Year's."

"That is a great idea!" Amy brought Vicki a cup of coffee. "Even if the teens can't contribute until winter break, they can help push through the final preparations. I'll call the high school in the morning and get the ball rolling."

The group settled into a comfortable silence as everyone tucked into their plates. Finally, Nancy glanced at the clock. "Well, I suppose we should talk about the book, at least a little." Everyone laughed, and then Bev raised her hand.

"Actually, before we get started, I have some exciting news to share."

"A new grandbaby?" Nancy asked.

"Oh, no, not yet. Another month to go. I've decided to go back to work."

Melinda was surprised. "Aren't you and Clyde still farming? I mean, you have the cows, even if you don't plant crops anymore."

"Well, truth be told, we could use the money," Bev admitted. "And it's been a few years since I retired from teaching. I miss getting out of the house. That's why I decided to join book club."

Sam frowned. "But full time? At your age?"

"Oh, you mean *our* age? You're still chugging along. I've signed up as a substitute mail carrier for the Eagle River post office. Just found out yesterday, I'll be joining the force after the first of the year. It's just a few days each week, filling in for the regular drivers."

"Aren't you worried about the weather?" Vicki asked. "When it's snowing, or if the wind's howling, like it is tonight. Won't that be some tough driving?"

"I thought about that, but decided I could handle it. Driving the gravel doesn't faze me. And our old beater car runs like a top, even in sub-zero temperatures."

"You have to use your own vehicle?" Shelby was surprised.

"They all do," Bev explained. "But we get mileage on top of our pay. It's a pretty sweet deal."

"Well, I'd say congratulations are in order." Sam raised his mug of cider. After the applause died away, he turned back to the business at hand.

"As for this book we read, the real reason we're here, I've seen several movie and TV versions, but never sat down and read the source material. Amy, this was a great choice."

"It's rather short, so I thought we could easily finish it in time. Not to mention, it's perfect for the season."

As everyone chimed in with their opinions, Melinda looked around the table. Sam was partially right; they were here to discuss what they had read.

But that wasn't the only, or even the best, part of book club. The friendships were what mattered most. Even little Francesca was enjoying herself, eagerly accepting treats so she would sit through the group's debate about character development and symbolism.

Melinda was surprised by Bev's news, but energized, too. Even though Bev was in her early sixties, she was embracing change and looking forward. A new year would soon arrive. What might Melinda accomplish if she did the same?

* 14 *

Melinda swept her hand through the brooder box, much to the dismay of the hen snoozing inside. Nothing.

"Sorry, girlie, just checking." The next nest appeared empty, except for a generous mound of straw. Melinda felt around carefully, determined not to give up. Success!

"Well, that's four so far. Pansy, what do you have over there?"

Pansy cocked her head and glared at Melinda.

"Hmmm. You're in one of your moods, but I shouldn't be surprised. If I wasn't so desperate, I wouldn't even ask. But one of our best customers called, and I don't want to disappoint her. Especially this close to Christmas."

Melinda had inherited Horace's list of regular egg buyers and, spring through fall, the wall phone in the kitchen rang regularly with someone seeking a dozen or two. She was happy to fill their orders, as the "egg money" always came in handy.

She'd even doubled her flock from eight to sixteen in the spring and broadened her little venture to include Prosper Hardware customers looking for farm-fresh eggs. The trucked-in ones were in such high demand, the refrigerated case regularly went empty before the next shipment arrived.

But the hens' production had decreased with the change in seasons, and the requests also rolled to a stop weeks ago.

Until Melinda came home to find Harriet's message on Horace's old answering machine.

Harriet Van Buren was in her eighties, and lived about six miles northwest of Melinda. Her husband passed away a decade ago, Horace had said, but she continued to refuse all pleas from family and friends to move to town. Melinda didn't know much else about her, other than she drove an old Cadillac and loved to spend a few minutes with Hobo whenever she picked up a dozen.

She had a sudden yearning for "real" eggs, Harriet had said, and the roads were getting bad. Would Melinda be a dear and bring them over?

Pansy squawked and spread her wings as Melinda approached. "I already told you, this is a sort-of-emergency. Not because of the roads, since they're fine. But I guess when you're Harriet's age, you don't like to drive when there's even a skim of snow on the gravel. What was I supposed to say? Nope, sorry, I don't do deliveries? Pansy, stop that!"

The cranky hen pecked Melinda's thick chore glove twice, but finally moved over.

One extra egg. Seven to go.

Melinda poked around for a few more minutes, then gave up. "Five will have to do, I guess. I wonder if she would like some Christmas cookies, too. If I'm going to drive over, I might as well make it worth the trip."

The eggs were carefully packed in a partial carton, and the cookies wrapped and added to the tote. Melinda changed into her cleanest farm boots, grabbed her purse, and started for the machine shed.

Lizzie fired up quickly despite the cold, and Hobo's shoulders slumped with disappointment as he watched Horace's old truck rumble down the lane. He never showed an interest in car rides, but Lizzie's appearance often signaled an adventure was about to start. And sometimes, she let him come along. But Melinda knew she was right to leave Hobo at home today. Harriet's farm would be foreign to him, and it was likely Harriet had a dog or two.

Lizzie's heater was temperamental, so Melinda was as bundled up as the eggs. With the defrost on high she puttered up the gravel, turned west on the blacktop, then headed north. A left turn, another mile, and there was the little creek Harriet had told her about.

Up a slight rise from the waterway sat a T-frame farmhouse whose white clapboards were even more faded than Melinda's. The yard light was just coming on, and a fat gray cat looked up from its perch on the wheelchair ramp when Lizzie turned up the short lane.

The remnants of a barn slumped east of the drive, and the shed across the way had seen better days. There was a sturdy garage, at least, and a barren garden plot behind. Far across the lawn, she spotted a small stand of apple trees, now gnarled and bare against the deepening sky.

Harriet must have been watching for her, as she was at the back porch door before Melinda could get out of the truck. "Oh, I can't thank you enough for coming over." Her voice was high-pitched but raspy. Harriet wore at least two cardigans over a faded button-down shirt, and her iron-gray hair was rather long, but recently combed.

Melinda felt a pang of guilt as she picked her way up the sidewalk. Sure, she had chores waiting at home, but this visit was probably the highlight of Harriet's day. "Well, I'm glad the girls still had a few eggs to offer. I'm sorry, but I only found five."

Harriet's wizened face fell, but then she smiled. "Oh, that's all right. It's five more than I had five minutes ago."

She laughed, and Melinda had to join in. It was easy to get caught up in life's worries, and miss the simple blessings that came your way. Like farm-fresh eggs in the middle of December.

"And there's cookies, too." Melinda hoped Harriet wouldn't be too proud to accept them. "I had so many, and I didn't want them to go to waste."

"Oh, bless you. I've been meaning to do some baking but, well, the days just seem to get away from me." She coughed into her sleeve. The entryway was colder than Melinda expected, but she reminded herself that not every enclosed porch had heat.

"There's a little snow, out there on the steps," Melinda said casually. "I see a broom there, in the corner. Would you like me to sweep up before I go?"

"Oh, it's no trouble. I'll get to it, maybe tomorrow. Here, come on in while I get your money. Would you like some tea? I bet you're frozen right through."

She wasn't, but suspected Harriet was well on her way. The kitchen was so cool, Melinda hated to remove her coat. But the room was flooded with the last rays of daylight, and scrubbed so clean that Melinda was instantly ashamed of the dirty dishes waiting in her own sink. She took one of the chairs at the small metal table while Harriet reached for tea bags and two mugs.

Melinda searched for something to say as she set the half-carton of eggs on the table. "I know you haven't started any cookies, but I see the oven's ajar. Are you baking bread?"

Harriet was startled. "Oh, goodness, I forgot." She closed the door, snapped off the temperature dial and reached for the kettle. "The water's hot."

"Here, let me help." Melinda brought over the mugs and tea. Once they were settled, she opened the container of cookies and slid them toward Harriet. The older woman stared at the treats with a mix of emotions on her face, but Melinda struggled to make them out. Especially since the overhead light wasn't on.

"Go ahead, have one," she said brightly. "Take as many as you like. They're yours."

"Are you sure?" Harriet reached for a cookie in the shape of a star, then lifted a paper napkin from the holder on the table. She broke off one corner and chewed slowly, savoring the sweet frosting. "Oh, it's so good! Reminds me of my mother's recipe."

"I have more at home. More cookies, of course, but not eggs. I can place a special order with the hens, if you like.

Maybe they can come up with a few more. You'll be first in line."

A soft bark came from the adjoining room, and an elderly dog padded in and leaned against Harriet. The lab mix's coat had probably been black once, but its muzzle was now completely covered in gray.

"Oh, Buster, my boy." Harriet stroked the dog's ears. "We have company, huh? It's a special occasion." She reached for another paper napkin. "Here, baby, let me wipe your eye."

"What a sweetheart. Is he sick?"

"Just a bit of a cold, I guess. It comes and goes."

Melinda was about to tell Harriet that Doc and Karen made house calls, if she didn't feel up to taking Buster to town. But as she looked around this too-quiet house, it all started to make sense. Harriet didn't have the money for a vet visit. Or much else, for that matter.

Harriet had been trying to warm the kitchen with the old electric stove, so she wouldn't have to turn up the furnace. The entrance into another porch was barricaded with a rolled rag rug; the other closed door, which Melinda guessed opened into a steep stairwell, had its bottom gap stuffed with old towels.

Around the corner, on the living room's mottled brown carpet, sat an unlit kerosene stove. None of the lamps were on, despite the waning day. A nest of worn-but-clean blankets on the drab couch showed where Buster spent his days.

"I like your house." Melinda chose her words carefully. "I'm guessing you've lived here a long time." There was a past-its-prime thermostat by the stairwell door. Melinda couldn't read it from her chair, but the gauge was farther down than it should be. "It's a bit chilly in here. Would you like me to turn up the heat a bit?"

"I'm just fine," Harriet said quickly. "You know, when I was a girl, all we had was a woodstove here in the kitchen and another in the front room. We managed. Of course, when Albert and I took over the house and put in the furnace, we really thought we were living the life."

"It's not still the same one, I hope."

"Oh, no, he put the new one in about thirty years ago."

"Does it work? I mean, like it should?"

Harriet looked at the floor. "Propane's awfully expensive these days." Then she raised her chin. "I have to ration what I have. And you know how those companies are, no one wants to bring out just a little, here and there. Oh, no, they all have a minimum charge and a delivery fee. My check only comes once a month."

"But it's December." Melinda leaned over the table. "And winter's just getting started. How are you going to make it through?"

"Same as I always have." Harriet smiled faintly. "On faith, and what little I have in my purse." She put a wrinkled hand on the table's edge and pushed herself up from her chair. "I'm sure you need to get going. I haven't paid you for the eggs yet." She unzipped her worn wallet, counted out some change and slid the coins across the table. When she reached for more, Melinda gently interrupted her.

"That's enough, that's fine."

"Two dollars a dozen, right?" Harriet frowned. "I would think I owe you at least twenty cents each, since I'm not buying in bulk."

"OK, I'll take a dollar for the five. And if I get any more, I'll call you. And bring them over."

"Oh, that would be wonderful. Thank you." Harriet didn't move to put the eggs in the refrigerator. Maybe she didn't want to open it just now, Melinda realized. Maybe there wasn't much inside.

They sat there, Melinda bursting with questions she didn't want to ask and Harriet didn't want to answer. "You have such a nice kitty." Melinda finally said, pointing toward the front porch. "A big gray one, out there on the ramp."

"That's Mouse." Harriet suddenly smiled. "Because of his color, you see. Hard to believe he was tiny once, when he was a kitten. Did you see Shadow and Midnight? They might be in the garage already, they have their own little door."

"So they like to come inside?"

"Garage only." Harriet shook her head. "Not the house. Oh, don't think I haven't tried!"

The women said their goodbyes, and Melinda hurried out to Lizzie with a heavy heart. Harriet was just one of so many elderly people living alone in the country, clinging to their way of life and trying to get by.

She thought of Horace and Wilbur, and how they had done the same. But the Schermann brothers had always had each other, still did. And while money was always tight, they were never as destitute as Harriet.

"There's stretching a dollar, and then there's this." Melinda watched for any sign of the cats as she carefully backed Lizzie around. "Well, I'm not going to stand by and do nothing. Not this time of year. Not ever."

By the time she passed Ed and Mabel's, a plan was forming in her mind. Harriet didn't have any children, as far as Melinda knew. What about other family? Did her neighbors check on her? A lack of money was hard enough. But a lack of human companionship was almost as bad.

Melinda and her neighbors had been searching for someone needing their help. And here was Harriet, just a few miles away, and in such desperate circumstances. They must be careful, approach Harriet in a way that wouldn't wound her pride. But unlike the Wildwoods, Melinda suspected Harriet was lonely enough to let someone give her a hand.

Ed and Mabel would know how to handle the situation. But there were evening chores to do first, and darkness fell over the farmyard before Melinda finished her rounds. Sunny and Stormy followed her back to the house as far as the picnic table, demanding a few more minutes of attention. Just before she bid them goodnight, headlights appeared on the gravel and came up her lane.

"We have a delivery! Sorry, boys, I have to go. I'd hoped to be here when it came. Finally, the mystery will be solved!"

What was inside the box wasn't in doubt; there were a few gifts for her mom and dad, and a little something for herself.

But the identity of her neighborhood's parcel-service driver had remained unknown, even though the ease of online shopping meant packages were dropped off on a regular basis. In keeping with the customs of this rural area, they were simply left on the unlocked front porch.

The first sticky note appeared several months ago, on a carton from a pet-supply chain. Melinda had been surprised, but then laughed when she read the comment about how cute the baby lambs were as they frolicked in the pasture. Later on, there were notes about the beautiful peonies along the drive, more comments about the sheep's personalities, and observations on the weather. Melinda now looked forward to the friendly notes as much as her purchases.

As it turned out, she wasn't the only one happy about this meeting. The brown truck's horn gave a friendly toot before it rolled to a stop. When the door opened and the interior light snapped on, Melinda saw a woman behind the wheel. Hobo, who had been missing just minutes ago, dashed around the garage and barked a friendly greeting.

"Melinda, it's so good to finally meet you! I'm Connie." She stuck out a gloved hand, and Melinda shook it eagerly.

"At last! I've so appreciated your notes. I've been hoping that one day, I'd be here when you came."

Connie was younger than Melinda would have expected, probably in her thirties. "I've had this route for over five years now." She found some treats for Hobo in the pocket of her brown parka. "The Schermanns rarely got a package, so it's been fun to get a peek at your spread now and then. You're doing wonders with this place. How are Horace and Wilbur these days?"

"Wilbur's memory is getting worse, of course." Melinda followed Connie around to the back of the truck. "Horace, though, he's doing really well. He wasn't crazy about the change at first, but he's settled in."

Connie handed Melinda her box. "I love the country, but it's no place for a ninety-year-old to be living alone. While my husband and I are over between Eagle River and Prosper now, I grew up around here, about five miles away. I'm so glad my route lets me visit the old neighborhood."

"You're loaded down like Santa, I see."

Connie laughed. "For sure, this is the busiest time of year. But it's my favorite, for that very reason. My sleigh has a few more stops tonight, but then it'll be time to head home. Have a great holiday! And I'm sure we'll meet again!"

She patted Hobo on the head, waved to Melinda, and climbed back in the van. Melinda put her box on the sidewalk and reached for Hobo's collar, then kept him close as Connie turned around, tooted her horn again, and headed toward the road.

"Well, I'd say we've had quite the exciting day," Melinda told Hobo when they reached the back steps. As she balanced the box on one hip and opened the door, she started to laugh. Only in an area this rural would someone living five miles away be considered a "neighbor."

"I guess that officially makes Harriet our neighbor, too. There has to be a way we can make her holidays brighter."

* 15 *

"It's just as well Liz and her family aren't coming for Christmas." Melinda studied the stack of unwrapped gifts still waiting under her tree. "I don't have even five minutes to get ready for guests."

She glanced at the clock on the dining-room wall, the one that used to hang in Grandma and Grandpa Foster's home. In one hour, she needed to be at Prosper Hardware to help construct the cat shelters and deliver them to farms around the area. Heavy snow was expected to arrive by nightfall, which only added to the volunteers' sense of urgency.

To top it off, she'd been on the run all weekend. Yesterday had been one of the busiest days of the season at the store, and then she'd hurried home to do chores before running back to town for a clean-up session at the community center.

Would they have it tolerable in time for New Year's Eve? Every completed task seemed to lead to three more. A simple cleaning had turned into a push to repaint the main space and fix up the kitchen. It was rewarding to see everyone's enthusiasm for the project, and reservations for the party were coming in at a steady rate, but Melinda was starting to worry their expectations were too high.

"One thing at a time," she reminded herself as she went into the downstairs bedroom. "At least I have plenty of wrapping paper."

The closet door always seemed to stick, and it made quite the racket when it finally gave way. Hobo, who had been fast asleep on his bolstered bed, looked up with curiosity in his eyes.

"Are you going to help me?" She almost wished he wouldn't, as time was ticking away. "OK, come on." The rustle of the paper rolls brought Hazel on the run from the kitchen, and Grace soon appeared around the half-closed stairwell door. "Girls, you too, I guess. Not like I have a choice."

Hobo helped ferry the unwrapped gifts to the table, but at least he was willing to remain on the floor. The cats insisted on being directly involved, and quickly moved from the chairs to the table's surface to bat at the rustling paper and attack the stack of bows waiting on one corner. Even a wadded-up scrap, tossed into the living room for an impromptu chase, bought Melinda only a minute or two of unassisted peace.

The paper was soon wrinkled, and she was too tired to keep her cuts perfectly straight. But it was just as well. Many of her gifts this year were handmade, and they were far from flawless.

Diane had tried to teach her daughter to knit, but Melinda cringed as she folded the thick scarves she'd crafted for Mark, Roger, and Uncle Frank. Miriam and Diane were no slaves to fashion, but Melinda had decided months ago that the men in her life definitely wouldn't care if the stitches were even, or if there was a loose loop here and there.

"This is what I call 'rustic chic,'" she told Hobo as she held up Mark's navy wrap for a final inspection. "See, the nubby texture hides all the mistakes. As long as it doesn't unravel, I'm good."

She reached for a roll of wrapping paper that wasn't too cute or bright. "He's been living in Austin for years, he's not prepared for this cold. I have no idea how long he'll stay, but I don't think he's going to be picky. Grace, no! That ribbon's not your toy. I need that!"

The calico knew she had contraband in her teeth, and beat a hasty retreat into the living room. Melinda dropped her scissors, fished a little stuffed bird out from under the coffee table, and found Grace hiding behind the couch.

"Here, let's trade." Grace growled, but let the ribbon go. "Oh, great, now it's all wrinkled and dusty. Forget it, I'll leave off the trimmings this time."

Prosper was quiet that afternoon, with only a few cars parked in front of the Watering Hole. Main Street offered a markedly different scene from yesterday morning, when over three hundred people showed up to protest the post office's possible closure and load up on stamps.

The line to get in the door had snaked along for blocks, and several attendees brought homemade signs expressing varying degrees of frustration over the federal government's proposal. It was getting late in the season to mail out holiday cards, but that didn't matter. The stamps would still be valid in the new year, and people had been eager to open their wallets for a good cause.

Prosper Hardware's back lot was full of vehicles when Melinda arrived. The store was closed on Sundays, so the volunteers gathered in the wood shop could be as noisy as they needed to be.

Sheets of stiff foam were spread over two of Bill's worktables, where they could be easily scored and snapped. The two sizes of plastic totes were stacked along one wall, ready to be nestled one inside the other. Bill had already rigged a drill with a router large enough to quickly cut the round openings.

Josh was inside the back door, leaning on the smaller worktable as he showed Bill a drawing of the dimensions. He looked up when Melinda came in, and his smile lit up his whole face.

It was bad enough that her heart did one of those silly little flips when she returned his greeting; even worse was that Bill saw the whole exchange. Thankfully, he only smirked and tucked his extra pencil behind one ear. "Here's what we can do," he told Josh. "Looks like we can get six long sides out of one sheet, and four bottoms, and then ..."

Karen and Melinda had decided on a mix of black, blue and gray bins, so their bulk purchase wouldn't unevenly deplete the Mason City home improvement store's inventory. Karen waved Melinda over to where she and Miriam were sorting the totes.

"Final count is thirty-two shelters, using sixty-four bins. We're trying to decide whether to match the colors up, big and small, or give them some variety."

"Overthinking, actually," Miriam said. "I doubt the kitties will mind which colors they get. By tonight, they'll be snug and warmer than ever before. What's it doing outside?"

"Nothing yet." Melinda tossed her coat on a nearby chair. "It's gloomy, but no snow. I'm really glad we could work this in before Christmas. The timing couldn't be better."

Eric came by with Frank and a few other helpers in tow. "Is the straw out back? We'll bring it in."

"You boys can unload those bales." Miriam's expression made it clear she was referring to everyone under the age of sixty. "Frank, you can hold the door, nothing more."

"Yes, ma'am. Bill says I get to run the router. I can't wait."

Miriam shook her head as the group moved on. "He loves to work with his hands, doesn't matter what it is."

"What's he going to do when you move?" Melinda wondered. "Will he have room for another shop?"

"I don't know. Our friends' ranch isn't exactly spacious, but I think for his well-being, as well as my own, it'll have to be a priority."

"Hey, can you grab that first stack of lids?" Karen asked Miriam. "Let's sort those next. Each house needs two: One large, one small."

Melinda felt a hand on her arm. It was Josh. "So, is Gertrude on board? Is she going to let us bring over a stack of these, free of charge?"

It had taken all of Melinda's powers of persuasion to get the caretaker of Prosper's stray-cat colony to take part in this project. Gertrude loved her cats, but she was as proud as she was poor.

"Yep, I'll deliver her eight on my last stop this afternoon. I told her we got carried away with the spirit of giving, and overbought supplies. And it's too much work to do returns this time of year, so ..."

"Excellent!" Josh beamed. "I knew you'd find a way to bring her around." His vet technician was trying to flag him down. "Sorry, gotta go, Norma needs something. Hey, can you meet me by the door in a few minutes with our list? I have the water bowls out in the truck."

"Sure. I'll be over in a bit."

The parking lot was calm and quiet compared to the organized chaos inside the store. Josh's work truck was pulled up just outside the back door.

"Oh, this is amazing!" Melinda clapped her hands as she counted the stacks of green plastic bowls. "There must be, what, at least twenty?"

"Twenty four, a full two dozen. Insulated cords, sturdy bases, exactly what we need. One for every location; two for the larger groups, like Gertrude's; and a few to spare. Auggie really came through, didn't he? He says he got a bulk discount, but still. Just goes to show what the love of an animal can do to turn someone around."

"Or three. He adores Mr. Checkers and Pebbles, but Chaplin? The two of them have something really special."

"That's for sure." Josh pulled blank stickers and a pen from his coat pocket. "Let's mark these by recipient so they're ready to go."

She glanced at the sky. "I'm glad things are going smoothly. We'll want all of these delivered before dark. I'll make three piles; one for me, one for Karen, one for you."

"Oh, we'll need four. Norma will take part of my route to save time. I have a ... I have something going on tonight. Need to get cleaned up and be ready by five, at the latest."

He was busy writing names on the stickers, but was that the only reason Josh suddenly turned away? Melinda sensed there was something else and, against her better judgement, pushed to find out what it was.

"So, you have plans, then?"

"Yeah, one of the neighbors decided to host a last-minute holiday party. Gretchen said she ..."

"Oh, how fun!" That came out a bit shrill, and Melinda tried to dial it down. "I could see Gretchen wanting to entertain this time of year. She ... certainly is stylish. I can imagine her house is beautifully decorated, and there'll be fabulous food and drinks. How nice of her to invite the whole neighborhood over. Should be a good time."

Josh looked down for a second. "Um, Gretchen's not the host. It's the Davidsons, at the other end of the block. She ... we ... well, she asked me to go with her."

So, that was it.

"I see." Melinda forced a smile. "Well, I'm glad Norma is able to help with delivery, then."

Josh wouldn't look at her.

"I think you have this all figured out." She handed him the list. "I'd better see if they need me inside."

The wood shop was messy with foam scraps and bits of straw, and abuzz with good cheer. Melinda felt pale and sick, but no one seemed to notice.

"Hey, there you are!" Bill's round face was ruddy with laughter as he and Eric broke the scored foam into sections. "Frank's not the only handy one in your family; you should see Miriam work that router, she's getting good at it." At the next table, Miriam repositioned her safety glasses as Karen held another tote steady.

Frank was at the shop radio, trying to sync his phone to the speakers. "Hey, Bill! What am I doing wrong?" he shouted over the roar of the drill. "We need some holiday tunes. But it won't play."

"Old people." Bill sighed, then called over his shoulder. "Frank, you gotta use that other cord. No, the smaller one."

Melinda hurried off to where the rest of the volunteers were assembling the shelters. As soon as a unit was ready, it was whisked away to be padded with a heaping mound of fresh straw. Blinking back tears, she reached for a few slabs of cut foam and put herself to work. Josh could do as he pleased; so could she. How he spent his time, and who he spent it with, was none of her concern. Or at least, it shouldn't be.

It was just one date; but if they were all neighbors and knew each other, why bother to go as a couple? Why wasn't it enough for Gretchen to just hang out with Josh at the party?

Melinda was sure she knew the answer. What she really wanted to know was, did Josh feel the same? Maybe he ...

She wasn't going to solve this problem today, so Melinda tried to set her confusion aside and focus on the tasks at hand. It was already after three, and the group pushed on to complete the shelters as fast as they could. The stacks of finished units were growing by the back door, and Miriam was already circling with a broom, trying to get a jump on tidying up.

"That's the last one!" Karen called out. The wood shop broke out in cheers and claps. "Thanks for your hard work. These look great, and we're just in time." She checked her phone. "The storm warning starts at six. Let's move out!"

There wasn't time to talk. Trucks and vans were loaded, the water bowls divided, and each location double-checked. Josh and Norma would take the western deliveries, as those were on their way back to Swanton. Karen had the northeast portion, and Melinda would travel a southeastern route before making her last delivery at Gertrude's.

"Santa would be proud," Miriam told her niece as Melinda mounted Lizzie's running board. "On Dasher, on Dancer ..."

Lizzie roared to life and lurched out of the parking lot. Melinda turned east on Main, scooted past the vet clinic and the water tower, and made her way out into the country. The first left took her over the old iron river bridge, and then she made a right on the gravel.

The wind was gaining strength, even in this low-lying area guarded by trees on one side and sloping fields on the other. She tried to focus on her mission, on how so many barn cats would benefit from their efforts, but her mind kept returning to Josh.

"It's one date, it's not like ... oh, why is it bothering me so much? Because I like him? Well, of course I do."

But as she rounded the last bend before her first stop, Melinda realized why she was so upset. She and Chase had dated for almost five months, and she had really cared about him. When he started hanging out with an old girlfriend, she'd been surprised, and hurt. But, as she'd finally discovered, she wasn't really jealous. It had been a wake-up call, a sign that even though Chase meant something to her, they weren't meant to be.

And now? The thought of Josh with Gretchen was like a hot knife straight into Melinda's chest. It cut deeper than she ever expected it would. What could she do about that? What *should* she do? Nothing, at least for now; because the name she was looking for was on the next mailbox.

A man in coveralls came out of the enclosed front porch, and bounded down the steps with a quick wave. He'd been watching for her, and the smile on his lined face told her all she needed to know. The plan she and Josh created was already doing good in the community. This farmer had surely had a hard year, and the future wasn't exactly bright; but there were people who cared, and he was grateful.

So was the teenaged girl who ran around the corner of the farmhouse, her coat barely zipped and her knit hat askew over her blonde curls. Three cats followed in her wake, their tails held high in anticipation.

The man was at Melinda's window now, and she rolled it down. "Just pull up by the barn, and I'll drop the tailgate." He glanced into the flatbed and gave a whistle of appreciation. "Look at those! Just what we need. The snow's rolling in within the hour, they say. Perfect timing!"

His daughter caught up with them, a black cat now curled in her arms. "They're here!" Melinda heard her tell the kitty. "Your Christmas houses are here!"

Three totes were soon lined up in a small room inside the barn, hidden away from any drafts. The family's five outdoor cats were all in attendance by then, too busy climbing over the totes and popping in and out of the entrances to pay any mind to the stranger in their midst. The girl filled the insulated water bowl and plugged it in, and her father fetched the cats' food dishes from another area of the barn. In a matter of minutes, there was a snug, cozy space where the cats could ride out winter in comfort.

Melinda left the father and his daughter standing by their barn, and returned their waves as she started down the lane. She gave Lizzie's horn a toot, and was laughing by the time she reached the road.

"Miriam was right, I do feel like one of Santa's elves. And those cats were so happy with their new homes." She glanced at her list. "OK, I need to take a left at the next corner."

Three more deliveries, and it was time to turn Lizzie back toward town. Melinda's final stop was the one that meant the most. She'd called Gertrude when she left the last farm, and the older woman was on her front stoop, wrapped in an old coat. Two cats rushed around the corner of the garage, their eyes alight with curiosity about this visitor, and two more met Melinda on the south side of the house as she carried the first shelter to the open back porch.

"Babies, get away!" Gertrude gently admonished the cats as they circled Melinda's feet. "She's brought us some very special gifts, and you need to let her pass."

As promised, Gertrude had cleared space for the new shelters. The old wooden boxes and drafty carriers were now stored under the porch's floor, and the worn boards had been swept clean. Melinda recognized many of the furry faces eager to give the shelters a test run, but was pleased there were no young kittens in the crowd. The last of Gertrude's colony had been neutered in October, and the population was steady for now. Until a new face showed up, hungry and cold, and was welcomed with open arms.

Gertrude scooped a small brown tabby off a metal chair. "Well, as you can see, we're all decked out for the holidays."

Melinda eyed the single strand of lights draped unevenly along the porch's eaves. "Yes, I see. They're so pretty."

"Got them down at the decoration swap. Makes things festive for the kitties." She tipped her gray curls toward the picture window, where her husband dozed in his lift chair. "We got our tree up and put some stockings on the mantel, and we quit there. We're just so busy."

Melinda just nodded. In truth, the elderly couple couldn't easily deck the halls, or do much of anything else considered manual labor. "There's nothing wrong with keeping it simple. Decorations are nice, but that's not what the season is really about."

Once the shelters were in place on the porch, Melinda brought around the heated water bowls and the insulated extension cord she'd purchased at Prosper Hardware.

"Oh, my, so many new things." Gertrude studied the much-improved situation with damp eyes as the cats continued their inspections. "I just hope this didn't cost too much."

"Everything was donated." Melinda shrugged, careful to not let this transaction carry even a hint of charity. "I'm just glad your kitties can use all of this stuff. We have so much of it, more than we really needed."

"You know, I've never seen that cat you were telling me about," Gertrude said as she walked Melinda back to the truck. "The black-and-white one, with the funny moustache. I've kept an eye out, but he hasn't turned up here."

Dark clouds were moving in from the west, and Melinda was still reeling from her conversation with Josh. But the holiday spirit now filled her heart, and she smiled despite the damp chill in the air. "And I don't think he ever will." She paused to open Lizzie's door. "Chaplin's moved up in the world; he's installed himself in a basket under Auggie's desk. He's found a good life, and he'll never be lonely again."

"Oh, bless his heart." Gertrude beamed, then picked up the large calico cat that had appeared at her feet. "Patches, this is your lucky day," Melinda heard her say. "I told you Santa Claus was real."

* 16 *

"Well, we're as ready as we can be." Jerry leaned back in his folding chair and looked out on Main Street, where a few flurries drifted down to the pavement. "All the lights are on; I called every property owner last night and reminded them to have their displays at full blast first thing this morning."

George looked up from his newspaper. "I thought those magazine people wouldn't be here until at least eleven. Vicki said they were flying into Minneapolis crazy-early, but it's a three-hour drive from the airport."

"Better safe than sorry." Frank lifted his mug from the sideboard and started for his usual seat. "This is our big moment; we don't want to drop the ball now. You know, it really is pretty; like a scene from a snow globe or something. Jerry, do you think the buildings' owners would keep everything lit around-the-clock until Christmas? It's less than a week away now."

"Oh, sure." Jerry rolled his eyes. "They'll think it's a great idea, as long as the city pays for the extra electricity. Which, as you know, we can't afford. They lit everything up for the festival, and then again today, but that's all I can promise. That was the deal."

"I wish I could, but I can't," Doc admitted. "Karen and I want to do some renovations to the clinic next year, so we're pinching every penny."

"As is everyone else around here." Melinda reached for the dust cloth and buffed the oak showcase to a shine. "Practical, affordable gifts top their lists, from what I've seen. Uncle Frank, I think we could sell a few more of those starter tool kits if we can get them in by the end of the week."

"I'm on it. Or I will be, once I finish my coffee."

"It does look lovely out there." Melinda took a moment to enjoy the view. "So peaceful."

George snorted. "Good thing our visitors weren't here Saturday. What a circus that was, between the crowds and all the media attention!"

Staff from the Swanton newspaper attended the stamp-in, as expected, but a van from the Mason City television station surprised everyone when it rolled up just after ten. The spectacle was near the top of both evening newscasts and, much to his delight, Jerry's off-the-cuff speech made the cut. The piece also included several seconds of Glenn behind the counter, chatting and laughing with his longtime customers.

"That went better than I thought it would," Melinda admitted. "George, what a great idea! Although I still can't figure out how the television station got wind of it."

"Didn't they get a press release?" Auggie asked, a little too quickly.

"No, Nancy kept it on the down-low. Word of mouth only, remember? We didn't want the regional office to find out ahead of time, to protect Glenn. Of course, the Swanton paper hears about everything around here; no one would question that." She sprayed a clean cloth with disinfectant and wiped the cash register's keys. "Just makes me wonder if someone called up to Mason City and tipped them off."

The men were suddenly silent. Melinda watched them out of the corner of her eye as she cleaned. When it became clear no one would own up to anything, at least not this morning, she changed the subject.

"Auggie, I have to admit, I'm proud of you for taking down your angry sign. Vicki's worked so hard to make today picture-perfect; lots of other people in town have, too."

"It's not angry. It just states the truth, is all."

"You talk about it like it still exists." Doc studied his friend, a smirk forming at the corner of his mouth. "I noticed that while the sign is gone, the posts are still there. Any chance it'll reappear anytime soon?"

"Oh, I don't know." But Auggie's tone made it clear he did. "Besides, the ground's too frozen now to pull the posts up. Guess they'll be out there until spring, at least. Hey, here comes Vicki now. And little Frankie."

"It's Francesca," Melinda reminded him as she ran to the door. With the leash in one hand and her other arm weighed down with bulging canvas totes, Vicki was overloaded this morning.

"Today's the big day!" Her smile was bright, thanks to her perfectly applied lipstick, but there were lines of fatigue around her eyes. For the hundredth time, Melinda hoped this unexpected opportunity would meet her friend's oversized expectations.

"I went with this evergreen sweater," she told Melinda, as the guys had offered quick greetings and then turned their discussion elsewhere. "Simple and chic, but dark enough it won't compete with the store's displays. I like your hair!"

"Oh, thanks." Melinda had taken five extra minutes to curl her strands before arranging them into their usual work ponytail. She'd added eyeliner and tinted lip balm this morning, too. The guys hadn't noticed any of it, which meant she'd achieved the understated polish she wanted. The magazine spread would be focused on Vicki's shop, of course, but you never knew who might come sailing through Prosper Hardware's door this afternoon.

"Well, two of my best part-timers are coming in early." Vicki began to recite her action plan. "We have that flash sale going on today, to draw more customers than a usual Monday. Angie whipped up some lovely gingerbread muffins and decorated cookies last night, they're like works of art."

"Ever wonder if you're going a bit overboard?" George was gentle, but cautious. "I mean, isn't the point to show the shop as it truly is? Anyone who sees this and wants to come here, aren't they going to be a little bit disappointed?"

Vicki flicked his concerns away with one freshly manicured hand. "Oh, that's not a problem. The feature won't publish for ten months, long enough that people won't expect the same exact experience. It's the feel of the photos that matter, not what is actually depicted in them."

"The concept is what's key," Melinda added. "Especially for this magazine. It's very aspirational." She reached down to greet Francesca, who sported a cream-colored sweater with a border of glittering snowflakes.

"They'll spend most of their time at Meadow Lane, of course," Vicki added, "but city hall's such a beautiful building, and on the historic register. That'll make for some good shots, too. I think they may pop in at the Watering Hole, as well as here, for more local color."

Auggie did the math, then crossed his arms. "What about me? Aren't you sending them down to the co-op?"

Vicki was caught off guard. "Sorry, I didn't think that was part of our agreement. I mean, we talked about it, but ..."

"Agreement?" Doc frowned. "What agreement is this?"

Auggie ignored him. "I would think it's best to include as many businesses as possible," he told Vicki.

Something in the newspaper caught George's eye, and the rest of the men started to discuss it with great gusto. When Vicki saw they were distracted, she turned to Auggie.

"I hear your concerns." There was a hint of defeat in her tone. "And I appreciate how the ... offensive item was removed in a timely manner. OK, fine, I'll make sure they stop by. Just remember to bring your list to the shop tomorrow, so we can have everything selected and wrapped by Friday. If you keep under the limit we discussed, I'll throw in free delivery to the co-op, too."

Auggie could be difficult, but he wasn't dumb. He had apparently bargained his way into every man's biggest holiday wish: A shopping-free Christmas, and a personal assistant to make sure every bow was perfectly in place.

The co-op, however, was going to be a hard sell to the magazine crew. Farmers in muddy coveralls didn't quite mesh with Vicki's vision. Melinda saw another, better opportunity.

"Why don't you make sure the cats are at the counter? Everyone loves animals; it would make for a cute photo or two. Or maybe an exterior shot of the tower, with the big star glowing at the top?"

"That would be really festive." Vicki tried to soothe Auggie's ruffled feathers. "I'm sure they want a few landscape shots to set the scene."

Jerry joined the conversation. "Nancy has two hours blocked out to show them around. I don't know about your cats, though. They add character to the place, but they're not always welcoming to strangers. I tried to pet Mr. Checkers the other day, and he slapped my hand away. With his claws out, I might add."

"Well, you have to do it right," Auggie insisted. "But I'll talk to them about it, see if they're willing to cooperate."

Vicki sighed. "I'll leave that up to you. But wherever the crew decides to go, whatever they want to see, we all need to stay on message: Prosper is quaint, and charming, and filled with friendly faces."

She gripped the leash tighter, and tried to keep Francesca from rushing Prosper Hardware's Christmas tree. "Whatever happens, no one can mention this mess with the post office, and what it would mean for our town. It's going to blow over," she added quickly. "By next fall, none of it's going to matter."

With a round of waves and goodbyes, she swooped Francesca into her arms and went next door. Jerry looked at Melinda and Auggie, and shook his head. "Well, I hope Vicki's Christmas wish comes true. It's at the top of my list, too."

***

A once-shiny black SUV pulled up to the curb just before noon. Its underbelly was coated with slush and muck, and the man departing from the driver's side was careful not to dirty his artfully distressed jeans. A wave of brown hair was slicked back from his forehead, which was surprisingly tan for this time of year.

Melinda was at the window, studying their visitors. The woman's pale-blond bob sported a razor-sharp cut, and her red coat was equally fashionable. Its skirted hem made an elegant twirl as she turned to chat with the photographer.

Esther, who had been replenishing the grocery aisle, now stood by the door, hands on hips. "Well, that must be them. No one around here drives a vehicle like that. Or wears that much black, unless there's a funeral."

"Who is that?" A woman edged around Esther for a better look. "Oh, my, it must be those magazine people." She brushed self-consciously at the front of her faded sweatshirt.

"Now, Marie," Esther warned her, "don't you duck your chin at those New York folks. We're just as good as them. In fact, I'd say we're better. Can you imagine what that coat must have cost? Why, you could outfit your whole family in new coveralls for what she paid, I'm sure."

Vicki appeared on the sidewalk, a green-plaid shawl artfully tossed over her shoulders. Melinda could see her friend's welcoming smile from inside the store, and the man and woman warmly returned Vicki's greetings as well as her handshake. The woman gestured around them and said something to Vicki, who beamed under whatever praise was offered.

"I think they're impressed with our decorating efforts," Melinda told the other women. "They actually seem excited to be here. I hope this goes well." Her phone buzzed in her pocket. "Hey, Nancy. Yeah, we just saw them pull up. Are you heading over to do the official greeting? Great. Good luck."

Esther and Marie lingered by the window long after their visitors followed Vicki inside Meadow Lane, as if waiting to see what might happen next. Melinda had to tap Esther on the shoulder to get her attention.

"Vicki reminded everyone again this morning that we are not to talk about the mess with the post office. We're only supposed to point out Prosper's obvious charm, how Meadow

Lane has been such a boost to our historic business district, and how this is a community where everyone rallies to help each other."

"And that's where Prosper Hardware comes in." Esther gave a nod of understanding. "Vicki's shop has the handmade and specialty items covered, and then people come next door for the nuts and bolts of life, if you will."

Melinda stared at her, then smiled. "Very good, Esther. You're prepared."

"Well, I have it all worked out. Once I see them coming down the sidewalk, I'll head for the other window so that when they walk in the door, I'll be rearranging the ornaments on the tree." She tipped her head in that direction. "See, if I'm over there and they snap a photo, they'll have good light. And we can probably get the antique sideboard in the background."

Bill joined them at the window. "Sounds like you'll be able to hit your mark. So, what's my part in this play?"

"Well, I guess you're the jack-of-all-trades guy," Melinda told him. "Master craftsman, keeper of the ice melt, the hip member of the coffee group, that sort of thing." She reached into her pocket for a folded scrap of paper. "I made these talking points last night. Miriam really wants me to highlight our family's history, how many years the store's been operating, all that stuff." She sighed as she studied it again.

Bill blinked. "So you're the spokesperson, then."

"I guess."

They'd been civil since that awkward conversation during the holiday open house. But their usual buddy-system banter was absent, and Melinda missed it.

Before she could say anything, he pointed behind them. "She's ready to go." A customer with an overflowing hand basket was at the counter. As Melinda went to ring up the woman's purchases, Bill disappeared into the wood shop.

What did he want her to say? *Sorry I'm related to Frank and Miriam, and you're not? Sorry I came home, and decided to stay?*

There was no time to think about it, as a man needed help in the plumbing aisle. His toilet was broken, and he wasn't sure if he'd found the right fitting. Melinda had learned a great deal in her time at Prosper Hardware, but Bill was the real expert. As she called back to the shop, she inwardly sighed over how the day seemed to be going downhill. She just hoped Meadow Lane could deliver on Vicki's promise of holiday cheer.

"What's going on now?" Esther pointed outside. Bethany, one of Vicki's part-timers, hurried to Prosper Hardware's door. Her coat had apparently been forgotten, but she had Francesca in her arms.

"Melinda! Oh, I hope you don't mind, but can you take her? Francesca is a very bad girl!"

The little dog mounted her defense with a snarling bark.

"She's chasing Pierre all over the place." Bethany was nearly out of breath, even though she'd only traveled a few yards. "He can hardly get a shot in before she grabs the hem of his jeans and growls. She's going to rip them, I know she is! And when Audrey was at the counter, right when they arrived? Francesca got on my chair, then climbed up there and bared her teeth, like she was guarding the place. She could ruin everything! We don't know what to do, and Arthur's at work."

"Sure, don't worry, it'll be fine. We'll look after her. Francesca!" Melinda clapped her hands. "Come behind the counter and help me, instead."

Now that she was among friendly faces, the Pomeranian seemed her usual happy self. Bethany let out a big sigh of relief. "Oh, thank you, thank you! We didn't want to bother Nancy, she's going to help Vicki show them around town in a little while."

"How's it going, otherwise?"

"They love the place, and I'm so glad. Audrey's already bought three things for herself. And oh, be sure to tell Frank, Pierre was floored by those weathervanes. He asked if custom designs were available. He's happy to pay extra, of course."

"A weathervane?" Esther snorted. "I doubt he has a barn, or even a house, for that matter. Where would he put it? On the roof of his condo building?"

"Who knows?" Bethany shrugged. "But I'm sure Frank would love a commissioned project."

It was mid-afternoon before Audrey and Pierre made their way to Prosper Hardware. While Melinda hustled Francesca upstairs to the storeroom, Esther got in position by the tree. Sure enough, Pierre snapped her photo. She floated off to stock the housewares aisle, where she could be out of sight but still hear everything that transpired.

"What a charming place!" Audrey told Melinda. "So rustic and yet refined, at the same time." One expensive leather glove fingered the carved edges of the oak showcase. "This piece is just breathtaking. I've never seen anything like it."

"My great-great-grandfather hauled it here from Cedar Falls in a horse-drawn wagon." Melinda had rightly assumed the cabinet would catch the writer's eye, and had her story straight. "They brought it through the front door, and it's been in this spot ever since. It's twelve feet, end to end, and solid oak."

Audrey scribbled in her notebook, and gave Melinda a grateful smile. The more details she had, the easier her job would be. "Vicki says you have quite the story, yourself. So, you really did it? You left the city behind and found your way home again? She mentioned a farm, and animals."

Melinda had those comments ready, too. She'd practiced them on Hobo, Grace and Hazel last night as they'd cuddled on the couch.

Esther nominated herself to show Pierre around the store, but Audrey lingered at the counter.

"You know, Vicki's little shop is just sublime, certainly worth the trip. Our readers will be so in love with what she's accomplished. But there's a larger story here. This town is full of strong women, ladies getting it done, day after day. Why, between Vicki, and yourself, and Nancy ..."

"Nancy's a powerhouse."

Audrey shook her head with genuine respect. "She's got her own empire there, across the street."

"It's too bad Aunt Miriam has the flu and couldn't be here today. Not only have she and Uncle Frank kept this store going, but she's the first person to step up when there's an important project or other need in the community."

The truth was, Miriam had no interest in the spotlight but didn't want to hurt Vicki's feelings. As Melinda talked about how Prosper Hardware was a local landmark, Bill ambled up the main aisle.

"So you're the fifth generation, right?" Audrey checked her notes. "How exciting! And one day, you'll be in charge. What do you envision for the future of Prosper Hardware? It'll all be in your hands."

Melinda tried to keep her smile bright as Bill leaned on the end of the counter. His expression made it clear he didn't share Audrey's enthusiasm.

"Yes, well, I'm going to have a lot of help. This is Bill Larsen, the other full-time employee. He runs the wood shop; he can make just about anything, for anyone. We always say: If you can draw it, Bill can build it." That, at least, brought a smile to his face.

"Sounds like you are quite the craftsman." Audrey seemed genuinely impressed. "You know, I have a friend upstate. Upstate New York, that is. He has his own sawmill and shop, turns out these fabulous tables and chairs, oh, anything you can think of. Hand-milled serving bowls are his signature piece. So, tell me: what are you working on, right now?"

Bill rubbed his hands together. "Well, every day's a little different, as you might expect. But today? A farmer east of town is putting a new steel door on his hog shed, and the current frame's almost rotted away. So I'm cutting lengths for that, and a new threshold, too. Everything has to be just right; those pigs, they're strong as well as smart."

Audrey listened intently as Bill explained the depth of the pigs' intellect. Pierre, however, had only one question. "What's the wi-fi password in here?"

"Oh, sorry," Melinda told him. "We don't have that. The library does, but I doubt the signal reaches across the street. It's the only one in town," she added before Pierre could ask.

"Really? I thought, if nothing else, the post office might have it. Since it's a public building."

Esther, who had trailed Pierre to the counter, widened her eyes at Melinda in alarm. Audrey was still distracted, at least, as Bill was now describing the dozens of interlocking pieces he'd cut for a new chicken coop last week.

"Oh, no, there's no wi-fi at the post office." Melinda tried to head Pierre off. And that was the truth. "Not much else there, either. It's really tiny, as you can see; not worth a stop."

"My grandparents live in a small village in Vermont." Pierre didn't seem willing to drop the conversation. "And there, the post office is the center of everything. It's where people gather. I'd bet this one's the same. It would make a few nice shots."

"Prosper Hardware is the hub of this town," Esther said quickly, and a little too loudly. "No one ever goes to the post office."

"Not for anything other than their mail," Melinda added. She could just imagine the scene next door: Glenn, with his weary face and defeated attitude, leaning on the counter as he grumbled about how the federal bean-counters were trying to destroy this town. If Pierre wanted more photos, she needed to send him somewhere else. Anywhere else.

"There's a really charming place, though, that you passed on the way in. The co-op has been in Prosper for a hundred years. It has that community feel you're looking for."

Audrey was listening now. "Oh, Vicki did mention that. I was surprised to hear you have a cooperative in town. I didn't think Prosper had a grocery store. I assumed this was the only place where ..."

"It's a different kind," Melinda explained. "For the farmers, and their grain."

"It's always full of characters." Bill leaned in, as if sharing a secret. "Everyone likes to hang out there."

"And there are cats," Esther added. "Three rescued strays, in fact. They love to lounge on the counter and greet their guests."

"They're so sweet," Melinda gushed, as she saw the light of interest in both visitors' eyes. "You have to meet them."

"Well, then, I think we've found our final stop." Audrey stuffed her notebook in her oversized leather tote. The bag was sleek and expensive and, for a moment, Melinda felt a pang of envy. She'd had one, too, in her past life. But it was as out of place in Prosper as Audrey, and Melinda had donated it long ago.

"That, and a stop for gas, and we'll be ready to head out," Pierre told Audrey, then turned to Melinda. "Where's the gas station? It must be on the east end of town, since I don't think we've seen it."

"There isn't one, sorry."

They stared at her with surprise, and maybe a bit of fear, in their eyes.

"You don't have one?" Audrey gasped. "How is that possible? How far ..."

"Swanton's south and west of here, about eight miles," Bill explained. "Or, since you'll be wanting to head north, there's a truck stop right before you hit the interstate. But that's about twenty miles."

When neither of them responded, Bill had to ask. "How low are you, anyway?"

"We can make it to Swanville," Pierre finally said, and Melinda felt too sorry for him to point out his mistake. "It's out of the way, but it'll have to do."

"The good news is, you don't have to drive all the way in," Esther explained, as if Swanton was a traffic-congested metropolis and not a town of ten thousand. "Too bad it's already afternoon; that place has the best breakfast pizza."

"But there's doughnuts," Bill was quick to point out. "There's always doughnuts."

"Yes, well, we'll have to get some of those." Audrey's tone indicated she'd rather starve than consume a fried pastry that had lingered on waxed paper for eight hours. She wrote down Melinda's cell number, in case she had any more questions about Prosper Hardware, then she and Pierre gushed their goodbyes and left.

"Well, that's done." Esther seemed deflated as she straightened the snow shovels in the display window. "Our fifteen minutes of fame are over."

"They sure are." Bill laughed. "And not a moment too soon. We can drop the welcome-wagon act, and get back to normal. Speaking of which, those pigs are waiting for their new door. I better get busy."

Melinda leaned over the counter. Esther was preoccupied, and there were no customers in the store. This was her chance. "Bill, I'm sorry if you felt left out today. I didn't mean to ... well, Miriam asked me to take her place."

"Never mind. You're family."

"But you are, too. Doesn't matter that we're not related. Frank and Miriam are always saying that, and they mean it."

"They do?" His eyes lit up. "Really?"

"Yes. And I agree. Look, I don't know what the future holds. But if this town can find a way to keep going, and this store keeps going with it ... I don't want to do this alone. I *can't* do this alone. You're always going to be needed around here. Please know that."

Bill mulled it over, then finally nodded. "Cool," was all he said, but he was smiling. "I'll be in the back."

* 17 *

Melinda's arms overflowed with totes and containers as she approached Scenic Vista's front entrance the following evening. A stiff wind swept through the parking lot on the edge of Elm Springs, and threatened to knock her off her feet. At least, she wasn't out there alone; a couple came up the sidewalk just then, and the man was quick to get the door.

"Thank you, so much," Melinda gasped. "I didn't want to make more trips than I had to."

"No problem. I bet you're celebrating Christmas tonight." He pointed at her packages as they all stomped the slush off their shoes. "You're loaded down, I see."

"You must have grandparents here," the woman said. "Who's your family?"

Melinda was caught off guard, but then a smile spread across her face. Yes, she did have family at this senior-living facility. They may not be true relatives, but she and the Schermanns had been brought together by chance and now, she couldn't imagine what her life would be like without them. It was too complicated for an easy reply, but the man and woman had cared enough to ask, so ...

"I'm here to visit Horace and Wilbur Schermann. They're ... extended family. Great-uncles."

"You're so fortunate." The man shook his head as he removed his gloves. "My mother is here, and we come often, but it's so hard to get the larger family together. Everyone is spread all over, and so busy. You must consider yourself blessed."

"I do." Melinda meant it. "Well, enjoy your visit. Merry Christmas!"

As she settled her totes on the lobby floor and tried to get organized, she thought about what the man had said. Frank and Miriam had no children, of course, but she had several cousins, aunts and uncles on the Foster side.

Other than the annual summer family reunion, she didn't see them very often. Grandma and Grandpa Foster had always hosted a large Christmas celebration at their farm, but that tradition had faded as they aged. Once they died, it stopped altogether.

But now, Melinda had her own farmhouse. There was plenty of room. More than once already, she'd hosted the Schermann clan for one reason or another. Why not her own extended family? It was too late for the holidays, but maybe in the spring ...

Scenic Vista's employees had gone all-out again this year, as obvious reminders of the season were visible in every room and waiting around every corner. The effect was cozy and cheerful, even if it was a bit overdone. A fire glowed in the gathering room's hearth, and a towering Christmas tree stood proudly by the main bank of windows. More faux greenery, in the form of oversized wreaths, crowded the halls. Garlands wrapped with glowing lights were draped over every entryway, and stockings marched along the edge of the nurses' station.

Her arms growing heavy, Melinda trudged down the main corridor and took the turn toward Horace and Wilbur's apartment. The unit had only one bedroom, with a sitting area and a tiny kitchen tucked along a wall, but it had a sweeping view of Scenic Vista's back yard. Birds and squirrels flocked to the feeders, and the apartment was perfectly positioned to view the sunrise. Kevin always said the place was perfect for two old farmers.

And there he was in the doorway. The blue eyes behind his glasses were so like those of his elderly uncles', there was no question they were related. "Goodness, is there anything still out in the sleigh? You must have packed the trunk full."

"Well, not really. This time of year, it's reserved for all the necessities: extra gloves and hats, blankets, water, and energy bars. Not to mention the shovel, spare boots ... if I ever get stranded, I'll be ready. But the back seat? Yeah, it was overflowing."

"Oh, country life." Kevin relieved her of two of her totes. "I remember it well. I miss our farm, it was a great place to grow up; but this time of year, I'm glad Mom and I are both in Mason City."

The apartment was decked out for Christmas, with a tabletop tree and a string of lights above the main window, but no one was inside. "Where's the party?"

"Oh, we reserved one of the community rooms." As they started down the hall, Kevin leaned in. "So, what's going on with this Josh guy? Have you talked to him?"

"Nope. Not since Sunday. And I don't intend to. At least, not for a while. It's only been two days."

"Uh-huh." Kevin didn't seem convinced.

"Hey." She slapped his arm. "I told you, I need to stay out of it. Look, it's probably just as well that he's ... well, whatever is going on."

"Dating someone else?"

She frowned.

"Sorry."

"I mean, we need to keep this professional. There's the clinics, of course, and the grants ..."

"Just stop it." Kevin rolled his eyes. "You're nuts about him, and I suspect he feels the same. I have a good feeling about it."

That made Melinda happier than she wanted to admit. "Well, thanks."

"I don't think you believe me." Kevin pretended to be hurt. "Did I ever tell you that Horace's grandma always claimed she had 'the sight,' as she called it? And I'm rather intuitive, myself. I'd say you have this locked down."

"This is a conversation for another time." Melinda had never heard that bit of Schermann family lore, and she was intrigued by both of Kevin's comments. But the community room was packed with familiar faces, and she couldn't wait to visit with some of her favorite people.

"I see Jack's here. I'm so glad he came." Kevin's boyfriend had been readily accepted by his mom and Uncle Horace. But Melinda raised an eyebrow when she saw Aunt Edith. "What does she think of all this?"

"I don't know if she gets it, but doesn't care," Kevin whispered, "or she's decided to ignore it. I introduced him as my friend, and she didn't ask any questions. Besides, her family's trying to talk her into selling her place and moving to a care facility, so she's up in arms about that."

Edith sat at the head of the large table, right where she preferred to be, immersed in what looked like a tense conversation with Jen and Dave, two of her grandchildren. The siblings were especially close to Kevin, and Melinda was glad they had both volunteered to bring Edith up from Hampton for this party.

Ada ambushed Melinda with a hug before she could even set down her totes. Kevin's mom was now in her early seventies, but still the baby of the eight Schermann siblings. Her roots continued to run deep in Melinda's rural neighborhood, even though she'd moved away fifty years ago.

"It's so good to see you! I talked to Mabel last night. Poor Harriet! What a shame to be rationing propane, and at this time of the year." Ada shivered. "She's a saint, no one deserves a helping hand more than she does."

"How do you know her?" Melinda was now accustomed to the ties that ran through her rural community, but this one gave her pause. "I don't think she goes to the Lutheran church down the road."

"Oh, no, she's Catholic," Ada explained. "The Prosper parish. But she grew up south of the blacktop, only a few miles from us. She went to school with ... let's see, Lydia, I believe. Or, no, maybe it was Emma ..."

Kevin sighed. "Mom, must we hear the bio of every resident of Fulton Township, past and present?"

Horace rose from his chair, slowly and carefully, and extended his hand to Melinda. She was pleased that his grip was still surprisingly strong for someone his age.

"There's the farmer." His grin was wide, but he didn't go in for a hug. Horace was as reserved as Ada was outgoing. "Glad you could join us."

"You're looking well. New shirt?"

He glanced down at his red plaid flannel. "Yep. Got fancy today, as we're going to have a special guest. I mean, other than yourself."

"Really? When is she ..."

Before Melinda could confirm her hunch, Horace gently poked Wilbur on the arm.

"Melinda's here. Want to say hello?"

Wilbur was comfortably folded into his chair, and didn't seem inclined to change that. But Melinda wasn't hurt by his simple nod. Dementia meant he was often living in the past, or at least confused about the present. Although she tried to visit the brothers at least once a month, Wilbur never recognized her.

With introductions done, Horace took his seat and motioned for Melinda to take one, too. "So. How are the roads? Any trouble getting here?"

"No, none at all." Horace was now content at Scenic Vista, but still hungry for details from the outside world. "The gravel's easily passable, except for some snow on the shoulder. We got about eight inches Sunday night. Of course, you have to watch for a little ice there, on the creek bridge."

"What's Hobo been up to these days?" Horace's casual tone belied how much he yearned for an update on his furry friend. "Is he leaving the Christmas tree alone?"

She assured him Hobo was being surprisingly good. Grace and Hazel, however, had never seen such a glittering tower of potential toys, and Melinda had finally removed all the breakable ornaments. While Hazel seemed content to nap on the tree skirt, headstrong Grace had launched herself inside the synthetic branches more than once.

Melinda had taken dozens of photos around the farm the past few days, knowing Horace would be eager for direct evidence of how everything, and everyone, was faring. There was even a video of Annie and some of the other sheep strolling across the pasture, baaaing their holiday greetings as they hoofed over the snow-dusted ground.

"Now, that's really something," Horace said softly. "To think you could make that, right there on your phone, and bring it here to show me. I'd really like to get down there sometime soon." Melinda knew, given the chance, he'd grab his old coat and go that very minute.

"I understand." She patted his arm. "But the weather's turning. Old Man Winter has arrived, and I'm afraid he plans to stay for a while."

"You're right. I suppose it'll have to wait until spring. Better to slip in the mud than fall on the ice."

"I brought you something that I think will make you feel closer to home." She reached into one of her totes and pulled out a large gift bag mounded with green tissue paper.

"Oh, you shouldn't have. I didn't get you anything."

"You've given me plenty! Don't worry, it wasn't expensive. In fact, it was free."

Horace's blue eyes lit up. "Really?" He loved nothing more than a bargain. "Well, in that case, I guess I'll accept it."

"Good. Because I don't have anywhere at the farm to put it. Not anywhere that's safe from Grace and Hazel's paws, at least."

"My, it's heavy." He pulled away the tissue paper while Melinda held the bag steady. "Hey, now, this looks familiar! Wherever did you find it?"

"At the decoration swap. It's not exact, but it's close. It lights up, see? I thought you and Wilbur might like it, that it would remind you of Christmases long ago."

Horace touched the ceramic church's glazed roof with a weathered hand. "It sure does. Brings back some really good times." He stared at the figurine for a moment, lost in his memories. "Well," he finally said. "Thank you. This is really special. And I know just where I'm going to put it, right there next to the television."

There was a commotion outside the door, and Ada hurried into the hall. Melinda had a hard time staying in her seat. "She's really coming tonight? Maggie is here?"

Horace smiled, and he suddenly looked decades younger. "Wendy promised to bring her. Oh, and there she is." Maggie entered the room cautiously, guided by her daughter's arm. Her white curls were in place, and she wore a glittering Christmas tree pin on her green cardigan. She was still pretty and elegant, but all Horace saw was the teenage girl who'd stolen his heart seventy years ago.

Maggie had given it back, however, and they'd parted ways. Until last summer, when Melinda helped Kevin and Ada track her down in Cedar Falls. She'd eventually married and had children, while Horace's life went in the opposite direction. She was now a widow, and Maggie and Horace talked on the phone at least once a week. In-person visits weren't as easy to arrange, but her daughters had brought her to see Horace a few times.

Melinda was quick to give up her chair so the lovebirds could sit together. "Just look at them." Ada shook her head. "I never knew this could be possible. Of course, until just a few months ago, I didn't know she even existed."

Kevin pointed at Horace and Maggie, who were already lost in conversation. "Best Christmas present ever, right there. Well, there's plenty to eat; we might as well dig in."

Melinda had made another batch of stollen, her confidence boosted by the praise of her friends and family for her earlier efforts. Horace instantly recognized it as his mother's recipe, and it pleased Melinda to see Anna's love of baking displayed elsewhere around the table. Ada passed a large tray of the family's sour-cream sugar cookies, while

Edith had recreated the date-filled spice cookies from their childhood.

"I want this recipe, too," Jen said after her first bite of stollen. "I can't wait to start my own holiday traditions, and all of these things will be on that list."

Jen was getting married next year, and Melinda had been honored to be invited. "I'll email it to you," she promised.

"I have the other ones written down for you already," Edith told Jen. "Of course, you'd better take them with you tonight. If I have to move, I might misplace them."

"You know it's for the best," Jen reminded her.

"Whatever." Edith turned to Melinda. "Mother used to buy the candied fruit for the stollen at your family's store, back when it was still called Prosper Mercantile. They got it in special for the holidays."

After more treats were passed around, Melinda found her way over to where Horace and his love were still side-by-side. Maggie gave her hand a warm squeeze. "My dear, I can't thank you enough for bringing us back together, after all this time."

"Oh, my pleasure. I'm so glad everything worked out."

"It just goes to show, love can be hard to find." She looked at Horace, and her eyes filled with happy tears. "And if you had it, but then lost it somewhere along the way? Well, it's easy to give up hope."

"I had," Horace admitted. "I wish I hadn't, but ..."

"We'll speak no more of it now," Maggie said gently. "It's water under the bridge." Melinda sensed them slipping back into their own, private world, and she was about to move on to visit with Dave. But then, Maggie leaned over with a secretive smile on her face.

"So, what about you? I hear there's a new man in your life."

Melinda's jaw dropped. Horace was trying his best to keep a straight face.

"How did ... wait!" She called down the table. "Kevin, what did you tell him?"

"Oh, enough. I didn't think it was a secret." He raised an eyebrow. "Or is it?"

Maggie laughed. "Good news travels fast."

"I'm not sure if it's all that good. More like, too soon to tell." She told them everything and, when she finished, Horace nodded slowly. "Sounds like you have a bit of competition there. What are you going to do about that?"

"I don't know." Melinda shrugged. "Wait and see what happens, I guess. If it's meant to be, it'll sort itself out on its own, right?"

Horace and Maggie exchanged an understanding glance. "Well, that's one way to look at it," Maggie said. "But sometimes, fate needs a good shove in the right direction."

"I didn't take that chance." Horace looked at the floor. "Don't get me wrong, I don't begrudge her any of her years with her husband. But the fact that I was a coward, that I didn't try harder?" He shook his head.

"Talk to him," Maggie pleaded. "It's a risk, to be sure. But do it for yourself. Don't be like me, all those years, wondering if I'd made the right choice. What if I had done things differently? That's a heavy burden to carry."

Melinda looked at Horace and Maggie, at the way they held hands, clinging to each other and whatever time they had left. They were right. Josh mattered to her; she needed to see this through, one way or another.

"OK," Melinda finally said. "I'll try. I don't know when, or how ..."

"Good." Horace nodded. "You do that. Now, why don't you pass those cookies my way again? I intend to eat at least three more."

✳ 18 ✳

"Merry Christmas!" Melinda called after the man as he started for the door. "Hope you can get that sink unclogged before your guests arrive on Friday."

Esther wandered over with a tote filled with packages of batteries and strings of lights. She set her bin on the counter with a heavy sigh. "I have only two days to get ready for the kids and grandkids, but it's not going to be enough. All the spare bedding needs to be washed, the bathrooms are a disaster, and I still haven't made that last batch of cookies."

"Can Bruce help out? I mean, he's retired now."

"Oh, he's *helping*. Helping drive me crazy. 'Honey, where are the air mattresses? I can't find the extension cords.'" Esther's mood was at odds with the frolicking puppies on her holiday sweatshirt. "I'd be better off handling everything myself. And I hate to say it, but Christmas doesn't mean as much as it used to."

Esther's mother passed away last year, right before the holiday. "Father Perkins has talked about starting a 'Blue Christmas' service for people who're hurting, for one reason or another. Too bad it's too late, this time around. I sure could use it."

"I'm so sorry." Melinda didn't know what else to say. "He should open them to everyone, regardless of faith, if he ever does. I'd bet half the town would show up, for one reason or another. This isn't always 'the most wonderful time of the year.' Everyone talks about how fun it is to shop, and wrap presents, and bake. But sometimes, it's too much."

Esther stared out at Main Street. The skies were too dark for early afternoon, a sign of more snow. "It's not just that I miss Mother. There are weeks of buildup before the holidays, then Christmas comes and goes so fast. And this year, we have that post-office thing hanging over our heads."

"All we can do is wait, I guess. No one expects to hear anything until at least after New Year's. I suppose there'll be more meetings."

"I wonder if it's even worth it, keeping up the fight." Esther slid her tote to the counter's edge. "The feds will do whatever they want. We made a stand; we can be proud of that. Well, I better get this stuff on the shelves. Miriam wants to put the decorations on clearance tomorrow already, right?

"Yep. Everyone's had their stuff up for a month, so we might as well. And most of our last-minute shoppers will be men. They won't pass up a deal on gear for next year."

Melinda had just started on a stack of returns when the bell jingled above the door. Glenn came in, seemingly lost in thought, and she was struck by how much he'd aged in just a few months. Everyone said the transition to retirement was as stressful as being laid off. She had yet to experience the first, but she knew all-too-well how awful the second could be.

"How's it going today?" She tried for a smile. "I bet it's busy over there."

"Yeah. Is Frank around?"

"No, sorry. Miriam's up in the office, and Bill's in the back. Is there something ..."

"Well, I guess you'll have to do." Glenn added his coat to the hall tree by the sideboard, as if he planned to stay. Melinda glanced at the clock; his half-hour lunch break had just started.

He pulled a folded paper from his jeans' pocket and approached the counter, gripping the page so tightly Melinda thought it might tear.

"What's on your list?"

"No, it's not that. Well, I need some toilet paper before I go, but, look, I've got something to say, something really important, and I need a trial run." He raised his chin, which hadn't seen a razor in several days. "I have it all worked out. I'm going to fight this post-office thing by bringing it down to a personal level."

Melinda stared at him. Between the meeting and the petition, the stamp-in and the efforts to bombard the postal service with calls and emails, wasn't that what the whole town had been doing for weeks?

"Yeah, I know." He answered the question on her face. "Everyone's been trying really hard, and I appreciate it. But there's one other thing I can do, on my own, to try to fix this."

"It's not your fault. Please don't think ..."

Glenn put a hand on the counter, and Melinda knew he had more to say.

"My retirement request gave the feds the gas they needed to start this fire, and it's time to put it out. If I withdraw my notice, they'll have to deal with me head-on. Lay me off, fire me, I don't give a damn anymore. The union will step in, I've already talked to my rep. Given my age and years of service, it'll get ugly fast."

"Are you sure the risk is worth it?"

"Absolutely."

The regional board had a meeting the next morning, and Glenn was going to show up and take a stand. "I'm going to offer to go part-time. And I don't mean I'll put in for a transfer. I'm talking about staying right here, and keeping our post office open for limited hours."

"Would they ... can they do that?"

"Well, it's the federal government, they pretty much do as they please." Glenn smirked. "Besides, it could tip the numbers in our favor."

Similar proposals had been successful in other small communities, he explained. The post office wouldn't have to worry about unloading an aging building that few buyers would want, and there would be some cost savings by continuing to serve Prosper's vast zip code out of a centralized location.

Glenn had been eager to retire, but now saw his days were better spent helping his community thrive, rather than fishing and traveling. At least for now.

"It may not be enough, but it's worth a try. Besides, we already have them running scared. They underestimated us, and that was a big mistake." He crossed his arms. "And after the meeting, I'm going to call every major media outlet in the state and tell them what I've done. But first, I need to make sure I have this just the way I want it."

Melinda tried not to get her hopes up, but Glenn's determination was contagious. She flagged down Esther, then texted Miriam and Bill to meet them at the register.

"Let's get a few more ears to hear this speech. And if it needs any polishing, I promise I'll help you get it just right."

* * *

Glenn's proposal was better than Melinda had hoped. It was personal and effective, and backed by enough data that it might merit a second glance from the postal authorities. Either way, helping Glenn rework his speech had raised her spirits, at least a little.

She left work an hour early that afternoon for another effort that was sure to ease her holiday blues.

"Helping others is always a good idea," she told Hobo as they watched the driveway from the kitchen windows. "It takes your mind off your troubles. I just hope Harriet doesn't think we've gone too far; we don't want to hurt her pride. Look, there's Karen!"

Hobo put his paws on the windowsill and barked, which brought Hazel and Grace on the run from the living room. He recognized Karen's work truck, which sometimes arrived at the farm with Pumpkin in the front seat. But not today.

"I'm sorry." Melinda patted him on the head. "It's pretty cold out. Pumpkin's a town dog, you know, she doesn't love to dash around in the snow as much as you do. But someday, when it's warmer, we'll have a play date. I promise."

She reached for her chore coat and purse, then pulled a pan of lasagna from the freezer. Hazel was only one step behind, her golden eyes wide with curiosity. "No, none for you. You girls will have to make do with your kibble, and there's plenty to go around. This is a special treat, for a special lady."

"Hey!" Karen popped through the kitchen door. "I didn't take off my boots, so I won't come all the way in. Anything I can carry?"

"Here." Melinda handed her the lasagna. "Take this, and I'll grab the cookies. Mabel just texted, said she and Ed are about to leave."

"She texts?" Karen was impressed. "Is that new?"

"Sort of. The grandkids have been on both of them to join the modern era. Mabel loves it now, but Ed is still dragging his feet. I wish I could have given you a better idea about what's wrong with Harriet's dog; I hope you have what you need."

The truck was still running, and it was cozy and warm inside. "Oh, I brought half the clinic along. But I do that, anyway. Sounds like a simple respiratory issue." They reached the road, and Karen turned north toward the creek. "So, Snarky Steve's on board, huh?"

Melinda laughed. "Yeah. I suppose I should stop referring to him in that way. He's nosy and opinionated, but I think his heart's in the right place. Or at least it was this time."

Her neighborhood's propane delivery driver hadn't hesitated when Melinda asked him to make a special trip to top off Harriet's tank. Even better, his supplier agreed to cover the cost as part of a program that helped senior citizens in rural areas.

"That's wonderful! Give people a chance to help someone less fortunate, and they're usually quick to get on board." Karen slowed for the creek's crossing. "Oh, there's one of the eagles! So they've decided to stay around this winter?"

"Looks like it. Ed and I have our fingers crossed that come spring, there'll be another little family to observe." Melinda tipped her head toward the shelterbelt east of the bridge. "Of course, we're still trying to keep it quiet, so ..."

Karen raised one gloved hand off the steering wheel. "Not a word. I hear all kinds of things when I'm on rounds. When you're crawling around in the straw with someone, trying to save their prize dairy cow, they really bare their souls. Doc likes to joke that we should tack on a surcharge for counseling services. So, you said Ed got ahold of Harriet's niece? Is she going to be there?"

"Yes to both." Melinda sighed with relief. "And she promised to keep a better eye on her aunt in the future. Sounds like Kelly wasn't the only one Harriet was keeping at arm's length; Ed said her neighbors suspected she could use help, but she dodged them at every turn."

"Old people want to be as independent as possible." Karen turned west on the blacktop. "They never want to admit when they're in a bind. But then, that's true of most people, when you think about it."

"Kelly insisted Harriet join her family for Christmas dinner, so she won't have to be alone. Here's the corner; take a right."

Steve's propane truck was already in Harriet's yard, expertly backed across the lawn toward the tank. A few other familiar vehicles were also in the row parked along the driveway. Harriet was surprised, and a bit overwhelmed, when her home was suddenly filled with so many people. Melinda explained her lasagna recipe made too much for her to eat on her own, and the other food donations were passed off as great deals too good to ignore.

When it came to Buster, however, Harriet was eager to let Karen give him a free exam. His respiratory issue was easily treatable, and Karen offered a full run of medicine as well as a promise to stop by next week.

Harriet even agreed to accept a few cat shelters to improve conditions in her garage, and Karen was confident she could convince her to bring the kitties to the first clinic of the spring.

Harriet fretted about the propane bill, of course, but cried tears of joy when Steve assured her his company had covered the cost.

"I think if her neighbors had picked up the tab, she wouldn't have wanted to accept it," Melinda told Karen once they were back in the truck, giddy with the spirit of giving. "I thought the assistance for her animals would be readily accepted, however, and I'm glad I was right."

"Her fur babies are her world. She'd rather go hungry than see her dear dog and cats want for anything." Ed and Mabel were still in the driveway, chatting with Helen and Will, and Karen tooted her horn in farewell before starting down the lane. "Did you have any idea about that neighborhood women's group? How cool is that?"

As a young bride, Harriet had joined a now-defunct social club for ladies in the area. Mabel's mother was its president for several decades, and the women had enthralled the rest of Harriet's visitors with their memories of days gone by.

"Just goes to show, people out here are connected in ways I never could have imagined." Melinda shook her head in wonder. "But the best part is, I think it reminded Harriet she's not alone out here, there are people all around her that care."

Karen cranked the radio, and they sang along with a few holiday standards on the way back to Melinda's farm. Just after they passed the last crossroads, Karen turned down the tunes. "So, have you talked to Josh lately?"

"No." Melinda's tone was sharper than it should have been. "No, I haven't," she tried again. "All the grant applications are done, as you know, I sent out the last one yesterday. I haven't had a reason to, and, well, I'm sure he's busy."

Karen was unusually quiet.

"Why?" Melinda turned to study her friend. "What is ... did he say something?"

When Karen slowed the truck and pulled to the shoulder, Melinda's heart began to pound in her ears. "What's wrong? Did something happen?"

"Well, yes, and no. He's fine," she added quickly, "but there's something ..."

"Oh, God." Melinda slid down in her seat. "Does this have anything to do with Gretchen?"

"Gretchen?" Karen's eyebrows shot up. "That attorney that lives on his street? She's a piece of work. You can't think he'd be interested in her!"

"Well, they went out Sunday night." Melinda crossed her arms. "They had a date. To a holiday party. He told me all about it, when we were sorting the water bowls in the parking lot. That's why Norma took part of his delivery route; he had to get home and get ready."

Karen frowned. "I talked to him yesterday. He said there was some party, but it was really boring. Now that you mention it, he did say she was there, but ..."

"Well, I know she was."

"Huh." Karen stared out the windshield.

"Wait. If that's not what you were talking about, then ... what were you going to say?"

Karen drummed her fingers on the steering wheel. "Do you remember all those weeks ago, the day Josh came out to your farm?"

Melinda blinked, caught off guard. "Sure, back before Thanksgiving."

"Well, I kind of ... sent him out there on purpose."

"I know. You and Doc were swamped that day."

"Uh, not really. Oh, sure, we had other patients, but I could have easily come over myself. I was at the Tomlinsons' that afternoon, only two miles away."

"You were?"

"Look. Doc and I talked it over, and we decided to ... play matchmaker, I guess."

Melinda's mouth fell open. "You're saying you set us up? Sort of a date, but not; a deworming date."

Then she burst out laughing. Karen's hand in this was one thing, but Doc? The thought of the two of them, conspiring in the clinic's office, make her shoulders shake.

"Yeah, well, it was the best we could come up with." Karen grinned. "It pushed the two of you together, didn't it? You were alone ... or the only people around, anyway. You had to talk to each other. We decided, why not?"

"What about the day we were going to have lunch, and you didn't show up?"

"That wasn't planned, I swear. I really did get behind on calls." Karen put the truck in gear, as a car was coming up behind them. They shouldn't sit there much longer. "Oh, and all that stuff about a formal partnership with Josh is true, too. We've discussed it, several times. And so far, our trial run's working out great."

The other vehicle passed by, and Karen pulled back out on the road. "Now, tell me the truth. If I'd suggested something more ... definitive, would you have been receptive to the idea? Or shut it down?"

Melinda rolled her eyes. "You got me there. Chase and I had just broken up, only a few weeks before. No, that was the last thing on my mind."

And now, she thought but didn't say, *I can't stop thinking about Josh.*

"I can't tell you what to do," Karen said as they turned up Melinda's lane. "But, well, I'm going to tell you what to do. Talk to him, tell him how you feel. I know you care about him."

"It's that obvious?" Melinda sighed.

"Well, yeah. And he thinks the world of you. If you don't say something, you'll always wonder what might have been."

"That's not ... you don't know that he ..." Melinda put her hands over her face. "You're starting to sound like Horace."

"*Horace?*" Karen put the truck in park and turned in her seat, her eyes wide. "He told you to speak up, didn't he? Wow, a ninety-year-old bachelor farmer and I agree on something in the romance department." She shook her head.

"Well, if you won't listen to me, then listen to him. When has he ever steered you wrong?"

"But what about Gretchen?"

"Oh, who cares about her?" Karen sneered and adjusted her knit cap, which was dusted with bits of old straw. "She's pretty and successful, and high-maintenance. You know some guys like that diva crap. She'll find someone else to sink her claws into."

"No, I mean, what if Josh is actually interested in her?" Melinda gathered up her things and reached for the door handle, suddenly eager to make her escape. Hobo was there by the front fender, waiting to greet her, and she had chores to do.

"That's the risk you take, I guess," Karen called after her, determined to have her say before Melinda shut her out.

"Just think about it, OK? If nothing else, Doc and I would hate to see our efforts go to waste."

* 19 *

Christmas Eve morning was cold but bright, and the coffee group's holiday plans were the main topic of discussion around Prosper Hardware's sideboard. Until Glenn arrived.

Melinda pointed at the coffeepot, but he offered his regrets. "Oh, sorry, I can't stay. Need to get next door. But I wanted all of you to know, I went to that meeting Thursday and gave my speech. It felt good, fighting for something I believe in. Two things, actually; this town, and my career."

He answered the questions forming on his friends' faces. "I don't know if it will help, but I can take comfort that I gave it a try."

George raised his mug in salute. "You spoke up; that's what matters."

"And we all appreciate it," Doc added. "You're as much a fixture of this town as the post office itself."

"Way to go, my friend." Jerry got up to shake Glenn's hand. "You know, I've always thought that when I get tired of playing mayor, or people tell me to quit, you might want to give it a go."

"Really?" Glenn was pleased.

"Absolutely." Frank grinned. "This town needs people like you. Always has, always will."

"Well, you certainly know how to make a guy feel good." Glenn didn't have time for a cup of brew, but he couldn't resist a few Christmas cookies for the road. "Merry Christmas, to each and every one of you."

Frank followed Glenn to the door as everyone offered their holiday wishes. "Let's get lunch next week, huh? Burgers at the Watering Hole will be a nice change from ham and turkey and the usual." Glenn heartily agreed, and there was a spring in his step as he started down the sidewalk.

Once he was gone, Prosper Hardware fell quiet.

"Aw, hell," Auggie finally said. "We're still screwed."

Jerry rubbed his face. "I know. What were we supposed to say? 'Hey, Glenn, glad you made a fool of yourself, but guess what? You're just one of thousands of postal employees, and the feds don't give a crap about you or this town.'"

"You don't think there's any chance?" The hint of hope in George's raspy voice made Melinda's heart break.

Frank and Jerry looked at each other and finally, Frank shook his head.

"Look, it would be great ... amazing, in fact, if Glenn could sway those mucky-mucks to give Prosper another chance. But you have to understand what we're dealing with. You think there's politics and drama here in town? You have no idea what goes on, higher up in the food chain."

"Even with the county, it's like pulling teeth to get anything done," Jerry grumbled. "Too many forms and reports, rounds of discussion."

He gestured at Main Street. "Why do you think the pavement's still not patched? Because it's part of a county highway, and there's not enough traffic to get it moved up the list. The state's worse, and the feds ..." He shook his head. "That's like trying to move a mountain."

"It's going to take a miracle." Bill had arrived at the tail end of the conversation and now leaned against the sideboard, fueling up for the day. "A Christmas miracle."

Doc decided he needed another cookie. "Well, I guess it's like Glenn said: We've done what we can. People around here always look out for each other, sure, but I'm really proud of how this whole area has rallied behind us."

"We need to keep that momentum going." Jerry nodded. "Community spirit and a willingness to work together are our best bets to keep this town afloat if the post office closes."

"And even if it doesn't." George wasn't ready to give up.

"I hate to sound like a Scrooge." Auggie crossed his arms. "But I think we need to prepare ourselves for the worst." He turned to Jerry. "How much time do we have? When might they make a final decision?"

Jerry shrugged. "No idea. Could be months yet, but could be sooner. The feds are notorious for playing their hands close to their vests. I'm hoping that, once Christmas is over, more information will come out. That's our best bet to see if our efforts are paying off at all."

"In the meantime, let's try to enjoy the holiday," Frank told his friends. "That's all we can do."

Uncle Frank was right. And before she could do that, Melinda had plenty to cross off her to-do list.

"I might as well get ready to open." She started for the counter. "Glenn's not the only one who'll be busy. I expect a significant percentage of our regular male customers to show up today."

"What's that supposed to mean?" Doc stared at her, but his eyes sparked with humor. "Are you saying men are procrastinators? That we don't like to shop?"

Jerry picked up the joke. "And we'll make the special ladies in our lives suffer through another set of towels?"

Auggie stayed silent, but Melinda could sense he was patting himself on the back. Thanks to his bargain with Vicki, his shopping was done.

"All I said was: it'll be busy today." Melinda pointed toward the housewares aisle. "And Jerry, just remember: We have a lovely selection of kitchen towels, in shades other than red and green, and potholders to match."

Aunt Miriam and Esther soon arrived to help with the last-minute shopping rush. Everyone knew Prosper Hardware would close at two, and the aisles were soon packed with shoppers. Frank, however, had quickly made himself scarce.

"I don't know where he went, but I know what he's doing," Miriam muttered to her niece in the few moments they had between checkouts. Even with Melinda running the register and Miriam sacking purchases, they could barely keep up.

"I bet he didn't have one gift bought until just a few days ago. And now, he's making a mad dash to fill up the sleigh."

"Someone else is in a hurry, too." Melinda pointed outside. "I don't know the last time I saw Karen run like that. I hope everything is OK."

Karen burst into Prosper Hardware, unwrapping her scarf with one hand and motioning to Melinda with the other. "I had to tell you!" She made it as far as the display of discounted decorations before she had to stop and take a breath. "We got it! We got the grant!"

"What? You're serious?" Melinda nearly knocked Aunt Miriam down as she scooted out from behind the counter. Several customers sidelined their shopping long enough to gape at the sight of two grown women jumping up and down, but Melinda had already forgotten anyone else was there. "When do we .... what are they ..."

"One thousand dollars!" Karen raised her arms in triumph. "I found out a few minutes ago. A letter's coming next week, but the foundation sent out emails this morning. This is the best Christmas gift we could have hoped for!"

Melinda put her fingers on her temples. "Think of all the medicine that will buy, surgical supplies ..."

"And we can cover the costs for people who can't afford to pay." Karen clapped her hands with glee. "Best of all, this is just the first app, the one from the fall."

"If we can get half of the rest of them ... even a third ..."

"This changes everything! It's life-changing, actually, for so many ..."

Miriam came over to offer her congratulations. "What wonderful news, and on Christmas Eve, no less." She took in Karen's disheveled appearance. "Goodness, did you run all the way from the clinic?"

"Oh, no." Karen laughed. "Just from my truck. I'm on the way to a call, and I have two more after that." She grabbed Melinda's arm. "We should tell Josh, right away!"

"He's closing early today," Melinda reminded her, "but I bet he'll be happy to take your call."

When Karen didn't respond, she blinked. "Oh."

"Yes." Karen nodded emphatically. "Go. Right now, if you can. Here's your chance."

"But we're swamped. Saturdays are always busy, and we're closing early, too. Miriam can't spare me until at least noon and even then, I don't know ..."

Melinda looked to her aunt for support, but Miriam raised an eyebrow and pointed at the door. During the afternoon she'd volunteered to build cat shelters, Miriam learned more than how to operate a router. Melinda and Josh's interactions had raised her curiosity and, when cornered, Melinda had told her everything.

"Hmm, I think Esther and I can manage," Miriam said over her shoulder as she turned away. "I'd say it's worth your time to drive over to Swanton, since you now have two bits of news to share."

"OK," Melinda told Karen. "Send me the email so I can have some talking points for at least one of the things I need to tell him."

Miriam was back with Melinda's coat, hat and gloves, and purse. "Here, I saved you a few minutes. Go on, before you lose your nerve."

Melinda passed the co-op and headed west toward the state highway. At the stop sign, she had to choose: turn left, and follow the main road; or keep straight on, the way toward home, staying on the blacktop until the outskirts of Swanton came into view. Josh's clinic was on the north side of town, so that way was shorter ...

"Left," she finally said with a sigh. "I need a few extra miles to pull myself together."

The state highway carried more vehicles than usual today. The weather was clear, and people were already on the way to their holiday destinations. She cranked the carols on the radio and gripped the steering wheel, and wished she felt as calm as the blue sky beyond her windshield.

Her emotions bounced here and there, up and down. Elation because of the grant; anxiety about trying to tell Josh how she felt; fear over what he might, or might not, say ...

"This is ridiculous! I'm a grown woman, for God's sake. It's not lunch time in the middle-school cafeteria, wishing some boy would ask me to the holiday dance." She shook her head as she idled at Swanton's first stop light.

"Besides, who says I have to say anything about *that* today? I'll tell him about the grant; that's it. Miriam and Karen don't have to know I chickened out. He'll be busy, there isn't going to be time to really talk."

It was an excuse, and she knew it. Why did this matter so much? Why couldn't she just say what she felt? She cared about Josh, of course, but was fear of rejection the only thing holding her back?

She needed to figure this out, and quick, as it was time to turn off the highway and drive the last blocks to the clinic. Whatever she said to Josh, whatever she told her friends and family, suddenly didn't matter as much as getting to the bottom of what was in her heart.

And then, Melinda knew why she was so afraid of what might happen next. She wasn't in Minneapolis anymore. Josh wasn't a friend-of-a-friend, three times removed; or someone she'd met on a random night out downtown.

Their lives were already intertwined, in all the usual ways of people living in small towns. She was all-in on the cat-clinic program, and wasn't willing to give that up. And he was a colleague, and probably a future business partner, of two of her friends.

If this went wrong, she wasn't going to be able to avoid Josh. Not the way she'd been able to avoid Chase. He lived in Meadville, an hour's drive away. It was one of the reasons their relationship had been difficult but, in the end, that distance turned out to be a blessing. Because when it was over, he was really gone. She had no reason to drive up there, he had no need to come to Prosper ... their end came on quick, and it hurt, but at least the cut had been clean.

And here was the clinic, the parking lot made even smaller by the mounds of bladed snow occupying its corners. Several vehicles were in the lot, clients working in a vet visit before the holiday or dropping off their pets for boarding over the long weekend.

"I guess I'll go in," she told herself, as if leaving was still an option. "I'll tell him about the clinic, we can celebrate, whatever. The rest of it ... well, we'll see what happens."

One look around the lobby, and Melinda's hope for privacy was long gone. A glittering Christmas tree took up a sizeable corner, and critters in various moods trailed by their humans seemed to take up every other bit of space. She had to smile at the poodle dancing in happy circles while his fur mom paid the bill. Norma came through the swinging door, carrier in hand, and the unhappy cat inside let out a nasty hiss when it saw its owner by the counter.

"He's not too happy," Norma told the woman. "It's been a tough morning, but he'll be fine. You're going to be in the doghouse, of course, but that'll pass."

Norma smiled when she spotted Melinda, then raised her eyebrows in surprise.

"Hey, there! What brings you our way?" She reached for a clipboard, which gave Melinda a moment to come up with an answer that wouldn't perk up the ears of everyone in the room.

"Oh, I just came by to talk to Josh." She leaned on the counter for support. "We got some really good news today, about the cat clinics. Is he wrapping up? If he's really busy, I can just ..."

"Yep, he is, but I'm sure he'll be glad to see you."

Norma got the woman's signature and traded a small sack for the clipboard. "Twice a day, for three days. We're closed tomorrow, and Doctor Vogel will be out of town, but be sure to call his cell if there's any change or you have questions."

She turned back to Melinda. "Good news, huh? From the grin on your face, I gather you'll want to tell him yourself." She tipped her head toward the hall. "He's in Exam Two, first door on the right."

The comfortable silence in the back of the clinic calmed Melinda's nerves. The room's door was partially open and there was Josh, in navy scrubs, with a black-and-white collie pup in his arms.

"Your dad will be here in a few minutes to take you home," he whispered to the little dog. "You'll be racing around again in no time."

Melinda's heart flipped over, and tears pricked the corners of her eyes. This scene, right here, held so much of why she was so drawn to Josh. He wasn't just handsome, although it was no wonder half the single women in town had him on their radar. He was attentive and caring. He was ...

What if he was too good to be true? No one was perfect, including Josh. Really, she needed to be more careful, not get her hopes up because ...

Too late. He saw her, standing there in the hallway, and his smile pushed all those doubts away. "Hey, you! What a surprise!" Then his face clouded. "Is everything OK?"

"Yes. Yes, it's fine." She let out a deep breath. No matter what happened in the future, or even the next five minutes, it would somehow sort itself out. "More than fine, actually. That's why I'm here. Karen came by the store, just now." She held up her phone. "We got the grant! The first one, from the fall. And it's a whole thousand dollars!"

Josh whooped so loud, the pup let out an excited bark.

"You're serious? Really?" He gave Melinda a high-five with his free hand. The puppy was squirming now, and Josh stopped celebrating long enough to put the little guy in his kennel. "Oh, wow, I was hoping for it, I thought we really had a chance. That report you compiled put us ahead of the pack, I'm sure of it!"

"I still can't believe it." Melinda bounced on her heels. "All of this started the day Karen and I stopped at the consignment shop outside Eagle River, looking for furniture for my house. They had so many cats, they were so sweet ... and by the time we got home, we had a plan all figured out."

Josh rubbed his hands together. "This is just the start. Maybe we can go to two clinics a month, there certainly is a need. I've been talking to another vet, over in Charles City, and I think she might be on board. More vets, more surgeries every time. There's so much we can do."

He leaned over the corner of the exam table and squeezed her arm. They stared at each other and, all of the sudden, she couldn't breathe. And it was wonderful.

"Sorry. I got carried away." Josh took a step back, slowly, as if forcing himself to move.

"Oh, I don't mind."

"No, I shouldn't have. It's not appropriate."

"I disagree." She raised her chin, felt the smile spread across her face. Josh looked so happy ... and so guilty. She almost burst out laughing. "I think it's entirely appropriate. In fact, I wouldn't mind if you did it again."

Josh stared at her. This time, there was something different in his gaze.

"Really? You sure?"

The door was already open, she might as well walk on through. "Yeah. But, I don't mean to put you on the spot, it's not like ..." She took a deep breath. "I have to know, though: what about Gretchen?"

"Gretchen?" He frowned, then began to laugh. "Oh, I see. The party, the other night. Well, she's persistent, I'll say that much for her. Really, she's not so bad. But she's not ..."

"I shouldn't have asked." Melinda started to backpedal. Maybe there was something between her and Josh, but it was a little early to draw boundaries. "Look, we're adults. What you do is your business."

"Well, sure." He slipped around the table. "But what if I said, I wouldn't mind if you made it your business?"

She had to smile at that. "Oh, I think I could try. I mean, if you think it's a good idea."

"I do. You know, I remember the first time I saw you. You came in the back door at city hall, at that first cat clinic." He laughed again, but there was only admiration in his voice. "You were in these grubby jeans and tee and an old ball cap. You had a scuffed-up carrier in each hand, and those cats were just *howling*."

Melinda shook her head. "They were from Gertrude's gang. It was a real struggle to get them there, but I was thrilled. It was a good start, at least."

"I turned to Karen, right then, and I said, who is *that*? I wanted to meet you. I thought, she's one tough lady. Not afraid to get her hands dirty, and the way you looked after those cats ..."

"You came over and asked if I needed help." She remembered thinking Josh was handsome, but that wasn't what brought her up short that day. "And when I turned around, I was so surprised."

Josh snorted. "Why?"

"I'd assumed you'd be old. I mean, so many people around here are. I was just so glad to hear that someone was willing to help. Karen and I had no idea if the clinics would be embraced, if people would participate. Some people thought we were crazy. But you didn't."

"No, I didn't. It was a brilliant idea. Still is. Tell you what. Let's have lunch again, sometime soon. And this time, let's not invite Karen."

Melinda tried to keep a straight face. If he only knew what Doc and Karen had been up to! But she'd keep her word. "I'd like that."

He reached for her hand. "And then, we'll just see where this goes. You're busy, I know. But do you think you could make a little time for me?"

"Absolutely."

"Do you have any to spare, like, right now?"

"Oh, I think so. Maybe a minute or two."

He kissed her, and everything else melted away. This felt right, and she was going to get out of the way and enjoy it.

The door flew open. "Josh, you have a call."

They each took a quick step back, but it was too late.

"Well, it's about time." Norma smiled, then pointed at Melinda. "That was a smooth move, saying you had something to tell him that couldn't wait. I don't let just anyone back here, you know."

"No, seriously, I wasn't making that up! The cat program got its first grant! Karen just found out today."

Norma let out a whoop. "That's fantastic! Hopefully, it's the first of many." She gestured at the phone on the counter. "Line three, Hugo's mom. A question about the antibiotics that went home today."

Melinda pulled on her knit cap as Josh picked up the call. "Doctor Vogel." He turned back long enough to give her a wink. "Hey, Jackie, how's he doing?"

Melinda floated into the hallway. If she hurried, she could be back to Prosper Hardware before the noon rush started. But she had to pause for a few moments to take it all in.

Yes, it was going to be a merry Christmas. Very merry, indeed.

* 20 *

Melinda's boots crunched through the skim of fresh snow on the back sidewalk. It was still dark, not even a faint line of pink on the eastern horizon. She switched on her headlamp, and its small beam bobbed ahead on her path to the barn.

"Wait until Sunny and Stormy see what I have," she told Hobo as she checked the plastic bucket's lid was still on tight. "It'll be like Christmas all over again."

The turkey scraps and gravy were piping hot from a spin in the microwave, but wouldn't stay that way long in this cold. Hobo wandered off, his nose to the snow, following the tracks of a rabbit that had crisscrossed the yard overnight.

She set the bucket down long enough to work the door's frosty iron latch. Once the pail was at his level, Hobo ran over to give it a good sniff. "No, you've had more than enough. And there's more in the house."

The screech of the door's hinges brought a chorus of "baaaas" from the sheep, who jostled at their feed bunks on the other side of the aisle fence.

Sunny and Stormy were already underfoot, their sharp eyes trained on the bucket as they demanded to be fed first. Once they were settled in the grain room, Melinda turned her attention to the sheep.

"Christmas comes and goes so fast, doesn't it?" She pried the lid off the oats bin and reached for the scoop. "It certainly was a silent night. Both of them were, actually. But there's nothing wrong with that."

Christmas Eve afternoon passed in a flash, between the crush of last-minute shoppers at Prosper Hardware and Melinda's elation over her mad-dash errand to Swanton. She'd hurried home to do chores, and made it to her parents' just in time for a quick supper and evening church services. Liz and her family weren't there, of course, but it was nice to have Mark around.

The holiday itself passed as quietly as the evening before. Frank and Miriam joined them for Christmas dinner and an afternoon of snacks, presents and good times.

Initially, Melinda had been disappointed this holiday wasn't going to be a repeat of last year's, when she had a houseful of guests and hosted her extended family's gathering. But she discovered there was something wonderful about not stressing over a menu, or having to scrub the farmhouse until it gleamed. Simply being present, she found, was enough.

There were still several wonderful moments, of course. The men in her family were all good sports about Melinda's knit scarves. And just before they tucked into the turkey, Mark tapped his fork on his wine glass. He had something to share, and it turned out to be very good news.

A college friend, now living in Chicago, played in a blues band seeing significant success. One of the guitar players had moved away, and Mark had been tapped to take his place. His buddy had a spare bedroom, which would do for now, and there were even a few leads on day jobs in the city. And just like that, Melinda's brother was as eager to leave home (for the second time) as he'd been to come back.

With the sheep and barn cats cared for, Melinda started for the chicken house. There were no extra treats for her feathered friends, but she expected to have a fresh supply that afternoon.

"Jessie's working her magic for you girls, probably right now. I better get to the house and get ready; it should be a busy day. And I have one last gift to give, even if there's no time to wrap it."

Grace and Hazel watched with wide eyes as Melinda carefully lifted the cat nativity's stable from the top of the bookcase. Once it was settled in a cardboard box, she reached for a roll of paper towels and swaddled each of the ceramic characters for their trip to town.

"I know, you're attached to them. Especially you, Grace. Or at least, you like to knock them around. But they should go to Gertrude; she doesn't have much for decorations and, after all, she's Prosper's unofficial cat lady."

With all the pieces tucked away, Melinda paused long enough to give each of her girls a loving pat on the head. "Do you realize how good you have it? Maybe not, but I do. I'm so blessed that you were meant to be my house babies. Sunny and Stormy were never going to move in. Believe me, I tried."

There wasn't time to stop at Gertrude's before work, but it was just as well. Her afternoon errand meant the spirit of giving would be alive for one extra day. As soon as Melinda arrived at Prosper's city limits, however, it was clear someone had already set his much of his holiday cheer aside.

Auggie's sign was back up along Main Street. Two spotlights were now installed in front of the display, ready to illuminate his in-your-face message through the long hours of darkness that marked this time of year. Santa, at least, still waved to everyone from the co-op's south lot, where the reindeer remained poised for liftoff.

Most of the coffee-group regulars were already gathered around the sideboard, recapping their holiday celebrations. Bill was still out of town, visiting his wife's family, and Doc wasn't expected back until that afternoon. Karen had been on call over the holiday, unable to make it back to her hometown, but had eagerly accepted Nancy's invitation for Christmas dinner.

Melinda deposited the last of the stollen on the sideboard, then removed her coat. Jerry had already finished his first cup of coffee, and was ready to get down to business.

"Now, who's bringing cookies and candy tomorrow? Frank? OK, good. George, can we count on you to be next? Let's space it out, now. It's important we don't get overwhelmed."

"Mary alone could keep us in cookies until at least next week," George told the group. "I don't know about the rest of you, but I plan to snack straight through from now until New Year's Eve. How are the party plans shaping up?"

"Those high-schoolers have been a great help," Frank said around a bite of stollen. "Where they get their energy is beyond me. They're on break all this week, of course, and I plan to keep them busy. Bill's going to rig the sound system, and we should be ready to go." He brushed the crumbs from his hands, then disappeared down the main aisle and into the wood shop.

"What's he up to?" Auggie wondered.

"Dunno." Jerry shrugged. "What I want to know is, what are *you* up to? I see the sign's back. Couldn't you have at least waited until after the New Year's party? Lots of people are coming into town for that."

"Which is exactly my point. It's going to fire people up, remind them we're still fighting for our future here in little Prosper. We need to make ourselves heard. This isn't the time to let up on the gas."

Frank reappeared with a wooden crate in his hands. "Melinda, I'm sorry I didn't get this to you yesterday. But I needed some time last night to finish up."

"This is for me?" She handed her mug to Jerry and lifted the lid on the crate, which now waited by her chair. "Oh, Uncle Frank, it's just perfect!"

The iron weathervane was painted a matte black. The main design echoed the lines of a barn, and there were two sheep shapes to one side of the structure. The other end showed a chicken and dog. And there, inside the open haymow door, were two outlines that were definitely feline.

"Sunny and Stormy are pretty small," Frank admitted. "I doubt you'll be able to see them, once it's up on the farmhouse's roof. But you'll know they're there, and that's what matters."

"How did you know I wanted one?" Melinda's eyes filled with happy tears. "I didn't want to ask, not yet, since it's been hard for you to keep up. This is incredible. I didn't know this much detail was even possible."

"I wasn't sure, myself, until I got started on it. It forced me to up my game."

The weathervane drew more compliments as it was passed around. "If you can do this," George said proudly, "you'll be able to recreate anything anyone asks for. Now the question is: does it come with free installation?"

"Oh, no," Melinda said quickly. "I don't want you up on the housetop, for anything. Dad, either. It'll have to wait until spring, and I'll hire a professional to do it."

The men drained their cups a second time, and the last of the stollen disappeared from the tray on the sideboard. As the others reached for their coats, Auggie strolled over to where Melinda was marking the Christmas decorations to eighty percent off.

"I'll wash up before I go, like usual. We'll be busy today, but Dan has things under control."

"Thanks. I need to get all these clearance signs updated before we open."

Auggie lingered, and Melinda sensed he wanted her full attention. "What's going on?"

He rocked on his heels. "Well, I have some news. Thought you'd want to be the first to know. As of Christmas Eve afternoon, Chaplin has a real home. No more hanging out at the co-op for him."

"Oh, that's ... is this good news? I mean, for you? That's great you found someone to take him, but won't you miss him?"

"Well, maybe a little, during the day." Auggie's brown eyes twinkled behind his dark-rimmed glasses. "You see, I'm the one that took him home. Jane and I talked it over, and she thought it was for the best. Mr. Checkers and Chaplin made their peace long ago, but Pebbles? She's queen of the concrete castle, and it's smart to get him out of her way, for good."

Melinda nodded. From the way Auggie beamed with happiness, she wasn't sure his wife had any say in the matter.

"I'm so glad! For Chaplin, of course. Did he get to take that donut bed with him?"

"Oh, no. I brought along his blanket, but I think Mr. Checkers wants the bed. Jane thought it was pretty beat up, anyway, and suggested we order Chaplin a few new things online."

Melinda knew what that meant. Auggie had probably spent a few hours, and a few hundred dollars, on beds, toys, and cat trees for his cherished friend.

"Well, you give Chaplin my congratulations on finding his forever home. And maybe, once things settle down, I'll swing by some day after work for a visit?"

"I'm sure he'd love that." Auggie was quiet for a moment. "I want to thank you again for ... helping me get Chaplin settled. That awful day, out there in the back lot, I was ... well, he just looked so familiar, you know? It brought back a lot of memories, I guess, and not all of them were good."

Auggie tried so hard to keep his smart-aleck, tough-guy reputation intact. Melinda had long ago realized it was his go-to defense against the painful parts of life. He waited now, hands in pockets, for her to say something. What he really wanted, she decided, was for her to promise to never tell anyone, especially the other guys, how Auggie Kleinsbach had bawled his eyes out over a stray cat.

It was such an easy gift to give, and she was willing to do just that.

"That's OK. I was glad to help. Chaplin's happy, and that's what matters. There's no need to dwell on the past, right?"

She pulled a stack of clearance tags off the nearest shelf. It was a signal their conversation was over, and she would keep her word.

"Sounds good," was all Auggie said. And with a grin, he started for the sideboard and gathered up the coffee mugs.

✳ 21 ✳

"What's it doing out there?" Vicki looked up from her clipboard when Melinda came through the community center's double doors. "Any snow yet?"

"I think it's just about to start." She shivered, despite the warmth of the spacious front room. The furnace had been kicked up in preparation for that night's celebration. "It's so damp, it just feels like snow. Auggie says we're not out of the woods yet. Just because the forecasters say ..."

Vicki closed her eyes and took a deep breath. "I'll stick with the official forecast until I have to do otherwise. A few inches, a little wind. Nothing too serious."

Emmett hurried past with a large bag of ice melt in his arms. "That's right. Not big enough to wreck our plans." He'd closed his barber shop at noon, which gave him plenty of time to help with last-minute party preparations. "Just a little Iowa winter weather to deal with. I'll salt the sidewalk and steps before the flakes can get started."

"I have a good feeling about this." Uncle Frank carefully dismounted his ladder and reached for another box of light bulbs. "This place is nothing like what it was two months ago, it's been totally transformed. We got some painting done, it's clean ... this is going to be a great party."

Vicki turned back to her list. "I'm glad we decorated at the start of the holiday season; it's saving us a ton of time now.

Melinda, how about you see if Nancy needs help? The coat racks are set up in the old front office over there; we just need to put the hangers out. Patricia is giving the kitchen and bathrooms one last scrub-down."

"How are things coming with the food?"

"Jessie's prepping everything now." Vicki tipped her head toward the Watering Hole. "She said Angie already brought in the cupcakes and cookies this morning. Bill will be here soon to finish the sound system. Betsy will help him get the tables and chairs set up, and we'll be good to go."

Nancy was grateful for an extra set of hands to get the coat room ready. She handed Melinda a stack of hangers with a sympathetic smile. "That's too bad about Josh, that he can't come to the party."

His ex-wife had called yesterday and offered to let him have Aiden overnight, and Josh had been delighted. While he'd seen his son at Christmas, most of his time had been spent with the rest of his family.

"Oh, it's fine." Melinda shrugged. She was a bit disappointed, even though she didn't want to admit it. This was New Year's Eve, after all, one of the most-romantic nights of the year. "It's more important he gets that one-on-one interaction with his son. I'm sure there'll be a few kids here tonight, especially early on, but Aiden wouldn't know any of them. It wouldn't be right to bring him here."

"It's good you see it that way. I'm just grateful my ex and I get along as well as we do. Not just for the kids' sake, but our own. I'm glad you and Josh are giving it a go, but I have a feeling you'll find yourself Number Three on his priority list. Between his son, and his practice, he's a busy guy."

Melinda sighed. "Yeah, I think you're right. I guess it's a good thing I'm not the clingy type, and that my life is overbooked, too."

"Neither of you has time for drama. That is sure to work in your favor."

Bill soon arrived, as did Jerry and the high-school students. Upbeat holiday tunes poured from the speakers angled in the corners, causing the volunteers to bob their heads and sing as they carried out their tasks. The hardwood floors received one last, careful sweep, and the tables and chairs were soon set up around the perimeter of the room.

Melinda was at the bank of front windows, adjusting the series of extension cords that powered the still-dazzling Christmas tree, when the scene outside caused her to take a closer look.

The snow was coming fast and furious now, accompanied by a blanket of fog. She could still see the lights on inside the Watering Hole, but the rest of the view was fading to gray.

Vicki wandered by with a spare string of lights, as she'd decided the vestibule needed a little more holiday glow.

"It's really coming down now," she said ominously. "Doesn't look good. I think the wind's picking up, too."

"I was thinking the same." Melinda's shoulders slumped. "But we can't call things off! It'd be a pain to issue refunds, and the food's already being prepared. Besides, it would be such a disappointment to pull the plug. People have been looking forward to this for weeks."

Only a few minutes later, her phone beeped in her jeans' pocket. She saw the others pause their work to check their screens, too. Nancy dropped her armload of paper tablecloths on the makeshift buffet, and read the bad news out loud. "A winter storm warning from four this afternoon until six in the morning. Eight to ten inches on the way, high winds ..."

"Dammit!" Jerry frowned. "Just what I was afraid of."

"I'd say the wind is already here." Emmett stomped off his boots on the front mat. His knit cap and the arms of his coat were dusted with icy pellets. "It's turned on us, just like that."

Frank crossed his arms. "The only person who's going to be remotely pleased about this is Auggie. He loves a party as much as anyone, but you know he prides himself on his forecasting skills."

"What do we do now?" Patricia asked. "All this work ..."

Nancy threw up her arms in frustration. "We'll just have to cancel, I don't see any way around it. Melinda, can you put a quick press release together? I'll run down to the office and get my laptop. Once you write something up, I'll get it online and send it out."

Frank reached for his coat. "I'll go tell Jessie."

"What will she do with all that food?" Vicki worried.

"They take their excess to the food pantry in Swanton," Melinda said. "But who knows if it's even worth the trip, in this weather? Besides, it's probably already closed for the holiday."

Bill snapped off the tunes. Despite Frank's freshly installed bulbs, a miserable gloom spread through the community center.

"Well, I guess this is the risk we take, trying to plan an event of this magnitude at this time of year." Jerry rubbed his eyes. "I'm really bummed about this. It's been years since Candace and I have gone out on New Year's Eve, I'm usually in bed long before the clock strikes. I was really looking forward to tonight."

Emmett crossed his arms. "This poor town can't catch a break! What are we supposed to do, just sit around and wait for Prosper to fade away?"

"We lose the post office, and we'll lose the school." Patricia had tears in her eyes. "And then it'll all go downhill from there."

Nancy put a hand on Patricia's arm. "We don't know what the future will bring," she said gently. "And we can't think about that right now. As for the party ... what if we just postponed it?"

"To when?" Frank frowned.

Jerry nodded slowly. "Nancy, that's a great idea! We could move it to next Friday. Oh, wait, there's basketball that night. How about that Saturday?"

"Doesn't that defeat the purpose?" Patricia asked. "New Year's Eve only happens once."

Melinda picked up her phone. "Yes, but the new *year* goes on. Let's see what the long-range forecast says. Hmm, it's supposed to be clear next weekend. Cold, but no snow."

"People around here aren't fazed by that, unless it's way below zero," Frank said. "It's still a risk, given the way the weather can change on a dime. But I think we should try."

Melinda looked around at the lights and decorations. "We can keep the new year theme, but the event's really more than that, anyway. This project is a big deal for the entire area; I would think curiosity alone would be enough to still draw a crowd."

"And people get bored, this time of year," Jerry added. "You're looking for any excuse to get out of the house for a few hours. Besides, I don't want to have to tell Delores we're canceling the party for good. Anyone else want to do it?"

No one moved.

"Well, that settles it." Nancy reached for her hat and coat. "We should still offer refunds, it's only fair. I think most people will still want to come, especially since everyone's going to get stuck at home tonight. Melinda, I guess that press release will be a little different than we thought. See what you can pull together; I'll be back in a few."

In a matter of minutes, a fresh plan took shape: The party would start at seven, as before, but wrap up by eleven. "Most of the people around here are old," Frank reminded Melinda when she balked at the time change.

"And the rest of them are early-risers. New Year's Eve will be long past by then; no one will expect to still be here when the clock strikes midnight."

The snow was intensifying, and everyone wanted to get home before dark. As the volunteers rushed to complete their half-finished tasks, Melinda and Nancy put together the press release. By the time the last email was sent, they were the only ones left at the now-silent community center.

"Just look at this place." Nancy nodded with satisfaction as they bundled up to face the storm.

"So much has been accomplished in a matter of weeks. This building used to be empty and dusty, a shell of its former self. Who would have ever thought it would get a second chance like this?"

"Nobody," Melinda said. "Well, except for Delores. You know what? I'm exhausted. I think a night curled up at home with my fur babies is just what I need."

It would feel good to get home, get her chores done, and pop a pizza in the oven. She'd find a movie to watch, or pick up the book club's January title, and settle in by the fire with Grace, Hazel and Hobo. Parties were fun, but they weren't the only way to celebrate New Year's Eve.

"Look at it this way," she told Nancy. "Since the party's been postponed, we have something to look forward to."

"You're right. We'll pick all this up next year." Nancy flipped the final light switch, and the room fell into darkness. "Let's go."

✳ 22 ✳

With several quick turns of her wrist, Esther rolled the last string of lights and packed them back in the plastic tote parked by the Christmas tree.

"I can't believe I'm saying this, but I'm ready to put these decorations away. It's Epiphany, after all. Out with the old, in with the new." A fresh Prosper Feed Co. calendar proclaimed the new year from its place of honor next to the sideboard. "Just look at that bright sun, and the sparkling snow. I'm ready for a clean sweep."

Melinda lifted the vintage garland from the front of the showcase and laid it on the counter. "Well, you're in the right place, then. The sweeping never ends around here. Once you get the tree down, there's some slushy mud there by the door. It's impossible to keep ahead of it."

"Oh, I'm talking about tackling more than the usual. Wash the inside of the front windows. Get every bit of dust out of the cubbyholes in apparel. I might even clear out the sideboard's drawers. You know, polish Prosper Hardware until it really shines."

Melinda knew she shouldn't be surprised by Esther's burst of motivation. Her sweatshirt showed winter at its best, with a smiling snowman surrounded by his feathered friends, and snowflake earrings sparkled in her ears. Even so, she saw a need to temper her friend's enthusiasm.

"I'm sure Miriam would love for you to scrub as much as possible. But I'd stay away from the sideboard. Auggie has his coffee supplies and paper plates exactly where he wants them. If you mess with his stuff, I think you'll regret it."

Miriam came down the stairs with a shipment of cereal in her arms. "Melinda's right. He hasn't worked here for forty years, but he takes his role as coffee guru seriously. On top of that, he's been especially puffed up the past few days. Predicting that New Year's Eve storm really put the wind in his sails."

"He'd be smart to give Old Man Winter the respect he deserves," Esther warned. "Bragging like that is just asking for it. We don't need a repeat of last year, that was terrible."

Melinda tucked the vintage garland into its original cardboard box and carefully secured the lid. It was too special, and too fragile, to toss in with the other decorations.

"I'm just glad the weather is going to stay clear through tomorrow night. This time, the party's actually going to happen."

While a few patrons had requested refunds, others snatched up their tickets. Jerry had been right; there wasn't much else going on this time of year, and people were eager for any excuse to get out for a few hours of fun.

Melinda's phone beeped, and she pulled it from her jeans' pocket. "Hey, Nancy ... what? Slow down ..."

"What in the world is going on out there?" Esther nearly dropped the ornament carton in her arms. Miriam joined her at the window, while Melinda put a hand over her other ear.

"Sorry, Esther's yelling about something, I didn't ..."

Her mouth fell open. "Are ... are you sure? You're positively sure?"

A huge grin spread across her face. "That's incredible! No, no, Miriam's here. She can call Frank, just reach out to the rest of the council. Oh, I can't believe it!"

Melinda was nearly breathless with excitement as she ran to the window. "It's the post office! It's staying open! Reduced hours, Nancy says, but we aren't going to lose it!"

Aunt Miriam's eyes filled with grateful tears. "Oh, thank you God! That explains what Glenn is up to. Or at least, why he's ... doing what he's doing."

"Is that some kind of dance?" Esther already had her coat on and was about to run outside. Melinda and Miriam didn't even bother with theirs. The three current customers abandoned their hand baskets by the counter and hurried for the door.

Sure enough, Glenn was in the middle of Main Street, gyrating like a football player who'd just scored the winning touchdown. Several residents were gathered around, watching the spectacle.

"Dear Lord," one woman gasped. "What's this all about?"

"He's lost his mind." A man slowly shook his head as he crossed his arms. "I think cabin fever's finally gotten to him. He's been a wreck lately, anyway. Maybe we need to call someone. Is Doc around?"

"Doc's a veterinarian," another man reminded him. "He can't help Glenn. And by the looks of it, I'm not sure anyone can."

"What you see, right there?" Aunt Miriam told the group. "That's pure, unadulterated joy. We just got word: The post office isn't going to close! The feds have dropped their plan!" The crowd was already growing, and Miriam's announcement was met with gasps and cheers.

"Well, then, Glenn's got something to celebrate!" one woman shouted. "We all do. I say, let's join him!"

"Someone's yelling in the back lot." Bill popped out Prosper Hardware's front door. "Couldn't make out what he was saying. What's going on?"

"Get your parka," Miriam ordered him with a smile. "There's a party to go to."

The throng of revelers had spilled into the middle of the road, and more residents were quick to join the celebration. Sam hurried out of his insurance office with a client in tow. Vicki appeared in Meadow Lane's doorway, then motioned for everyone inside to come out.

Several people ran out of the front door of the Watering Hole, cheering and hooting as they ran through the intersection. A horn blasted, and Melinda turned to see Auggie parking his truck as close to the group as he could get. Word certainly spread fast in a town this tiny. Especially when it was good.

"Just goes to show, you can't keep us down!" one man shouted. The crowd answered with a rousing round of cheers and applause.

Nancy burst out of city hall and waved her arms. "Everyone, please! Get out of the street!" But she was laughing, and the crowd good-naturedly complied with her request and shifted to the sidewalk.

"We did it!" Nancy exclaimed as she returned Melinda's hug. "Or I should say, Glenn did it. He poured his heart out at that departmental meeting, and I'm sure it tipped the scales in our favor."

Jerry soon arrived, so distracted that he barely had the car in park before he jumped out. He'd been at a county meeting in Swanton when Glenn called him with the news. Prosper's mayor had dashed out of the room so fast, the other area leaders assumed the worst and ran after him.

"Once I explained, the place just went nuts." Jerry stopped to catch his breath. "And then, I couldn't get down the hall, much less out to the car. Everyone was stopping me, wanting to congratulate us. I thought I'd never get away."

He turned to Nancy. "We'll need to get some remarks together, I'm sure the media will be calling as soon as they get wind of it."

"Speaking of a speech." Nancy nudged Jerry toward the front of the crowd. "I think Glenn wants you to join him."

Jerry shared what he knew about the post office's reduction of hours, and reminded everyone the changes wouldn't take effect until September, which was the start of the federal fiscal year.

"So, we have some time to adjust to the idea. But what matters is, our post office is going to stay open!" He waited for the cheers to ebb away before he continued. "It's a good day for Prosper, maybe one of the best we've ever had. But it's more than that. This is a good day for the common man, the little guy who sometimes feels like he can't make a difference."

At "little guy," Glenn grinned and playfully rubbed his rotund stomach, a move that drew chuckles from the crowd.

"OK, maybe you're not so little." Jerry clapped his friend on the shoulder. "But I know for sure you have made a difference. I think I speak for everyone here, and all over this part of the county, when I thank you for speaking up. You never gave up on our town, and we're behind you one-hundred percent."

Glenn doffed his knit cap and bowed, and the onlookers roared their approval. "I don't even know what to say. Other than ... thank you, everyone, for all your support these past few weeks. I didn't do this on my own, far from it." He took in a deep breath and let it out.

"Today's a good day. And tomorrow night? We're going to have the best party this little town has ever seen."

***

Melinda filled a platter with cookies, then elbowed her way through the crowded community center to add it to the array of sweets on one of the buffet tables.

"Just look at this crowd!" Angie shuffled the serving trays to make room. "Everyone came hungry, but that's exactly what we hoped for." She filched a mint-walnut cookie from the newest plate of goodies. "I'll help eat these up; looks like the chocolate-macadamia ones are going the fastest."

Melinda wanted to help, too. "I can understand why. They're all delicious. This night is shaping up to be wonderful advertising for your bakery business. Your phone's going to ring off the hook."

Jessie brought out another tray of cheese and crackers and added it to the adjoining table, which was packed with plates of sandwiches and vats of chili. "There's no better publicity than positive word-of-mouth. And to think, we were so disappointed when that blizzard blew in and ruined our New Year's Eve plans. Little did we know, a week later, we'd have so much more to celebrate!"

"It was meant to be." Melinda admired how a fresh coat of paint and a deep cleaning had transformed the abandoned bank into such a welcoming space. "Everything's falling into place. I'd say it's definitely been a happy new year so far."

"Especially for you." Angie raised an eyebrow. "Look who just walked in the door." Josh only made it a few feet into the crowd before someone stopped him to say hello.

"Oh, my." Jessie gave Melinda a nod of approval. "When did this start?"

"Two weeks ago, I guess." She couldn't keep the smile off her face.

"Officially," Angie interjected. "It's about time the two of you got together. Well, looks like we need to put out more punch."

"I think Doug could use some more ice." Jessie's husband had a bar set up in a corner by the kitchen. "Let's get everything restocked and get back to socializing."

Bill had created a makeshift DJ station in the alcove by the stairwell, and was spinning a mix of holiday tunes and upbeat favorites. A few revelers made use of the dance floor, which was simply a cleared space under the south windows, but most of the crowd was more focused on conversation than busting a move.

The Christmas tree still glowed in the bank of front windows, and the strings of clear lights strung along the walls added to the festive feel. Outside, the lighted trees and snowflakes remained on the lamp posts along Main Street, defying the calendar as well as the cold.

The volunteer fire department had yet to find the time to take them down, and it seemed appropriate to leave the town's only official decorations up for tonight's celebration. Auggie had followed suit, and the massive star still shone at the top of the co-op's highest tower.

He had, however, removed his massive protest sign. Or at least, most of it.

"I'm leaving the posts up," he told Melinda as he helped himself to a cup of chili. "At least for now. Who knows when we'll have another crisis that requires me to speak up? The old sign might come in handy yet. Paint's cheap, you know."

After running a few more trays of food to the buffet, Melinda found her way to Josh.

"Sorry I'm late," he said. "My last surgery ran over, and by the time I got home and ..."

"Don't worry about it. I can entertain myself." She reached for his hand. "Of course, it's even better now that you're here. But seriously, go ahead and mingle."

After Josh moved on, Melinda joined Nancy and Vicki near the Christmas tree.

"You won't believe how many people are dropping money into that donation box." Vicki tipped her head at the small table just inside the double doors.

"They've already paid for their tickets, so it's all gravy. Just think what we can do with that extra money. It would be wonderful to get a stainless-steel range for the kitchen, maybe some window blinds ..."

"I'm sure we can get by with what we have, for now," Nancy said. "We have some of the cosmetic stuff covered already, thanks to our plans for this party. But the building needs some work; who knows what we'll find?"

"I know, I know." Vicki rolled her eyes, but she was smiling. "A girl can dream, though."

"So, what's the plan?" Melinda took a sip of her white wine. "Is Jerry really going to speak right before ten? Do a New Year's toast, the whole thing?"

"He sure is." Nancy nodded. "He hates to get up in front of a crowd, but he worked on his comments for weeks and said he's not about to toss them in the trash. A few changes here and there, and they're still appropriate."

There was a commotion at the entrance. Melinda peered through the crowd and saw Delores come through the vestibule. She was greeted by a smattering of polite applause from those nearby, and gave a queenly wave in return.

A woman helped Delores manage her coat and cane, and the way was cleared for the community center's elderly benefactress to select a comfortable, sturdy chair.

As Melinda studied the smiling faces around her, she realized that nearly every person who'd become a part of her new life was in this room. A cluster in one corner contained many of her neighbors, and by the grins on the faces of John Olson and his wife, Ed was in the middle of one of his stories. Melinda's parents were already there, talking with Frank and Miriam.

"How's your mom doing now that Mark's moved out?" Nancy asked.

"Great, actually. He only left two days ago, so I think they're both still trying to get back to their regular routine. He seems happy with his decision, and it's a great opportunity. I think that's going a long way toward smoothing things over."

Vicki's husband wandered over with a beer in his hand. "Melinda, I guess congratulations are in order. My spies tell me you've taken the area's most-eligible bachelor off the market. Is that true?"

She turned to Vicki, who was laughing.

"Oh, you can't blame her for all of it," Arthur said with a smirk. "She told me, of course. But I first heard about it at the bank. Two of our young ladies were gossiping in the breakroom. They seemed pretty disappointed."

"Well, it's impossible to keep anything private around here. But, just to clarify: We're not serious, OK? We'll just have to see how it goes."

"I don't know," Nancy teased. "He's perfect for you. I've got a good feeling about this one."

"Oh, so you didn't before?"

Nancy changed the subject. "There's Richard." She took her wine glass off the nearby table. "I need to talk to him about the furnace upgrades. The bids came in yesterday but, with all the excitement, I never gave him a call."

Melinda was chatting with Karen and other members of the book club when her phone beeped. It was a text from Josh. *Meet me in the entryway.*

"What's going on? Is everything OK?"

"Just got a call. A horse south of town got his hoof stuck in a fence. Doesn't sound serious, they got him out and it's probably just a sprain. But they don't want to wait until tomorrow, just in case."

Josh had graciously offered to cover any Prosper clinic calls that night, so Doc and Karen could fully enjoy the party. After all, it was their town's future that had been in jeopardy.

"Then you need to go." Melinda pointed at Josh's pressed khakis and button-down shirt. "But can you go like that?"

Josh already had his coat in hand. "My work gear's out in the truck. I have a key, I'll stop at the clinic and change." He was about to turn away, then stopped.

"Happy new year." He kissed her, gently but quickly, then started for the door.

"Same to you," she called after him. And with a wave, he was gone.

"It's too bad Josh had to leave." Vicki sighed when Melinda told her what happened. "It would have been so romantic. He could have kissed you just as ... well, as the clock struck ten. On January seventh."

Melinda was laughing now. "Doesn't have quite the same ring to it, huh?"

A shrill whistle cut through the music and laughter, and Bill turned off the tunes. Jerry stepped to the now-clear dance floor, microphone in hand.

"I want to start out by thanking all of you for coming. We decided we weren't going to let a little blizzard ruin our fun, and we're glad you could join us for what has to be the latest New Year's Eve party on record."

He raised his plastic cup of beer, and the room erupted in cheers and applause. "Before we get too far along, I want to introduce you all to Delores Eklund. It's her generous donation that's made this entire project possible."

Delores stepped forward to a round of applause. She welcomed everyone to the celebration and explained how the plan for the community center came to life.

Then, she threw in a little retired-teacher guilt trip for good measure.

"My donation got this ball rolling, but the work's not done. We need more cash. I know you all paid to get in here, but there's a box over by the door. Let's see you fill it up before you leave."

Jerry raised his eyebrows at Nancy, who quickly took the microphone out of the older woman's grasp. "Thank you, Delores, for your ... motivational message. And now, I'll turn things back over to our mayor."

Auggie was at Nancy's elbow. "I have something to say."

"When doesn't he?" Vicki muttered to Melinda as Auggie snatched the microphone away.

"We all want to keep up the community spirit this town has shown in the past few months. There's something I've been noodling on for a while and I decided, what the heck? Tonight's as good of a time as any to tell you about it."

"He's going off script, for sure," Melinda whispered back. "Look at Jerry's face. No clue."

Auggie's brown eyes flashed behind his glasses as he nodded at Delores. "Along with this new community center, we'll have something else to celebrate this year. There's going to be a change down at the co-op, come spring."

Gasps and exclamations echoed through the room. "Nope, I'm not retiring! You can't get rid of me that easily. Instead, I'm going to add something. Out back, where we have the diesel for the tractors, we're going to put in another pump. We're going to start offering gas for everyone else."

This was met with hoots and cheers, then thunderous applause. Miriam gripped Melinda's arm.

"A gas station, right here in town? Can you believe it? It's not really one, I know, but this will mean so much to the community. The last one closed thirty years ago."

Melinda was as thrilled as anyone else. "This is

astounding! Not just his plan, but that he was able to keep it to himself this long. I didn't think that was possible."

"We're going to start small," Auggie told the crowd. "We already have a supplier, so I figured, why not? It's been in the back of my mind for some time, but when all this mess with the feds came up ..."

That observation was met with groans.

"I know, I was worried, too. But Glenn took care of that for us, didn't he?" Glenn, who stood near the bar, raised his glass to acknowledge the roar of approval.

"And now that we know the post office is saved, and our town is no longer under a cloud of gloom, I've decided this is the perfect time to expand. We already have one new business in town." Auggie pointed at Vicki, who beamed and nodded her thanks. "Who's to say what might happen next?"

Then he turned to Jerry, who was grinning from ear to ear. "I know we all stand on tradition around here, me included. The town's sign is perfect as-is, and I'm not saying we should paint it over. But it occurred to me that Prosper may no longer be "The Great Little Town That Didn't."

He turned back to the crowd, and raised a fist in triumph. "We're really 'The Great Little Town That *Did It!*'"

A wave of euphoria swept through the community center. The partygoers cheered, stomped on the floor, and raised their hands in victory as the celebration went on for several minutes.

Jerry let the room settle down before he shook Auggie's hand and took the microphone.

"Wow." He gave Auggie a grin. "I don't think I can top that. We're going to have a little countdown at ten, so I'll keep the rest of my comments brief. I'll start with Glenn."

He pointed at his friend. "Everyone's been saying that Glen's a hero, and I agree. He saw a need in this community, and he stood up for what he believed in. He won't speak tonight; believe me, I tried to talk him into it. But if you ask him, I'm sure he'll tell you exactly what he thinks about the whole mess. I say, let's have a round of applause for Glenn."

After the cheers died away, Jerry looked around at the faces in the crowd. "But Glenn's not the only hero who's here tonight."

He gestured around the community center, then toward the post office down the street.

"We never could have done any of this, in here or out there, without every single one of you. If you signed that petition, you're a hero. If you volunteered to take it around to your neighbors, whether they lived one house away or one mile away, you're a hero, too. Every person who called to file a complaint, who emailed the postal service in protest, who got up at that public meeting and defended our right to have efficient mail service and keep our community strong ... you're *my* hero. Every single one of you."

"Thank you, Mayor Jerry!" a man shouted in the back.

"No, don't thank me. Thank your friends, your neighbors, your family. In fact, right now, I want everyone to turn and congratulate those around you. There have been hard times before, and they'll come again. But we've always stuck together in this town, and we will continue to do just that."

Jerry gave everyone a few minutes to hug and shake hands, then checked the oversized clock on the far wall. It was an old, grand timepiece that had been left behind when the bank closed a decade ago. But Richard and Emmett had cleaned it, polished it, and reset its mechanism so it ticked like new.

Jerry nodded at Bill, then turned back to the crowd.

"Now, I know we're seven days, or should I say, *nights*, late on this thing." The familiar strains of a holiday standard drifted from the speakers.

"But let's have a verse of 'Auld Lang Syne,' just for kicks." He raised his glass. "Happy new year!"

The crowd took up the song, and Melinda's emotions got the best of her. It was almost too much, this rush of feeling. She loved this town, her family and friends, and her new life here. It had taken a long time for the dust to settle, but she knew this for sure: she was where she was supposed to be.

Just as the revelers rolled into the last stanza, she saw Jerry reach for his phone. What was he doing? Answering an email during this special moment?

The music faded and the crowd burst into applause and shouts of "happy new year!" And then, Melinda thought she heard something outside.

A bell ringing, sweet and clear. Miriam heard it, too, and craned her neck to see around the Christmas tree and out the front windows. Then came a chorus of bells, and their chimes echoed from one end of town to the other.

"What's that?" someone asked.

"Church bells are ringing! Everywhere! Can you hear them?"

"Oh, how lovely!"

The crowd shifted toward the front of the building. Diane joined her sister and daughter by the windows, and Nancy soon appeared out of the throng.

"Jerry wanted it to be a surprise. You probably didn't notice, but Father Perkins slipped out about ten minutes ago. There's someone at the other churches, too. Jerry texted everyone when it was time."

A man pulled his coat off its hanger and started for the door. "I'm going outside, this is too good to miss!" Others soon followed. Some stopped for their winter-weather gear, but many of them were too overwhelmed with emotion to bother with coats and hats.

"Let's go." Miriam guided Diane and Melinda to the coat racks. "I don't want to miss this."

There was no room left to stand on the community center's steps. People gathered in clusters up and down the sidewalk, in awe of the bells as they rang on and on. Frank and Roger soon joined the family huddle.

Melinda looked over, aghast. Was Uncle Frank crying? Miriam certainly was. And then, she couldn't be sure, not anymore, as tears of joy began to roll down her own face.

Diane put an arm around her daughter. "Better late than never. Happy new year, honey."

Aunt Miriam soon joined their hug. "This is a night we'll never forget! Oh, how I wish Mom and Dad could be here for this moment."

"They are," Diane told her sister. "You know they are. All the time."

"Listen to them ring!" Uncle Frank had wiped his eyes and regained some of his usual good cheer. "Jerry must have told them to really whoop it up. Good thing we don't have a police department, or they'd probably get on us for disturbing the peace."

"Well, for once, it's good to be so small," Roger said with a laugh. "Happy new year, everybody!"

"I think it's going to be a good one." Melinda hugged her dad. "We're so blessed, and our future is bright."

The bells pealed again and again, and their sweet notes echoed down Prosper's Main Street and up into a cold, clear sky. Their tones rang out into the darkness, and blanketed the silent, snow-swaddled fields in a song of new beginnings, a song of hope.

And on the edge of town, high on the co-op's tallest tower, a blazing star shined through the night.

WHAT'S NEXT

More to come! In case you haven't already heard, "The Blessed Season" isn't going to be the end of this series. Look for Book 9, "Daffodil Season," to arrive in spring 2021. Read on for a sneak peek!

Recipes: Visit fremontcreekpress.com and click on the "Extras" tab to enjoy all the recipes inspired by the series. For "Blessed Season," you'll find a German holiday tradition, a savory appetizer, and a special Christmas cookie!

Stay in touch: Be sure to sign up for the email list when you visit the website (you'll find it under the "Connect" tab). That's the best way to find out when "Daffodil Season" will be available for pre-order.

Thanks for reading!
Melanie

SNEAK PEEK: DAFFODIL SEASON

Late February: Melinda's farm

Melinda shoved the next cardboard box to the side, and a plume of dust rose from the storage room's floorboards.

"Did you find them yet?" Diane wanted to know. "There's some crates over here, but none of them seem to be what we're looking for."

Melinda's first answer came in the form of a sneeze. Grace, who was sniffing the box's worn corners, looked up in alarm. "Nope," Melinda finally said. "This one's marked 'tax forms.' I doubt they're in here."

Aunt Miriam stood by the bank of windows inside the wide east dormer, taking down the dust-crusted curtains with careful hands.

"Goodness, these things could stand up by themselves! I can't believe how much there is to sort through. I thought the Schermanns made a clean sweep of the place last spring, before the auction."

"Well, yes and no." Melinda sat back on her heels and took a break to rub Hazel's ears. "They did what they could in a few days, but they had to focus on the furniture and other items for the sale. Between that, and dividing family heirlooms, a bunch of random stuff was left behind."

"Are you sure Ada doesn't have the club's records?" Diane pushed a few stray hairs out of her face. "And they're not at Mabel's ... she's sure of it?"

Melinda couldn't resist the lure of local history, and word that a women's society had flourished for decades in Fulton Township piqued her interest. As it turned out, Anna Schermann had been as active in the club as Mabel's mother. Ada recalled once seeing a box of club-meeting minutes upstairs at the farmhouse. It was a sketchy memory, but Melinda was eager to verify it if she could.

"No, she checked again last night. Went through everything in the cedar chest, the other boxes she took home. Nothing."

Diane gently displaced Grace on her way to the windows, a move that earned a growl of disapproval. "Excuse me, Princess Grace! Look at that bright sunshine. Another few days of this weather, and the rest of the snow should be gone. Sure, we'll get a little more, but maybe we've turned that last corner."

Miriam's face broke into a wide smile. "Spring's not here yet, but it's on its way. Can you feel it?"

Melinda glanced at the storage room's dingy plaster ceiling and tossed up a quick prayer. "As long as I don't feel anything dripping on my head, I'll be grateful. Dave patched this section of the roof last year, but I'm sure a few more shingles are about to let go." She crossed her arms and looked around at the clutter. "This is just one more reminder that I have a ton of real spring cleaning to do, in rooms I actually use. Maybe this is a wild goose chase; something happened to the records, they were thrown away ..."

Miriam chuckled. "Oh, I can't imagine Horace and Wilbur tossing anything out."

"I need a break." Diane lowered herself to a wooden crate by the boarded-up north window. Hazel was eager to make the leap into Diane's lap. "Honey, you'll get everything done, you always do."

"Look at it this way." Miriam reached for an empty plastic sack. "You don't have to wash these old curtains, at least. They're off to the burn barrel."

"That's true." Melinda gazed out at the bare branches of the front yard's maple tree. It would be several weeks before the tiny, tender leaves would show their faces, but her mom and aunt were right: Spring would come again, as it always did. "I'm glad I'm tossing those curtains. The windows need a good cleaning, but there's already more light in here."

Miriam made her way to the room's only chair and tested its stability before she took a seat. "Oh, my knees. And this little scavenger hunt is nothing like what Frank and I will face when we move."

"We'll help," Diane promised. "You know we will."

"I wanted to make a dent in things over the winter, but never got it done." She looked at her sister, and then her niece. "And now, we'll have even less time to box stuff up."

"What do you mean?" Melinda frowned. "I thought you weren't planning to close on the new house until at least May."

"We aren't, our friends aren't moving until April." Miriam leaned forward, as if sharing a secret. "I wanted the two of you to be the first to know: Frank and I are going on vacation!"

"What?" Diane was floored. "But you never ..."

"And that's exactly why we're going to go. Neither of us is getting any younger."

Melinda shrugged. "A long weekend might be just what you need. Chicago is always fun. Minneapolis is, too, but you've been there several times. Kansas City ..."

"Oh, we're going much farther than that." Miriam's eyes sparkled with excitement. "Girls, we're off to Hawaii! For two whole weeks!"

Diane blinked, unable to speak. Melinda finally found the words.

"Two weeks?" She swallowed. "You're ... going to be gone for two weeks?"

"Oh, it'll be closer to three. I mean, as far as being away from the store. We'll need some days to pack, and then rest up when we get back. We're still trying to decide between two itineraries, but the plan is to ship out in late March."

She squeezed Melinda's arm. "And honey, we have you to thank for this opportunity. Bill's responsible, and your parents can help out, but having you back here is making this possible. We know we can trust you to run the store while we're away."

Melinda widened her eyes at her mom. "Sure. Of course."
"I think it's a wonderful plan." Diane plastered on a bright smile. "You're right, Roger and I will chip in. Don't worry about a thing! You two are overdue for a break."

Miriam hurried over to hug her sister. "Oh, thank you! This is going to be the trip of a lifetime." She studied the storage room with renewed energy, and zeroed in on an old dresser slumped against the far wall. "Ladies, those records have to be here somewhere. Let's get back at it."

"What are we going to do?" Melinda whispered to her mom after Miriam moved on. "What about the accounts, ordering supplies? I don't even know ..."

Diane took a deep breath. "We'll figure it out. At least we have a month's notice. I can't believe I'm saying this, but I'm no longer in a hurry for spring to arrive."

"Daffodil Season" arrives in spring 2021.
Visit the "Connect" tab at fremontcreekpress.com
and sign up for the email newsletter to find out
when Book 9 will be available!

ABOUT THE BOOKS

Don't miss any of the titles
in this heartwarming rural fiction series

Melinda is at a crossroads when the "for rent" sign beckons her down a dusty gravel lane. Facing forty, single and downsized from her stellar career at a big-city ad agency, she's struggling to start over when a phone call brings her home to rural Iowa.

She moves to the country, takes on a rundown farm and its headstrong animals, and lands behind the counter of her family's hardware store in the community of Prosper, whose motto is "The Great Little Town That Didn't." And just like the sprawling garden she tends under the summer sun, Melinda begins to thrive. But when storm clouds arrive on her horizon, can she hold on to the new life she's worked so hard to create?

BOOK 2

BOOK 3

BOOK 4

Songbird Season

BY MELANIE LAGESCHULTE

BOOK 5

The **Bright Season**

BY MELANIE LAGESCHULTE

BOOK 6

Turning Season

BY MELANIE LAGESCHULTE

BOOK 7

The **Blessed Season**

BY MELANIE LAGESCHULTE

BOOK 8

Daffodil Season

BY MELANIE LAGESCHULTE

BOOK 9

Look for Book 9 in spring 2021! For more information on all the titles, visit fremont creekpress.com

* * *

A TIN TRAIN CHRISTMAS

The toy train was everything two boys could want: colorful, shiny, and the perfect vehicle for their imaginations. But was it meant to be theirs? Revisit Horace's childhood for this special holiday short story inspired by the "Growing Season" series!

Made in the USA
Coppell, TX
20 January 2023

11457551R00152